# HEAVY WEATHER

When Lord Tilbury, founder of the Mammoth Publishing Company, receives a letter from Galahad Threepwood stating he will no longer be submitting his sensationally scandalous memoir for publication, he sees the prospect of a small fortune slipping from his grasp. So Tilbury decides to travel to Blandings Castle and steal the manuscript. But he isn't the only one after it — seemingly everyone is scrambling to nab the memoir for their own reasons. Meanwhile, Lord Emsworth suspects Sir Gregory Parsloe-Parsloe of scheming to nobble his pride and joy, that noble Berkshire sow Empress of Blandings, at the upcoming Agricultural Show . . .

P. G. WODEHOUSE

# HEAVY WEATHER

*Complete and Unabridged*

# ULVERSCROFT
*Leicester*

First published in Great Britain in 1933 by
Herbert Jenkins
London


This Ulverscroft Edition
published 2018
by arrangement with
Rogers, Coleridge & White Literary Agency
London

A catalogue record for this book is available
from the British Library.


ISBN 978-1-4448-3953-1


Published by
F. A. Thorpe (Publishing)
Anstey, Leicestershire

Set by Words & Graphics Ltd.
Anstey, Leicestershire
Printed and bound in Great Britain by
T. J. International Ltd., Padstow, Cornwall

This book is printed on acid-free paper

# 1

Sunshine pierced the haze that enveloped London. It came down Fleet Street, turned to the right, stopped at the premises of the Mammoth Publishing Company, and, entering through an upper window, beamed pleasantly upon Lord Tilbury, founder and proprietor of that vast factory of popular literature, as he sat reading the batch of weekly papers which his secretary had placed on the desk for his inspection. Among the secrets of this great man's success was the fact that he kept a personal eye on all the firm's products.

Considering what a pleasant rarity sunshine in London is, one might have expected the man behind the Mammoth to beam back. Instead, he merely pressed the buzzer. His secretary appeared. He pointed silently. The secretary drew the shade, and the sunshine, having called without an appointment, was excluded.

'I beg your pardon, Lord Tilbury . . . '

'Well?'

'A Lady Julia Fish has just rung up on the telephone.'

'Well?'

'She says she would like to see you this morning.'

Lord Tilbury frowned. He remembered Lady Julia Fish as an agreeable hotel acquaintance during his recent holiday at Biarritz. But this was Tilbury House, and at Tilbury House he did not desire the company of hotel acquaintances, however agreeable.

'Did she say what she wanted?'

'No, Lord Tilbury.'

'All right.'

The secretary withdrew. Lord Tilbury returned to his reading.

The particular periodical which had happened to come to hand was the current number of that admirable children's paper, *Tiny Tots*, and for some moments he scanned its pages with an attempt at his usual conscientious thoroughness. But it was plain that his heart was not in his work. The Adventures of Pinky, Winky, and Pop in Slumberland made little impression upon him. He passed on to a thoughtful article by Laura J. Smedley on what a wee girlie can do to help mother, but it was evident that for once Laura J. had failed to grip. Presently with a grunt he threw the paper down and for the third time since it had arrived by the morning post picked up a letter which lay on the desk. He already knew it by heart, so there was no real necessity for him to read it again, but the human tendency to twist the knife in the wound is universal.

It was a brief letter. Its writer's eighteenth-century ancestors, who believed in filling their twelve sheets when they took pen in hand, would have winced at the sight of it. But for all its brevity it had ruined Lord Tilbury's day.

It ran as follows:

2

Blandings Castle, Shropshire.

Dear Sir,

Enclosed find cheque for the advance you paid me on those Reminiscences of mine.

I have been thinking it over, and have decided not to publish them, after all.

Yours truly,
G. Threepwood.

'Cor!' said Lord Tilbury, an ejaculation to which he was much addicted in times of mental stress.

He rose from his chair and began to pace the room. Always Napoleonic of aspect, being short and square and stumpy and about twenty-five pounds overweight, he looked now like a Napoleon taking his morning walk at St Helena.

And yet, oddly enough, there were men in England who would have whooped with joy at the sight of that letter. Some of them might even have gone to the length of lighting bonfires and roasting oxen whole for the tenantry about it. Those few words over that signature would have spread happiness in every county from Cumberland to Cornwall. So true is it that in this world everything depends on the point of view.

When, some months before, the news had got about that the Hon. Galahad Threepwood, brother of the Earl of Emsworth and as sprightly an old gentleman as was ever thrown out of a Victorian music-hall, was engaged in writing the recollections of his colourful career as a man about town in the nineties, the shock to the many now highly respectable members of the governing classes who in their hot youth had shared it was severe. All over the country decorous Dukes and steady Viscounts, who had once sown wild oats in the society of the young Galahad, sat quivering in their slippers at the thought of what long-cupboarded skeletons those Reminiscences might disclose.

They knew their Gally, and their imagination allowed them to picture with a crystal clearness the sort of book he would be likely to produce. It would, they felt in their ageing bones, be essentially one of those of which the critics say 'A veritable storehouse of diverting anecdote.' To not a few — Lord Emsworth's nearest neighbour, Sir Gregory Parsloe-Parsloe of Matchingham Hall, was one of them — it was as if the Recording Angel had suddenly decided to rush into print.

Lord Tilbury, however, had looked on the thing from a different angle. He knew — no man better — what big money there was in this type of literature. The circulation of his nasty little paper, *Society Spice*, proved that. Even though Percy Pilbeam, its nasty little editor, had handed in his portfolio and gone off to start a Private Inquiry Agency, it was still a gold-mine. He had known Gally Threepwood in the old days — not intimately, but quite well enough to cause him now to hasten to acquire all rights to the story of his life, sight unseen. It seemed to him that the book could not fail to be the *succes de scandale* of the year.

4

Acute, therefore, as had been the consternation of the Dukes and Viscounts on learning that the dead past was about to be disinterred, it paled in comparison with that of Lord Tilbury on suddenly receiving this intimation that it was not. There is a tender spot in all great men. Achilles had his heel. With Lord Tilbury it was his pocket. He hated to see money get away from him, and out of this book of Gally Threepwood's he had been looking forward to making a small fortune.

Little wonder, then, that he mourned and was unable to concentrate on *Tiny Tots*. He was still mourning when his secretary entered bearing a slip of paper.

*Name* — Lady Julia Fish.
*Business* — Personal.

Lord Tilbury snorted irritably. At a time like this! 'Tell her I'm . . . '

And then there flashed into his mind a sudden recollection of something he had heard somebody say about this Lady Julia Fish. The words 'Blandings Castle' seemed to be connected with it. He turned to the desk and took up *Debrett's Peerage*, searching among the E's for 'Emsworth, Earl of 'Emsworth.'

Yes, there it was. Lady Julia Fish had been born Lady Julia Threepwood. She was a sister of the perjured Galahad.

That altered things. Here, he perceived, was an admirable opportunity of working off some of his stored-up venom. His knowledge of life told

5

him that the woman would not be calling unless she wanted to get something out of him. To inform her in person that she was most certainly not going to get it would be balm to his lacerated feelings.

'Ask her to come up,' he said.

Lady Julia Fish was a handsome middle-aged woman of the large blonde type, of a personality both breezy and commanding. She came into the room a few moments later like a galleon under sail, her resolute chin and her china-blue eyes proclaiming a supreme confidence in her ability to get anything she wanted out of anyone. And Lord Tilbury, having bowed stiffly, stood regarding her with a pop-eyed hostility. Even setting aside her loathsome family connexions, there was a patronizing good humour about her manner which he resented. And certainly, if Lady Julia Fish's manner had a fault, it was that it resembled a little too closely that of the great lady of a village amusedly trying to make friends with the backward child of one of her tenants.

'Well, well, well,' she said, not actually patting Lord Tilbury on the head but conveying the impression that she might see fit to do so at any moment, 'you're looking very bonny. Biarritz did you good.'

Lord Tilbury, with the geniality of a trapped wolf, admitted to being in robust health.

'So this is where you get out all those jolly little papers of yours, is it? I must say I'm impressed. Quite awe-inspiring, all that ritual on the threshold. Admirals in the Swiss Navy making you fill up forms with your name and business, and small boys in buttons eyeing you as if anything you said might be used in evidence against you.'

'What *is* your business?' asked Lord Tilbury.

'The practical note!' said Lady Julia, with indulgent approval. 'How stimulating that is. Time is money, and all that. Quite. Well, cutting the preamble, I want a job for Ronnie.'

Lord Tilbury looked like a trapped wolf who had thought as much.

'Ronnie?' he said coldly.

'My son. Didn't you meet him at Biarritz? He was there. Small and pink.'

Lord Tilbury drew in breath for the delivery of the nasty blow. 'I regret . . . '

'I know what you're going to say. You're very crowded here. Fearful congestion, and so on. Well, Ronnie won't take up much room. And I shouldn't think he could do any actual harm to a solidly established concern like this. Surely you could let him mess about at *something*!' Why, Sir Gregory Parsloe, our neighbour down in Shropshire, told me that you were employing his nephew, Monty. And while I would be the last woman to claim Ronnie is a mental giant, at least he's brighter than young Monty Bodkin.'

A quiver ran through Lord Tilbury's stocky form. This woman had unbared his secret shame. A man who prided himself on never letting himself be worked for jobs, he had had a few weeks before a brief moment of madness when, under the softening influence of a particularly good public dinner, he had yielded to the request of the banqueter on his left that he should find a place at Tilbury House for his nephew.

He had regretted the lapse next morning. He had regretted it more on seeing the nephew. And he had not ceased to regret it now.

'That,' he said tensely, 'has nothing to do with the case.'

'I don't see why. Swallowing camels and straining at gnats is what I should call it.'

'Nothing,' repeated Lord Tilbury, 'to do with the case.'

He was beginning to feel that this interview was not working out as he had anticipated. He had meant to be strong, brusque, decisive — the man of iron. And here this woman had got him arguing and explaining — almost in a position of defending himself.

Like so many people who came into contact with her, he began to feel that there was something disagreeably hypnotic about Lady Julia Fish.

'But what do you want your son to work here *for?*' he asked, realizing as he spoke that a man of iron ought to have scorned to put such a question.

Lady Julia considered.

'Oh, a pittance. Whatever the dole is you give your slaves.' Lord Tilbury made himself clearer.

'I mean, why? Has he shown any aptitude for journalism?' This seemed to amuse Lady Julia.

'My dear man,' she said, tickled by the quaint conceit, 'no member of my family has ever shown any aptitude for anything except eating and sleeping.'

'Then why do you want him to join my staff?'

'Well, primarily, to distract his mind.'

'What!'

'To distract his . . . well, yes, I suppose in a loose way you could call it a mind.'

'I don't understand you.'

'Well, it's like this. The poor half-wit is trying to marry a chorus-girl, and it seemed to me that if he were safe at Tilbury House, inking his nose and getting bustled about by editors and people, it might take his mind off the tender passion.'

Lord Tilbury drew a long, deep, rasping breath. The weakness had passed. He could be strong now. This outrageous insult to the business he loved had shattered the spell which those china-blue eyes and that confident manner had been weaving about him. He spoke curtly, placing his thumbs in the armholes of his waistcoat to lend emphasis to his remarks.

'I fear you have mistaken the functions of Tilbury House, Lady Julia.'

'I beg your pardon?'

'We publish newspapers, magazines, weekly journals. We are not a Home for the Lovelorn.' There was a brief silence.

'I see,' said Lady Julia. She looked at him inquiringly. 'You sound very stuffy,' she went on. 'Not your old merry Biarritz self at all. Did your breakfast disagree with you this morning?'

'Cor!'

'Something's the matter. Why, at Biarritz you were known as Sunny Jim.'

Lord Tilbury was ill attuned to badinage.

'Yes,' he said. 'Something is the matter. If you

9

really wish to know, I am scarcely in a frame of mind today to go out of my way to oblige members of your family. After what has occurred.'

'What has occurred?'

'Your brother Galahad . . . ' Lord Tilbury choked. 'Look at this,' he said.

He extended the letter rather in the manner of one anxious to rid himself of a snake which has somehow come into his possession. Lady Julia scrutinized it with languid interest.

'It's monstrous. Abominable. He accepted the contract, and he ought to fulfil it. At the very least, in common decency, he might have given his reasons for behaving in this utterly treacherous and unethical way. But does he? Not at all. Explanations? None. Apologies? Regrets? Oh dear, no. He merely 'decides not to publish' In all my thirty years of . . . '

Lady Julia was never a very good listener.

'Odd,' she said, handing the letter back. 'My brother Galahad is a man who moves in a mysterious way his wonders to perform. A quite unaccountable mentality. I knew he was writing this book, of course, but I have no notion whatever why he has had this sudden change of heart. Perhaps some Duke who doesn't want to see himself in the 'Peers I Have Been Thrown Out of Public-Houses With' chapter has been threatening to take him for a ride.'

'Cor!'

'Or some Earl with a guilty conscience. Or a Baronet. 'Society Scribe Bumped Off By Baronets' — that would make a good headline for one of your papers.'

'This is not a joking matter.'

'Well, at any rate, my dear man, it's no good savaging *me*. I'm not responsible for Galahad's eccentricities. I'm simply an innocent widow-woman trying to wangle a cushy job for her only son. Coming back to which, I rather gather from what you said just now that you do not intend to set Ronnie punching the clock?'

Lord Tilbury shook from stem to stern. His eyes gleamed balefully. Nature in the raw is seldom mild.

'I absolutely and positively refuse to employ your son at Tilbury House in any capacity whatsoever.'

'Well, that's a fair answer to a fair question, and seems to close the discussion.'

Lady Julia rose.

'Too bad about Gally's little effort,' she said silkily. 'You'll lose a lot of money, won't you? There's a mint of it in a really indiscreet book of Reminiscences. They tell me that Lady Wensleydale's *Sixty Years Near The Knuckle In Mayfair*, or whatever it was called, sold a hundred thousand copies. And, knowing Gally, I'll bet he would have started remembering where old Jane Wensleydale left off. *Good morning, Lord Tilbury. So nice to have seen you again.'*

The door closed. The proprietor of the Mammoth sat staring before him, his agony too keen to permit him even to say 'Cor!'

# 2

The spasm passed. Presently life seemed to steal back to that rigid form. It would be too much to say that Lord Tilbury became himself, but at least he began to function once more. Though pain and anguish rack the brow, the world's work has to be done. Like a convalescent reaching for his barley-water, he stretched out a shaking hand and took up *Tiny Tots* again.

And here it would be agreeable to leave him — the good man restoring his *morale* with refreshing draughts at the fount of wholesome literature. But this happy ending was not to be. Once more it was to be proved that this was not Lord Tilbury's lucky morning. Scarcely had he begun to read, when his eyes suddenly protruded from their sockets, his stout body underwent a strong convulsion, and from his parted lips there proceeded a loud snort. It was as if a viper had sprung from between the pages and bitten him on the chin.

And this was odd, because *Tiny Tots* is a journal not as a rule provocative of violent expressions of feeling. Ably edited by that well-known writer of tales for the young, the Rev. Aubrey Sellick, it strives always to take the sane middle course. Its editorial page, in particular, is a model of non-partisan moderation. And yet, amazingly, it was this same editorial page which had just made Lord

Tilbury's blood-pressure hit a new high.

It occurred to him that mental strain might have affected his eyesight. He blinked and took another look.

No, there it was, just as before.

### UNCLE WOGGLY TO HIS CHICKS

*Well, chickabiddies, how are you all? Minding what Nursie says and eating your spinach like good little men? That's right. I know the stuff tastes like a motorman's glove, but they say there's iron in it, and that's what puts hair on the chest.*

Lord Tilbury, having taken time out to make a noise like a leaking siphon, resumed his reading.

*Well, now let's get down to it. This week, my dear little souls, Uncle Woggly is going to put you on to a good thing. We all want to make a spot of easy money these hard times, don't we? Well, here's the lowdown, straight from the horse's mouth. All you have to do is to get hold of some mug and lure him into betting that a quart whisky bottle holds a quart of whisky.*

*Sounds rummy, what? I mean, that's what you would naturally think it would hold. So does the mug. But it isn't. It's really more, and I'll tell you why.*

*First you fill the bottle. This gives you your quart. Then you shove the cork in. And then — follow me closely here — you turn the bottle upside down and you'll find there's a sort of bulging-in part at the bottom. Well, slosh some whisky into that, and there you are. Because the bot, is now holding more than a quart and you scoop the stakes.*

*I have to acknowledge a sweet little letter from Frankie Kendon (Hendon) about his canary which goes tweet-tweet-tweet. Also one from Muriel Poot (Stow-in-the-Wold), who is going to lose her shirt if she ever bets anyone she knows how to spell 'tortoise' . . .*

Lord Tilbury had read enough. There was some good stuff further on about Willy Waters (Ponders End) and his cat Miggles, but he did not wait for it. He pressed the buzzer emotionally.

'*Tots!*' he cried, choking. '*Tiny Tots!* Who is editing *Tiny Tots* now?'

'Mr Sellick is the regular editor, Lord Tilbury,' replied his secretary, who knew everything and wore horn-rimmed spectacles to prove it, 'but he is away on his vacation. In his absence, the assistant editor is in charge of the paper, Mr Bodkin.'

'Bodkin!'

So loud was Lord Tilbury's voice and so sharply did his eyes bulge that the secretary recoiled a step, as if something had hit her.

'That popinjay!' said Lord Tilbury, in a strange, low, grating voice. 'I might have guessed it. I might have foreseen something like this. Send Mr Bodkin here at once.'

It was a judgement, he felt. This was what

came of going to public dinners and allowing yourself to depart from the principles of a lifetime. One false step, one moment of weakness when there were wheedling snakes of Baronets at your elbow, and what a harvest, what a reckoning!

He leaned back in his chair, tapping the desk with a paper-knife. He had just broken this, when there was a knock at the door and his young subordinate entered.

'Good morning, good morning, good morning,' said the latter affably. 'Want to see me about something?'

Monty Bodkin was rather an attractive popinjay, as popinjays go. He was tall and slender and lissom, and many people considered him quite good-looking. But not Lord Tilbury. He had disapproved of his appearance from their first meeting, thinking him much too well dressed, much too carefully groomed, and much too much like what he actually was, a member in good standing of the Drones Club. The proprietor of the Mammoth Publishing Company could not have put into words his ideal of a young journalist, but it would have been something rather shaggy, preferably with spectacles, certainly not wearing spats. And while Monty Bodkin was not actually spatted at the moment, there did undoubtedly hover about him a sort of spat aura.

'Ha!' said Lord Tilbury, sighting him.

He stared bleakly. His demeanour now was that of a Napoleon who, suffering from toothache, sees his way to taking it out on one of

15

his minor Marshals.

'Come in,' he growled.

'Shut the door,' he grunted.

'And don't grin like that,' he snarled. 'What the devil are you grinning for?'

The words were proof of the deeps of misunderstanding which yawned between the assistant editor of *Tiny Tots* and himself. Certainly something was splitting Monty Bodkin's face in a rather noticeable manner, but the latter could have taken his oath it was an ingratiating smile. He had intended it for an ingratiating smile, and unless something had gone extremely wrong with the works in the process of assembling it, that is what it should have come out as.

However, being a sweet-tempered popinjay and always anxious to oblige, he switched it off. He was feeling a little puzzled. The atmosphere seemed to him to lack chumminess, and he was at a loss to account for it.

'Nice day,' he observed tentatively. 'Never mind the day.'

'Right ho. Heard from Uncle Gregory lately?'

'Never mind your Uncle Gregory.'

'Right ho.'

'And don't say 'Right ho.''

'Right ho,' said Monty dutifully.

'Read this.'

Monty took the proffered copy of *Tots*.

'You want me to read aloud to you?' he said, feeling that this was matter.

'You need not trouble. I have already seen the passage in question. Here, where I am pointing.'

16

'Oh, ah, yes. Uncle Woggly. Right ho.'

'Will you stop saying 'Right ho'! . . . Well?'

'Eh?'

'You wrote that, I take it?'

'Oh, rather.'

'Cor!'

Monty was now definitely perplexed. He could conceal it from himself no longer that there was ill-will in the air. Lord Tilbury's had never been an elfin personality, but he had always been a good deal more winsome than this.

A possible solution of his employer's emotion occurred to him.

'You aren't worrying about it not being accurate, are you? Because that's quite all right I had it on the highest authority — from an old boy called Galahad Threepwood. Lord Emsworth's brother. You wouldn't have heard of him, of course, but he was a great lad about the metropolis at one time, and you can rely absolutely on anything he says about whisky bottles.'

He broke off, puzzled once more. He could not understand what had caused his companion to strike the desk in that violent manner.

'What the devil do you mean, you wretched imbecile,' demanded Lord Tilbury, speaking a little indistinctly, for he was sucking his fist, 'by putting stuff of this sort in *Tiny Tots?*'

'You don't like it?' said Monty groping.

'How do you suppose the mothers who read that drivel to their children will feel?' Monty was concerned. This opened up a new line of thought.

'Wrong tone, do you think?'

'Mugs . . . Betting . . . Whisky . . . You have probably lost us ten thousand subscribers.'

'I say, that never occurred to me. Yes, by Jove, I see what you mean now. Unfortunate slip, what? May quite easily cause alarm and despondency. Yes, yes, yes, to be sure. Oh, yes, indeed. Well, I can only say I'm sorry.'

'You can not only say you are sorry,' said Lord Tilbury, correcting this view, 'you can go to the cashier, draw a month's salary, get to blazes out of here, and never let me see your face in the building again.'

Monty's concern increased.

'But this sounds like the sack. Don't tell me that what you are hinting at is the sack?'

Speech failed Lord Tilbury. He jerked his thumb doorwards. And such was the magic of his personality that Monty found himself a moment later with his fingers on the handle. It's cold hardness seemed to wake him from a trance. He halted, making a sort of Custer's Last Stand.

'Reflect!' he said.

Lord Tilbury busied himself with his papers.

'Uncle Gregory won't like this,' said Monty reproachfully.

Lord Tilbury quivered for an instant as if somebody had stuck a bradawl into him, but preserved an aloof silence.

'Well, he won't, you know.' Monty had no wish to be severe, but he felt compelled to point this out. 'He takes all the trouble to get me a job, I mean to say, and now this happens. Oh, no, don't deceive yourself, Uncle Gregory will be vexed.'

'Get out,' said Lord Tilbury.

Monty fondled the door handle for a space, marshalling his thoughts. He had that to say which he rather fancied would melt the other's heart a goodish bit, but he was not quite sure how to begin.

'Haven't you gone?' said Lord Tilbury. Monty reassured him.

'Not yet. The fact is, there's something I rather wanted to call to your attention. You don't know it, but for private and personal reasons I particularly want to hold this *Tiny Tots* job for a year. There are wheels within wheels. It's a sort of bet, as a matter of fact.

Have you ever met a girl called Gertrude Butterwick? . . . However, it's a long story and I won't bother you with it now. But you can take it from me that there definitely are wheels within wheels and unless I continue in your employment, till somewhere around the middle of next June, my life will be a blank and all my hopes and dreams shattered. So how about it? Would you, on second thoughts, taking this into consideration, feel disposed to postpone the rash act till then? If you've any doubts as to my doing my bit, dismiss them. I would work like the dickens. First at the office, last to come away, and solid, selfless service all the time — no clock-watching, no folding of the hands in . . . '

'Get OUT!' said Lord Tilbury.

There was a silence.

'You will not reconsider?'

19

'No.'

'You are not to be moved?'

'No.'

Monty Bodkin drew himself up.

'Oh, right ho,' he said stiffly. 'Now we know where we are. Now we know where we stand. If that is the attitude you take, I suppose there is nothing to be done about it. Since you have no heart, no sympathy, no feeling, no bowels — of compassion, I mean — I have no alternative but to shove off. I have only two things to say to you, Lord Tilbury. One is that you have ruined a man's life. The other is Pip-pip.'

He passed from the room, erect and dignified, like some young aristocrat of the French Revolution stepping into the tumbril. Lord Tilbury's secretary removed her ear from the door just in time to avoid a nasty flesh-wound.

★　★　★

A month's salary in his pocket, chagrin in his heart, and in his soul that urgent desire for a quick one which comes to young men at times like this, Monty Bodkin stood hesitating in the doorway of Tilbury House. And Fate, watching him, found itself compelled to do a bit of swift thinking.

'Now, shall I,' mused Fate, 'send this sufferer to have his snort at the Bunch of Grapes round the corner? Or shall I put him in a taxi and shoot him off to the Drones Club, where he will meet his old friend, Hugo Carmody, with momentous results?'

It was no light decision to have to make. Much depended on it. It would affect the destinies of Ronald Fish and his betrothed, Sue Brown; of Clarence, ninth Earl of Emsworth, and his pig, Empress of Blandings; of Lord Tilbury, of the Mammoth Publishing Company; of Sir Gregory Parsloe-Parsloe, Bart, of Matchingham Hall; and of that unpleasant little man, Percy Pilbeam, late editor of *Society Spice* and now proprietor of the Argus Private Inquiry Agency.

'H'm!' said Fate.

'Oh, dash it!' said Fate. 'Let's make it the Drones.'

And so it came about that Monty, some twenty minutes later, was seated in the club smoking-room, side by side with young Mr Carmody, sipping a Lizard's Breath and relating the story of his shattered career.

'Turfed out!' he concluded, with a bitter laugh. 'Driven into the snow! Well, that's Life, I suppose.'

Hugo Carmody was not unsympathetic, but he had a fair mind and privately considered that Lord Tilbury had acted with great good sense. Obviously, felt Hugo, the whole secret of success, if you were running a business and had Monty Bodkin working for you, was to get rid of him at the earliest possible moment.

'Tough,' he said. 'Still, what do you want with a job? You're rolling in the stuff.'

Monty admitted that he was not unblessed with this world's goods, but said that that was not the point.

'Money's got nothing to do with it. It was

holding down the job that mattered. There are wheels within wheels. I'll tell you all about it, shall I?'

'No thanks.'

'Just as you like. Another spot? Waiter, two more spots.'

'Anyway,' said Hugo, with a kindly desire to point out the bright side, 'if you hadn't got fired now, you'd have been bound to have got fired sooner or later, what? I mean to say, I don't see how you could ever have been much good to a concern like the Mammoth, unless they had used you as a paperweight. And I'll bet you were all wrong about that whisky bottle.'

Monty's spirit had been a good deal reduced by recent happenings, but he could not let this pass.

'I'll bet I wasn't,' he said warmly. 'I had the information straight from an authoritative source. Lord Emsworth's brother, old Gally Threepwood. My Uncle Gregory's place in Shropshire is only about a couple of miles from Blandings, and when I was a kid I used to be popping in and out all the time, and one day old Gally drew me aside . . . ' Hugo was interested.

'Your Uncle Gregory? Would that be Sir Gregory Parsloe?'

'Yes.'

'Well, well. I never knew you were Parsloe's nephew.'

'Why, have you met him?'

'Of course I've met him. I've been down at Blandings all the summer.'

'Not really? Oh, but, of course, I was

22

forgetting. You and Ronnie Fish have always been pals, haven't you? You were staying with him?'

'No. I was secretarying for old Emsworth. A nice, soft job. I've chucked it now.'

'I thought a fellow called Baxter was his secretary.'

'My dear chap, you aren't abreast. Baxter left ages ago.'

Monty sighed, as a young man will who is made to realize that time is passing.

'Yes,' he agreed, 'I've lost touch with Blandings a bit. It must be three years since I was there. Somehow, ever since this business of going to the South of France in the summer started, I've never seemed to be able to get down. How are they all? Is old Emsworth much about the same?'

'What was he like when you used to infest the place?'

'Oh, a mild, dreamy, absent-minded sort of old bird. Talked about nothing but roses and pumpkins.'

'Then he is much about the same, except that now he talks about nothing but pigs.'

'Pigs, eh?'

'His Empress of Blandings won the silver medal in the Fat Pigs class at last year's Shropshire Agricultural Show, and is confidently expected to repeat this year. This gives the ninth Earl's conversation a porcine trend.'

'How's old Gally?'

'Still going strong.'

'And Beach?'

'Buttling away as hard as ever.'

'Well, well, well,' said Monty sentimentally. 'The old spot certainly doesn't seem to have changed much since ... Good Lord!' he exclaimed abruptly, spilling the remains of his cocktail over his trousers and in his emotion not noticing it. He had been electrified by a sudden idea.

Although since his arrival at the Drones we have seen Monty Bodkin relaxed, at his ease, chatting of this and that, he had never forgotten that he had just lost a job and that, owing to there being wheels within wheels, it was imperative that he secure another. And a bright light had just flashed upon him.

Minds like Monty Bodkin's may not always work at express speed, but they are subject to the same subconscious processes as those of more brain-burdened men. Right from the moment when Hugo had mentioned that he had been acting as secretary to the Earl of Emsworth, he had had a sort of nebulous idea that there was a big and important message wrapped up in this information. If only he could locate it. His subconscious mind had been having a go at the problem ever since, and now it passed the solution up to headquarters.

He quivered with excitement.

'Just a second,' he said. 'Let's get this straight. You say you were old Emsworth's secretary.'

'Yes.'

'And you've been fired?'

'I have not been fired,' said Hugo Carmody with justifiable annoyance. 'I've resigned. If you

24

really want to know, I'm engaged to Lord Emsworth's niece, and I'm taking her down to Worcestershire in about half an hour to meet the head of the clan.'

Monty was too preoccupied to offer felicitations.

'When did you leave?'

'Day before yesterday.'

'Anybody been engaged to take your place?'

'Not that I know of.'

'Hugo,' said Monty earnestly, 'I'm going to get that job. I'm going to phone straight off to my uncle Gregory to snaffle it for me without delay.'

Hugo looked at him commiseratingly. It was painful to him to be in the position of having to throw spanners into an old friend's daydreams, but he felt the poor chap ought to be told the truth.

'I shouldn't count too much on Sir G. Parsloe getting you jobs with old Emsworth,' he said. 'As I remarked before, you aren't quite abreast of modern Blandings history. Relations between Blandings Castle and Matchingham Hall are a bit strained just at the moment. Not long ago your uncle did the dirty on old Emsworth by luring his pig-man away from him.'

'Oh, a little thing like that . . . '

'Well, try this one. Lord Emsworth has a fixed idea that your uncle is plotting to nobble Empress of Blandings.'

'What! Why?'

'He's got it all worked out. Your uncle owns a pig called Pride of Matchingham, and with the Empress out of the way it would probably cop the silver medal at the Show. So when the Empress was stolen the other day . . . '

'Stolen! Who stole her?'

'Ronnie.'

Monty's head, never strong, was beginning to swim.

'What Ronnie? Do you mean Ronnie Fish?'

'That's right. It's a complicated story. Ronnie's engaged to a girl, and he can't marry her unless old Emsworth coughs up his money.'

'He's Ronnie's trustee?'

'Yes.'

'Trustees are tough eggs,' said Monty thoughtfully. 'I had one till I was twenty-five, and it used to take me weeks of patient spadework to extract so much as a tenner from the man.'

'So, in order to ingratiate himself with old Emsworth, Ronnie pinched his pig.'

Once more Monty became conscious of that swimming sensation. He could not follow this.

'But why-?'

'Quite simple. His idea was to kidnap the pig, hide it somewhere for a day or two, and then pretend to find it and so win the old boy's gratitude. After which, to have put the bite on him would have been an easy task. It was a very sound scheme indeed. Of course, it all went wrong. Any scheme of Ronnie's would.'

'What went wrong?'

'Well, various unforeseen events occurred, and in the end the animal was discovered in a caravan belonging to Baxter. I told you it was a little complicated,' said Hugo kindly, noting the strained expression on his friend's face.

Monty agreed, but on one point he found himself reasonably clear.

'Then old Emsworth must have known that my uncle didn't steal the pig? I mean, if it was found in Baxter's . . . '

'Not at all. He thinks Baxter was working for your uncle. I tell you once more, as I was saying at the beginning, that, taking it by and large, I don't think I'd rely too much on Sir Gregory's pull, if I were you.'

Monty chewed his lip thoughtfully.

'There's no harm in trying.'

'Oh, have a shot, by all means. I'm only saying it isn't one of those stone-cold certainties that old Emsworth will engage you as his secretary purely out of love for Sir G. Parsloe.' Hugo looked at the clock, and rose. 'I've got to be going,' he said, 'if I don't want to miss that train.'

Monty accompanied him to the front steps, and Hugo hailed a cab.

'It might work,' said Monty pensively.

'Oh, rather. Certainly.'

'They might have had a what-is-it — a reconciliation by this time.'

'I didn't see any signs of it when I left. And now I must really rush,' said Hugo, getting into the cab. 'Oh, by the way,' he added, leaning out of the window, 'there's just one thing. If you do go to Blandings, you'll find the second prettiest girl in England there. Keep well away, is my advice.'

'Eh?'

'Ronnie's fiancee. They're both at the Castle, and if you exhibit too much enthusiasm about

27

her he is extremely apt to strangle you with his bare hands. Personally,' said Hugo. 'I regard jealousy as a mug's game, my view being that where there is thingummy there should be what-d'you-call-it. Perfect love, ditto trust. But Ronnie belongs more to the Othello or green-eyed monster school of thought. He was so jealous of a fellow called Pilbeam that he went so far on one occasion as to wreck a restaurant when he found him apparently dining with Sue in it. Oh, yes, a bird of strong feelings and keen sensibilities, old Ronnie.'

'How do you mean apparently dining?'

'She was really dining with me. Blameless Hugo. But Ronnie didn't know that. He discovered Sue in conversation with this Pilbeam — you'll find him at the Castle too, . . . '

'Sue?' said Monty.

'Her name's Sue. Sue Brown.'

'What!'

'Sue Brown.'

'Not Sue Brown? You don't mean a girl called Sue Brown who was in the chorus at the Regal?'

'That's the one. You seem to know her.'

'Know her? I should say I do know her. Certainly I know her. I haven't seen her for about a couple of years, but at one time . . . Dear old Sue! Good old Sue! One of the sweetest things on earth, old Sue. You don't often come across such a ripper. Why . . . '

Hugo shook his head deprecatingly.

'Precisely the spirit against which I am warning you. Just the very tone you would do well to avoid. I think we may say that it is an excellent thing that your chances of getting to Blandings Castle are so remote. I should hate to read in my morning paper that your swollen body had been found floating in the lake.'

For some moments after the cab had rolled away. Monty remained in deep thought on the steps. The news that Sue Brown, of all people, was at Blandings Castle had certainly made the prospect of securing employment there additionally attractive. It would be great seeing old Sue again.

As for all that pig business, he refused to allow himself to be discouraged. Probably much exaggerated. An excellent fellow, Hugo Carmody, one of the best, but always inclined to make a good story out of everything.

Full of optimism, Monty Bodkin went along the passage to the telephone-room.

'I want a trunk call,' he said. 'Matchingham 8–3.'

# 3

Some twenty-four hours after Monty Bodkin had put in his longdistance call to Matchingham 8–3, an observant bird, winging its way over Blandings Castle and taking a bird's-eye view of its parks, gardens, and messuages, would have noticed a couple walking up and down the terrace which fronts the main entrance of that stately home of England. And narrowing its gaze and shading its eyes with a claw, for the morning sun was strong, it would have seen that one of the pair was a small, sturdy young man of pink complexion, the other an extremely pretty girl in a green linen dress with a Quaker collar. Ronald Overbury Fish was saying good-bye to his Sue preparatory to driving in to Market Blandings and taking the twelve-forty train east. He was going to Norfolk to be best man at the wedding of his cousin George.

He did not anticipate that the parting would be a long one, for he expected to return on the morrow. Nevertheless, he felt constrained to give Sue a few words of advice as to her deportment during his absence.

First and foremost, he urged, she must use every feminine wile to fascinate his Uncle Clarence.

'Right,' said Sue. She was a tiny girl, with an enchanting smile and big blue eyes. These last were now sparkling with ready intelligence. She followed his reasoning perfectly. Lord Emsworth, though he had promised Ronnie his money, had not yet given it to him and might conceivably change his mind. Obviously, therefore, he must be fascinated. The task, moreoever, would not be a distasteful one. In the brief time during which she had had the pleasure of his acquaintance, she had grown very fond of that mild and dreamy peer.

'Right,' she said.

'Keep surging round him like glue.'

'Right,' said Sue.

'In fact, I think you had better go and talk pig to him the moment I've left.'

'Right,' said Sue.

'And about Aunt Constance . . . ' said Ronnie.

He paused, frowning. He always frowned when he thought of his aunt, Lady Constance Keeble.

When Ronald Fish, the Last of the Fishes, only son of Lady Julia Fish, and nephew to Clarence, ninth Earl of Emsworth, had announced that a marriage had been arranged and would shortly take place between himself and a unit of the Regal Theatre chorus, he had had what might be called a mixed Press. Some of the notices were good, others not.

Beach, the Castle butler, who had fostered for eighteen years a semi-paternal attitude towards Ronnie and had fallen in love with Sue at first sight, liked the idea. So did the Hon. Galahad Threepwood, who when a dashing young man about town in the nineties had wanted to marry Sue's mother. As for Lord Emsworth himself, he had said 'Oh, ah?' in an absent voice on hearing the news and had gone on thinking about pigs.

It was, as so often happens on these occasions, from the female side of the family that the jarring note had proceeded. Women are seldom without their class prejudices. Their views on the importance of Rank diverge from those of the poet Burns. We have seen how Lady Julia felt about the match. The disapproval of her sister Constance was equally pronounced. She grieved over this blot which was about to be splashed upon the escutcheon of a proud family, and let the world see that she grieved. She sighed a good deal, and when she was not sighing kept her lips tightly pressed together.

So now when Ronnie mentioned her name, he frowned. 'About Aunt Constance . . . '

He was going on to add that, should his Aunt Constance have the nerve during his absence to put on dog and do any of that haughty County stuff to his betrothed, the latter would be well advised to kick her in the face; when there emerged from the house a young man with marcelled hair, a shifty expression, and a small and repellent moustache. He stood for an instant on the threshold, hesitated, caught Ronnie's eye, smiled weakly, and disappeared again. Ronnie stood gazing tensely at the spot where he had been.

'Little blighter!' he growled, grinding his teeth gently. The sight of P. Frobisher Pilbeam always tended to wake the fiend that slept in Ronald Fish. 'Looking for you, I suppose!'

Sue started nervously.

'Oh, I shouldn't think so. We've hardly spoken for days.'

'He doesn't ever bother you now?'

'Oh, no.'

'What's he doing here, anyway? I thought he'd left.'

'I suppose Lord Emsworth asked him to stay on. What *does* he matter?'

'He used to send you flowers!'

'I know, but . . . '

'He trailed you to that restaurant that night.'

'I know. But surely you aren't worried about him any longer?'

'Me?' said Ronnie.

'No! Of course not.'

He spoke a little gruffly, for he was embarrassed. It is always embarrassing for a young man of sensibility to realize that he is making a priceless ass of himself. He knew perfectly well that there was nothing between Sue and this Pilbeam perisher and never had been anything. And yet the sight of him about the place could make him flush and scowl and get all throaty.

Of course, the whole trouble with him was that where Sue was concerned he suffered from an inferiority complex. He found it so difficult to believe that a girl like her could really care for a bird so short and pink as himself. He was always afraid that one of these days it would suddenly dawn upon her what a mistake she had made in supposing herself to be in love with him and would race off and fall in love with somebody else. Not Pilbeam, of course, but suppose somebody tall and lissom came along . . .

Sue was pressing her point. She wanted this thing settled and out of the way. The only cloud on her happiness was that tendency of her Ronald's towards jealousy, to which Hugo Carmody had alluded so feelingly in his conversation with Monty Bodkin. Jealousy when two people had come together and knew that they loved one another always seemed to her silly and incomprehensible. She had the frank, uncomplicated mind of a child.

'You promise you won't worry about him again?'

'Absolutely not.'

'Nor about anybody else?'

'Positively not. Couldn't possibly happen again.' He paused. 'The only thing is,' he said broodingly, 'I *am* so dashed short!'

'You're just the right height.'

'And pink.'

'My favourite colour. You're a precious little pink cherub, and I love you.'

'You really do?'

'Of course I do.'

'But suppose you changed your mind?'

'You are a chump, Ronnie.'

'I know I'm a chump, but I still say — Suppose you changed your mind?'

'It's much more likely that you'll change yours.'

'What!'

'Suppose when your mother arrives she talks you over?'

'What absolute rot!'

34

'I don't imagine she will approve of me.'

'Of course she'll approve of you.'

'Lady Constance doesn't.'

Ronnie uttered a spirited cry.

'Aunt Constance! I was trying to think who it was we were talking about when that Pilbeam blister came to a head. Listen. If Aunt Constance tries to come the old aristocrat over you while I'm away, punch her in the eye. Don't put up for a moment with any pursed-lip-and-lorgnette stuff.'

'And what do I do when your mother reaches for her lorgnette?'

'Oh, you won't have anything of that sort from Mother.'

'Hasn't she got a lorgnette?'

'Mother's all right.'

'Not like Lady Constance?'

'A bit, to look at. But quite different, really. Aunt Constance is straight Queen Elizabeth. Mother's a cheery soul.'

'She'll try to talk you over, all the same.'

'She won't.'

'She will. 'Ronald, my dear boy, really! This absurd infatuation. Most extraordinary!' I can feel it in my bones.'

'Mother couldn't talk like that if you paid her. I keep telling you she's a genial egg.'

'She won't like me.'

'Of course she'll like you. Don't be . . . what the dickens is that word.'

Sue was biting her lip with her small, very white tooth. Her blue eyes had clouded.

'I wish you weren't going away, Ronnie.'

'It's only for tonight.'

'Have you really got to go?'

'Afraid so. Can't very well let poor old George down. He's relying on me. Besides, I want to watch his work at the altar rails. Pick up some hints on technique which'll come in useful when you and I . . . '

'If ever we do.'

'Do stop talking like that,' begged Ronnie.

'I'm sorry. But I do wish you hadn't got to go away. I'm scared. It's this place. It's so big and old. It makes me feel like a puppy that's got into a cathedral.'

Ronnie turned and gave his boyhood home an appraising glance.

'I suppose it is a fairly decent-sized old shack,' he admitted, having run his eye up to the battlements and back again. 'I never really gave the thing much thought before, but, now you mention it, I have seen smaller places. But there's nothing about it to scare anybody.'

'There is, if you were born and brought up in a villa in the suburbs. I feel that at any moment all the ghosts of your ancestors will come popping out, pointing at me and shouting 'What business have *you* here, you little rat?' '

'They'd better not let me catch them at it,' said Ronnie warmly. 'Don't be so . . . what on earth is that word? I know it begins with an m. You mustn't feel like that. You've gone like a breeze here. Uncle Clarence likes you. Uncle Gally likes you. Everybody likes you — except Aunt Constance. And a fat lot we care what Aunt Constance thinks, what?'

36

'I keep worrying about your mother.'

'And I keep telling you . . . '

'I know. But I've got that funny feeling you get sometimes that things are going to happen. Trouble, trouble. A dark lady coming over the water.'

'Mother's fair.'

'It doesn't make it any better. I've got that presentiment.'

'Well, I don't see why you should. Everything's gone without a hitch so far.'

'That's just what I mean. I've been so frightfully happy, and I feel that all the beastly things that spoil happiness are just biding their time. Waiting. They can't do nothin' till Martin gets here!'

'Eh?'

'I was thinking of a thing one of the girls used to play on her gramophone in the dressing-room, the last show I was in. It was about a man who goes to a haunted house, and demon cats keep coming in, each bigger and more horrible than the last, and as each one comes in it says to the others, 'Shall we start in on him now?' and they shake their heads and say, 'Not yet. We can't do nothin' till Martin gets here.' Well, I can't help feeling that Martin soon will be here.'

Ronnie had found the word for which he had been searching. 'Morbid. I knew it began with an *m*. Don't be so dashed morbid!'

Sue gave herself a little shake, like a dog coming out of a pond. She put her arm in Ronnie's and gave it a squeeze. 'I suppose it is morbid.'

'Of course it is.'

'Everything may be all right.'

'Everything's going to be fine. Mother will be crazy about you. She won't be able to help herself. Because of all the . . . '

On the verge of becoming lyrical, Ronnie broke off abruptly. The Castle car had just come round the corner from the stables with Voules, the chauffeur, at the helm.

'I didn't know it was as late as that,' said Ronnie discontentedly.

The car drew up beside them, and he eyed Voules with a touch of austerity. It was not that he disliked the chauffeur, a man whom he had known since his boyhood and one with whom he had many a time played village cricket. It was simply that there are moments when a fellow wishes to be free from observation, and one of these is when he is about to bid farewell to his affianced.

However, there was good stuff in Ronald Fish. Ignoring the chauffeur's eye, which betrayed a disposition to be roguish, he gathered his loved one to him and, his face now a pretty cerise, kissed her with all a Fish's passion. This done, he entered the car, leaned out of the window, waved, went on waving, and continued to wave till Sue was out of sight. Then, sitting down, he gazed straight before him, breathing a little heavily through the nostrils.

Sue, having lingered until the car had turned the corner of the drive and was hidden by a clump of rhododendrons, walked pensively back to the terrace.

The August sun was now blazing down in all its imperious majesty. Insects were chirping sleepily in the grass, and the hum of bees in the lavender borders united with the sun and the chirping to engender sloth. A little wistfully Sue looked past the shrubbery at the cedar-shaded lawn where the Hon. Galahad Threepwood, thoughtfully sipping a whisky and soda, lay back in a deep chair, cool and at his ease. There was another chair beside him, and she knew that he had placed it there for her.

But duty is duty, no matter how warm the sun and drowsy the drone of insects. Ronnie had asked her to go and talk pig to Lord Emsworth, and the task must be performed.

She descended the broad stone steps and, turning westward, made for the corner of the estate sacred to that noble Berkshire sow, Empress of Blandings.

* * *

The boudoir of the Empress was situated in a little meadow, dappled with buttercups and daisies, round two sides of which there flowed in a silver semicircle the stream which fed the lake. Lord Emsworth, as his custom was, had pottered off there directly after breakfast, and now, at half past twelve, he was still standing, in company with his pig-man Pirbright, draped bonelessly over the rail of the sty, his mild eyes beaming with the light of a holy devotion.

From time to time he sniffed sensuously. Elsewhere throughout this fair domain the air was fragrant with the myriad scents of high summer, but not where Lord Emsworth was doing his sniffing. Within a liberal radius of the Empress's headquarters other scents could not compete. This splendid animal diffused an aroma which was both distinctive and arresting. Attractive, too, if you liked that sort of thing, as Lord Emsworth did.

Between Empress of Blandings and these two human beings who ministered to her comfort there was a sharp contrast in physique. Lord Emsworth was tall and thin and scraggy, Pirbright tall and thin and scraggier. The Empress, on the other hand, could have passed in a dim light for a captive balloon, fully inflated and about to make its trial trip. The modern craze for slimming had found no votary in her. She liked her meals large and regular, and had never done a reducing exercise in her life. Watching her now as she tucked into a sort of hash of bran, acorns, potatoes, linseed, and swill, the ninth Earl of Emsworth felt his heart leap up in much the same way as that of the poet Wordsworth used to do when he beheld a rainbow in the sky.

'What a picture, Pirbright!' he said reverently.

'Ur, m'lord.'

She's bound to win. Can't help herself.'

'Yur, m'lord.'

'Unless . . . We mustn't let her get stolen again, Pirbright.'

'Nur, m'lord.'

Lord Emsworth adjusted his pince-nez thoughtfully. The ecstatic pig-gleam had faded from his eyes. His face was darkened by a cloud of concern. He was thinking of that bad Baronet, Sir Gregory Parsloe.

The theft of the Empress and the subsequent discovery of her in his ex-secretary Baxter's caravan had at first mystified Lord Emsworth completely. Why Baxter, though a recognised eccentric, should have been going about Shropshire stealing pigs seemed to him a problem incapable of solution.

But calm reflection had brought the answer to the riddle. Obviously the fellow had been a minion in the pay of Sir Gregory, operating throughout under orders from the Big Shot. And what was disquieting him now was the conviction that the danger was not yet past. Baffled once, the Baronet, he felt, was crouching for another spring. With two weeks still to pass before the Agricultural Show, there was ample time for his subtle brain to conceive another hideous plot. At any moment, in short, the bounder was liable to come sneaking in, mask on face and poison-needle in hand, intent on nobbling the favourite.

His eyes roamed the paddock. It was a lonely spot, far from human habitation. A pig, assaulted here by Baronet, might well cry for help unheard.

'Do you think she's safe in this sty, Pirbright?' he asked anxiously. 'I fear we ought to move her to that new one by the kitchen garden. It's near your cottage.'

What repy the Vice-President in charge of Pigs would have made to this suggestion — whether it

would have been an 'Ur,' a 'Yur,' or a 'Nur' —
will never be known. For at this moment there
appeared a figure at the sight of whom he
touched his forelock and receded respectfully
into the background.

Lord Emsworth, whose pince-nez had fallen
off, put them on again and peered mildly, like a
sheep looking over a fence.

'Ah, Connie, my dear.'

There had been times when the sudden advent
of his sister, Lady Constance Keeble, at a
moment when he was drooping his long body
over the rail of the Empress's sanctum, would
have caused him agitationand discomfort. She
had a way of appearing from nowhere and
upbraiding him for expending on pigs time
which had better have been devoted to
correspondence connected with the business of
the estate. But for the last two days, since the
departure of that young fellow Carmondy, he
had had no secretary; and a man can't be
expected to attend to his correspondence
without a secretary. His conscience, accordingly,
was clear, and he spoke with none of that
irritable defensiveness, as of some wild creature
at bay, which he sometimes displayed on these
occasions.

'Ah, Connie, my dear, you are just in time
to give me your advice. I was saying to
Pirbright . . . '

Lady Constance did not wait for the sentence
to be completed. In her dealings with the head
of the family, she was always inclined to infuse
into her manner a suggestion of a rather

short-tempered nurse with a rather fat-headed child.

'Never mind what you were saying to Pirbright. Do you know what time it is?'

Lord Emsworth did not. He never did. Beyond a vague idea that when it got too dark for him to see the Empress at a range of four feet, it was getting on for dinner-time, he took little account of the hours.

'It's nearly one, and we have people coming to lunch at half-past.'

Lord Emsworth assimilated this.

'Lunch? Oh, ah, yes. Yes, of course. Lunch, to be sure. Yes. Lunch. You think I ought to come in and wash my hands?'

'And your face. It's covered with mud. And change those clothes. And those shoes. And put on a clean collar. Really, Clarence, you're as much trouble as a baby. Why you want to waste your time staring at beastly pigs, I can't imagine.'

Lord Emsworth accompanied her across the paddock, but his face — there was hardly any mud on it at all, really, just a couple of splashes or so — was sullen and mutinous. This was not the first time his sister had alluded in this offensive manner to one whom he regarded as the supreme ornament of her sex and species. Beastly pigs, indeed! He pondered moodily on the curious inability of his immediate circle to appreciate the importance of the Empress in the scheme of things. Not one of them seemed to have the sagacity to realize her true worth.

Well, yes, one, perhaps. That little girl

what-was-her-name, who was going to marry his nephew Ronald, had always displayed a pleasing interest in the silver medallist.

'Nice girl,' he said, following this train of thought to its conclusion.

'What *are* you talking about, Clarence?' asked Lady Constance wearily.

'Who is a nice girl?'

'That little girl of Ronald's. I've forgotten her name. Smith, is it?'

'Brown,' said Lady Constance shortly.

'That's right, Brown. Nice girl.'

'You are entitled to your opinion, I suppose,' said Lady Constance.

They walked on in silence for some moments.

'While we are on the subject of Miss Brown,' said Lady Constance, speaking the name as she always did with her teeth rather tightly clenched and a stony look in her eyes, 'I forgot to tell you that I had a letter from Julia this morning.'

'*Did you?*' said Lord Emsworth, giving the matter some two-fifty-sevenths of his attention. 'Capital, capital. Who,' he asked politely, 'is Julia?'

Lady Constance was within easy reach of his head and could quite comfortably have hit it, but she refrained. *Noblesse oblige.*

'*Julia?*' she said, with a rising inflection. 'There's only one Julia in our family.'

'Oh, you mean Julia?' said Lord Emsworth, enlightened. 'And what had Julia got to say for herself? She's at Biarritz, isn't she?' he said, making a great mental effort. 'Having a good time, I hope?'

44

'She's in London.'

'Oh, yes?'

'And she is coming here tomorrow by the two forty-five.'

Lord Emsworth's vague detachment vanished. His sister Julia was not a woman to whose visits he looked forward with joyous enthusiasm.

'Why?' he asked, with a strong note of complaint in his voice. 'It is the only good train in the afternoon, and gets her here in plenty of time for dinner.'

'I mean, why is she coming?'

It would be too much to say that Lady Constance snorted. Women of her upbringing do not snort. But she certainly sniffed.

'Well, really!' she said. 'Does it strike you as so odd that a mother whose only son has announced his intention of marrying a ballet-girl should wish to see her?'

Lord Emsworth considered this.

'Not ballet-girl. Chorus-girl, I understood.'

'It's the same thing.'

'I don't think so,' said Lord Emsworth doubtfully. 'I must ask Galahad.' A sudden idea struck him. 'Don't you like this Smith girl?'

'Brown.'

'Don't you like this Brown girl?'

'I do not.'

'Don't you want her to marry Ronald?'

'I should have thought I had made my views on that matter sufficiently clear. I think the whole thing deplorable. I am not a snob . . . '

'But you are,' said Lord Emsworth, cleverly putting his finger on the flaw in her reasoning.

45

Lady Constance bridled.

'Well, if it is snobbish to prefer your nephew to marry in his own class . . .'

'Galahad would have married her mother thirty years ago if he hadn't been shipped off to South Africa.'

'Galahad was — and is — capable of anything.'

'I can remember her mother,' said Lord Emsworth meditatively. 'Galahad took me to the Tivoli once, when she was singing there. Dolly Henderson. A little bit of a thing in pink tights, with the jolliest smile you ever saw. Made you think of spring mornings. The gallery joined in the chorus, I recollect. Bless my soul, how did it go? Turn turn tumpty turn . . . Or was it Umpty tiddly tiddly pum?'

'Never mind how it went,' said Lady Constance. One reminiscencer in the family, she considered, was quite enough. 'And we are not talking of the girl's mother. The only thing I have to say about Miss Brown's mother is that I wish she had never had a daughter.'

'Well, I like her,' said Lord Emsworth stoutly. 'A very sweet, pretty, nice-mannered little thing, and extremely sound on pigs. I was saying so to young Pilbeam only yesterday.'

'Pilbeam!' cried Lady Constance.

She spoke with feeling, for the name had reminded her of another grievance. She had been wanting to get to the bottom of this Pilbeam mystery for days. About that young man's presence at the Castle there seemed to her something almost uncanny. She had no

46

recollection of his arrival. It was as if he had materialized out of thin air. And being a conventional hostess, with a conventional hostess's dislike of the irregular, she objected to finding that visitors with horrible moustaches, certainly not invited by herself, had suddenly begun to pervade the home like an escape of gas.

'Who is that nasty little man?' she demanded.

'He's an investigator.'

'A *what?*'

'A private investigator. He investigates privately.' There was a touch of quiet pride in Lord Emsworth's voice. He was sixty years old, and this was the first time he had ever found himself in the romantic role of an employer of private investigators. 'He runs the something detective agency. The Argus. That's it. The Argus Private Inquiry Agency.'

Lady Constance breathed emotionally.

'Ballet-girls . . . Detectives . . . I wonder you don't invite a few skittle-sharps here.'

Lord Emsworth said he did not know any skittle-sharps.

'And is one permitted to ask what a private detective is doing as a guest at Blandings Castle?'

'I got him down to investigate that mystery of the Empress's disappearance.'

'Well, that idiotic pig of yours has been back in her sty for days. What possible reason can there be for this man staying on?'

'Ah, that was Galahad's idea. It was Galahad's suggestion that he should stay on till after the Agricultural Show. He thought it would be a

47

good thing to have somebody like that handy in case Parsloe tried any more of his tricks.'

'Clarence!'

'And I consider,' went on Lord Emsworth firmly, 'that he was quite right. I know it was Baxter who actually stole my pig, and you will no doubt say that Baxter is notoriously potty. But Galahad feels — and I feel — that it was not primarily his pottiness that led him to steal the Empress. We both think that Parsloe was behind the whole thing. And Galahad maintains — and I agree with him — that it is only a question of time before he makes another attempt. So the more watchers we have on the place the better. Especially if they have trained minds and are used to mixing with criminals, like Pilbeam.'

'Clarence, you're insane!'

'No, I am not insane,' retorted Lord Emsworth warmly. 'I know Parsloe. And Galahad knows Parsloe. You should read some of the stories about him in Galahad's book — thoroughly well documented stories, he assures me, showing the sort of man he was when Galahad used to go about London with him in their young days. Are you aware that in the year 1894 Parsloe filled Galahad's dog Towser up with steak and onions just before the big Rat contest, so that his own terrier Banjo should win? A fellow who stuck at nothing to attain his ends. And he's just the same today. Hasn't changed a bit. Look at the way he stole that man Wellbeloved away from me — the chap who used to be my pig-man before Pirbright. Fellow capable of that is capable of anything.'

Lady Constance spurned the grass with a frenzied foot. She would have preferred to kick her brother with it, but one has one's breeding.

'You are a perfect imbecile about Sir Gregory,' she cried. 'You ought to be ashamed of yourself. So ought Galahad, if it were possible for him to be ashamed of anything. You are behaving like a couple of half-witted children. I hate this idiotic quarrel. If there's one thing that's detestable in the country, it is being on bad terms with one's neighbours.'

'I don't care how bad terms I'm on with Parsloe.'

'Well, I do. And that is why I was so glad to oblige him when he rang up about his nephew.'

'Eh?'

'I was delighted to have the chance of proving to him that there was at least one sane person in Blandings Castle.'

'Nephew? What nephew?'

'Young Montague Bodkin. You ought to remember him. He was here often enough when he was a boy.'

'Bodkin? Bodkin? Bodkin?'

'Oh, for pity's sake, Clarence, don't keep saying 'Bodkin' as if you were a parrot. If you have forgotten him, as you forget everything that happened more than ten minutes ago, it does not matter in the least. The point is that Sir Gregory asked me as a personal favour to engage him as your secretary . . . '

Lord Emsworth was a mild man, but he could be stirred.

'Well, I'm dashed! Well, I'm hanged! The man

steals my pig-man and engineers the theft of my pig, and he has the nerve.'

' . . . and I said I should be delighted.'

'What!'

'I said I should be delighted.'

'You don't mean you've done it?'

'Certainly. It's all arranged.'

'You mean you're letting a nephew of Parsloe's loose in Blandings Castle, with two weeks to go before the Agricultural Show?'

'He arrives tomorrow by the two-forty-five,' said Lady Constance.

And as she had thrown her bomb and seen it explode and had now reached the front door and had no wish to waste her time listening to futile protests, she swept into the house and left Lord Emsworth standing.

He remained standing for perhaps a minute. Then the imperative necessity of sharing this awful news with a cooler, wiser mind than his own stirred him to life and activity. His face drawn, his long legs trembling beneath him, he hurried towards the lawn where his brother Galahad, whisky and soda in hand, reclined in his deckchair.

# 4

Cooled by the shade of the cedar, refreshed by the contents of the amber glass in which ice tinkled so musically when he lifted it to his lips, the Hon. Galahad, at the moment of Lord Emsworth's arrival, had achieved a Nirvana-like repose. Storms might be raging elsewhere in the grounds of Blandings Castle, but there on the lawn there was peace — the perfect unruffled peace which in this world seems to come only to those who have done nothing whatever to deserve it.

The Hon. Galahad Threepwood, in his fifty-seventh year, was a dapper little gentleman on whose grey but still thickly-covered head the weight of a consistently misspent life rested lightly. His flannel suit sat jauntily upon his wiry frame, a black-rimmed monocle gleamed jauntily in his eye. Everything about this Musketeer of the nineties was jaunty. It was a standing mystery to all who knew him that one who had had such an extraordinarily good time all his life should, in the evening of that life, be so superbly robust. Wan contemporaries who had once painted a gas-lit London red in his company and were now doomed to an existence of dry toast, Vichy water, and German cure resorts felt very strongly on this point. A man of his antecedents, they considered, ought by rights to be rounding off his career in a bath-chair instead of flitting about the place, still chaffing head waiters as of old and calling for the wine list without a tremor.

A little cock-sparrow of a man. One of the Old Guard which dies but does not surrender. Sitting there under the cedar, he looked as if he were just making ready to go to some dance-hall of the days when dance-halls were dance-halls, from which in the quiet dawn it would take at least three waiters, two commissionaires and a policeman to eject him.

In a world so full of beautiful things, where he felt we should all be as happy as kings, the spectacle of his agitated brother shocked the Hon. Galahad.

'Good God, Clarence! You look like a bereaved tapeworm. What's the matter?'

Lord Emsworth fluttered for a moment, speechless. Then he found words.

'Galahad, the worst has happened!'

'Eh?'

'Parsloe has struck!'

'Struck? You mean he's been biffing you?'

'No, no, no. I mean it has happened just as you warned me. He has been too clever for us. He has got round Connie and persuaded her to engage his nephew as my new secretary.'

The Hon. Galahad removed his monocle, and began to polish it thoughtfully. He could understand his companion's concern now.

'She told me so only a moment ago. You see what this means? He is determined to work a mischief on the Empress, and now he has contrived to insinuate an accomplice into the

52

very heart of the home. I see it all,' said Lord Emsworth, his voice soaring to the upper register. 'He failed with Baxter, and now he is trying again with this young Bodkin.'

'Bodkin? Young Monty Bodkin?'

'Yes. What are we to do, Galahad?' said Lord Emsworth.

He trembled. It would have pained the immaculate Monty, could he have known that his prospective employer was picturing him at this moment as a furtive, shifty-eyed, rat-like person of the gangster type, liable at the first opportunity to sneak into the sties of innocent pigs and plant pineapple bombs in their bran-mash.

The Hon. Galahad replaced his monocle.

'Monty Bodkin?' he said, refreshing himself with a sip from his glass. 'I remember him well. Nice boy. Not at all the sort of fellow who would nobble pigs. Wait a minute, Clarence. This wants thinking over.'

He mused awhile.

'No,' he said, 'you can dismiss young Bodkin as a hostile force altogether.'

'What!'

'Put him right out of your mind,' insisted the Hon. Galahad. 'Parsloe isn't planning to strike through him at all.'

'But, Galahad . . . '

'No. Take it from me. Can't you see for yourself that the thing's much too obvious, much too straightforward, not young Parsloe's proper form at all? Reason it out. He must know that we would suspect a nephew of his. Then why is it worth his while to get him into the place? Shall I tell you, Clarence?'

'Do,' said Lord Emsworth feebly, gaping like a fish.

As the head of the family was standing up and he was sitting down, it was impossible for the Hon. Galahad to tap him meaningly on the shoulder. He prodded him meaningly in the leg.

'Because,' he said, 'he *wants* us to suspect him.'

'Wants us to suspect him?'

'Wants us to,' said the Hon. Galahad. 'He hopes by introducing Monty Bodkin into the place to get us watching him, following his every movement, keeping our eyes glued on to him, so that when the real accomplice acts we shall be looking in the wrong direction.'

'God bless my soul!' said Lord Emsworth, appalled.

'Oh, it's all right,' said the Hon. Galahad soothingly. 'A cunning scheme, but we're too smart to fall for it. We see through it and are prepared.' He gave Lord Emsworth's leg another significant prod. 'Shall I tell you what is going to happen, Clarence?'

'Do,' said Lord Emsworth.

'I can read Parsloe's mind like a book. A day or two after young Monty's arrival, there will be a mysterious stranger sneaking about the grounds in the vicinity of the Empress's sty. He will be there because Parsloe, taking it for granted that our attention will be riveted on young Monty, will imagine that the coast is clear.'

'God bless my soul!'

'And apparently the coast will be clear. We must arrange that. From now on, Clarence, you must not loaf about the Empress openly. You must conceal yourself in the background. And you must instruct Pirbright to conceal himself in the background. This fellow must be led to suppose that vigilance has been relaxed. By these means, we shall catch him red-handed.'

In Lord Emsworth's eye, as he gazed at his brother, there was the reverential look of a disciple at the feet of his master. He had always known, he told himself, that as a practical adviser in matters having to do with the seamier side of life the other was unsurpassed. It was the result, he supposed of the environment in which he had spent his formative years. Membership of the old Pelican Club might not elevate a man socially, but there was no doubt about its educative properties. If it dulled the moral sense, it undoubtedly sharpened the intellect.

'You have taken a great weight off my mind, Galahad,' he said. 'I feel sure you are perfectly right. The only mistake I think you make is in supposing that this young Bodkin is harmless. I am convinced that he will require watching.'

'Well, watch him, then, if it will make you any happier.'

'It will,' said Lord Emsworth decidedly. 'And meanwhile I will be giving Pirbright his instructions.'

'Tell him to lurk.'

'Exactly.'

'Some rude disguise such as a tree or a pail of

potato-peel would help.'

Lord Emsworth reflected.

'I don't think Pirbright could disguise himself as a tree.'

'Nonsense. What do you pay him for?'

Lord Emsworth continued dubious. Only God, he seemed to be feeling, can make a tree. 'Well, at any rate, tell him to lurk.'

'Oh, he shall certainly lurk.'

'From now on . . . ' began the Hon. Galahad, and broke off to wave at some object in his companion's rear. The latter turned.

'Ah, that nice little Smith girl,' he said.

Sue had appeared on the edge of the lawn. Lord Emsworth beamed vaguely in her direction.

'By the way, Galahad,' he said, 'is a chorus-girl the same as a ballet-girl?'

'Certainly not. Different thing altogether.'

'I thought so,' said Lord Emsworth. 'Connie's an ass.'

He pottered away, and Sue crossed the turf to where the Hon. Galahad sat.

The author of the Reminiscences scanned her affectionately through his monocle. Amazing, he was thinking, how like her mother she was. He noticed it more every day. Dolly's walk, and just that way of tilting her chin and smiling at you that Dolly had had. For an instant the years fell away from the Hon. Galahad Threepwood, and something that was not of this world went whispering through the garden.

Sue stood looking down at him. She placed a maternal finger on top of his head, and began to

56

twist the grey hair round it.

'Well, young Gally.'

'Well, young Sue.'

'You look very comfortable.'

'I am comfortable.'

'You won't be long. The luncheon gong will be going in a minute.'

The Hon. Galahad sighed. There was always something, he reflected.

'What a curse meals are! Don't let's go in.'

'I'm going in, all right. My good child, I'm starving.'

'Pure imagination.'

'Do you mean to say you're not hungry, Gally?'

'Of course I'm not. No healthy person really needs food. If people would only stick to drinking, doctors would go out of business. I can state you a case that proves it. Old Freddie Potts in the year '98.'

'Old Freddie Potts in the year '98, did you say, Mister Bones?'

'Old Freddie Potts in the year '98,' repeated the Hon. Galahad firmly. 'He lived almost entirely on Scotch whisky, and in the year '98 this prudent habit saved him from an exceedingly unpleasant attack of hedgehog poisoning.'

'What poisoning?'

'Hedgehog poisoning. It was down in the south of France that it happened. Freddie had gone to stay with his brother Eustace at his villa at Grasse. Practically a teetotaller, this brother, and in consequence passionately addicted to food.'

57

'Still, I can't see why he wanted to eat hedgehogs.'

'He did not want to eat hedgehogs. Nothing was farther from his intentions. But on the second day of old Freddie's visit he gave his chef twenty francs to go to market and buy a chicken for dinner, and the chef, wandering along, happened to see a dead hedgehog lying in the road. It had been there some days, as a matter of fact, but this was the first time he had noticed it. So, feeling that here was where he pouched twenty francs . . . '

'I wish you wouldn't tell me stories like this just before lunch.'

'If it puts you off your food, so much the better. Bring the roses to your cheeks. Well, as I was saying, the chef, who was a thrifty sort of chap and knew that he could make a dainty dinner dish out of his old grandmother, if allowed to mess about with a few sauces, added the twenty francs to his savings and gave Freddie and Eustace the hedgehog next day *en casserole*. Mark the sequel. At two-thirty prompt, Eustace, the teetotaller, turned nile-green, started groaning like a lost soul, and continued to do so for the remainder of the week, when he was pronounced out of danger. Freddie, on the other hand, his system having been healthfully pickled in alcohol, throve on the dish and finished it up cold next day.'

'I call that the most disgusting story I ever heard.'

'The most moral story you ever heard. If I had my way, it would be carved up in letters of gold

58

over the door of every school and college in the kingdom, as a warning to the young. Well, what have you been doing with yourself all the morning, my dear? I expected you earlier.'

'I was talking to my precious Ronnie most of the time. He went off to catch his train about half an hour ago.'

'Ah, yes, he's going to young George Fish's wedding, isn't he? I could tell you a good story about George Fish's father, the Bishop.'

'If it's like the one about old Freddie Potts, I don't want to hear it. Well, after that I went to look for Lord Emsworth, because I had promised Ronnie to talk pig to him. But I saw Lady Constance with him, so I kept away. And then I came to see you, and found you talking together. You seemed to be having a very earnest conversation about something.'

The Hon. Galahad chuckled.

'Clarence has got the wind up, poor chap. About that pig of his. He thinks Parsloe is trying to put it on the spot or kidnap it.'

Sue looked round cautiously.

'You know who stole it that first time, don't you, Gally?'

'Baxter, wasn't it? The thing was found in his caravan.

'It was Ronnie.'

'What!' This was news to the Hon. Galahad. 'That young Fish?' She gave his hair a tug.

'You are not to call him 'that young Fish'.'

'I apologize. But what on earth did he do it for?'

'He was going to find it and bring it back. So

59

as to make Lord Emsworth grateful, you see.'

'You don't mean that young cloth-head had the intelligence to think up a scheme like that?' said the Hon. Galahad, amazed.

'And I won't have you calling my darling Ronnie a cloth-head either. He's very clever. As a matter of fact, though, he says he got the idea from you.'

'From me?'

'He says you told him you once stole a pig.'

'That's right,' said the Hon. Galahad. 'Puffy Benger and I stole old Wivenhoe's pig the night of the Bachelors' Ball at Hammer's Easton in the year '95. We put it in Plug Basham's bedroom. I never heard what happened when Plug met it. No doubt they found some formula. Wivenhoe, I remember, was rather annoyed about the affair. He was a good deal like Clarence in that respect. Worshipped his pig.'

'What makes Lord Emsworth think that Sir Gregory is going to hurt the Empress?'

'Apparently Connie has gone and engaged his nephew as Clarence's secretary, and he thinks it's a plot. So do I. But personally, as I told Clarence, I feel that Parsloe is using young Monty Bodkin purely as a cat's paw.'

'Monty Bodkin!'

'The nephew. I'm convinced, from what I remember of him, that he isn't at all the sort of fellow . . . '

'Oh, Gally!' cried Sue.

'Eh?'

'Monty Bodkin coming here?' Sue stared in dismay.

'Oh, Gally, what a mess! Oh, I knew something was going to happen. I told Ronnie so, I've been feeling it for days.'

'My dear child, what's the matter with you? What's wrong with young Bodkin coming here?'

'I used to be engaged to him!' said Sue.

★   ★   ★

It seemed to the Hon. Galahad that advancing years and the comparative abstinence of his later life must have dulled his once keen quickness at the uptake. Sue's face had lost its colour, and anxiety and alarm were clouding her pretty eyes, and he could make nothing of it.

'Were you?' he said. 'When was that?'

'Two years ago . . . Two and a half . . . Three . . . I can't remember. Before I met Ronnie. But what does that matter? I tell you I used to be engaged to him.'

The Hon. Galahad was still fogged.

'But what's your trouble? What's all the agitation about? Why does it upset you so much, the idea of meeting him again? Painful associations, do you mean? Embarrassing? Don't want to awake agonizing memories in the fellow's bosom?'

'Of course not. It isn't that. It's Ronnie.'

'Why Ronnie?'

'He's so jealous. You know how jealous he is.'

The Hon. Galahad began to understand.

'He can't help it, poor darling. It's just the way he is. He makes himself miserable about nothing. So what *will he* do when Monty arrives? I know

61

Monty so well. He won't mean any harm, but he'll come bounding in, all hearty and bubbling, and start talking of old times.

'Do you remember — ?'

'I say, Sue, old girl, I wonder if you've forgotten-?' . . .

'Ugh! It will drive poor Ronnie crazy.'

The Hon. Galahad nodded.

'I see what you mean. That touch of Auld Lang Syne *is* disturbing.'

'Why, he tries to pretend he isn't, but Ronnie's jealous even of Pilbeam.'

Once more the Hon. Galahad nodded. A grave nod. He quite realized that a man who could be jealous of the proprietor of the Argus Inquiry Agency was not a man lightly to be introduced to former fiancés, especially of the type of Monty Bodkin.

'We must give this matter a little earnest consideration,' he said thoughtfully. 'You wouldn't consider taking a firm line and telling Ronnie to go and boil his head and not make a young fool of himself, if he starts kicking up a fuss?'

'But you don't understand,' wailed Sue. 'He won't kick up a fuss. Ronnie isn't like that. He'll just get very stiff and cold and polite and suffer in a sort of awful Eton and Cambridge silence. And nothing I do will make him any better.'

An idea struck the Hon. Galahad.

'You're sure you really are in love with this young Fish?'

'I wish you wouldn't . . . '

'I'm sorry. I forgot. But you are?'

'Of course I am. There's nobody in the world for me but Ronnie. I've told you that before. I suppose what you're wondering is how I came to be engaged to Monty? Looking back, I can't think myself. He's a dear, of course, and when you're about seventeen, you're so flattered at finding that anyone wants to marry you that it seems wrong to refuse him. But it never amounted to anything. It only lasted a couple of weeks, anyhow. But Ronnie will imagine it was one of the world's great romances. He'll brood on it, and worry himself ill, wondering whether I'm still not pining for Monty. He's just like a kid in that way. It'll spoil everything.'

'And we may take it as pretty certain that Monty will let it out?'

'Of course he will. He's a babbler.'

'Yes, that's how I remember him. One of those fellows you can count on to say the wrong thing. Reminds me rather of a man I used to know in the old days called Bagshott. Boko Bagshott, we called him. Took a girl to supper once at the Garden. Supper scarcely concluded when angry old gentleman plunges into the room and starts shaking his list in Boko's face. Boko rises with chivalrous gesture. 'Have no fear, sir. I am a man of honour. I will marry your daughter.' 'Daughter?' says old gentleman, foaming a little at the mouth. 'Damn it, that's my wife.' Took all Boko's tact to pass it off, I believe.'

He pondered, staring thoughtfully through his black-rimmed monocle at a spider which was doing its trapeze act from an overhanging bough.

'Well, it's quite simple, of course.'

'Simple!'

'Presents no difficulties of any sort, now that one gives it one's full attention. Ronnie won't be back from that wedding till late tomorrow evening. You must run up to London first thing in the morning and warn young Monty how the land lies. Tell him that when he arrives here he must meet you as a stranger. Pitch it strong. Explain about Ronnie's unfortunate failing. Drive it well into his head that your whole happiness depends on him pretending he's never met you before, and I should think you would have no trouble whatever. I wouldn't call Monty Bodkin particularly bright, but he ought to be able to handle a thing like that, if you make it perfectly clear to him what he's got to do.'

She drew a deep breath.

'You're wonderful, Gally darling.'

'Experienced,' corrected the Hon. Galahad modestly.

'But can I do it? I mean, the trains.'

'On your head. Eight-fifty from Market Blandings gets you to London about noon. Interview Monty between then and two-thirty. Catch the two forty-five back, and you get to Market Blandings somewhere around a quarter to seven. Take the station taxi, stop it half-way up the drive, get out and walk the rest, and you'll be in your room with an hour to dress for dinner, and not a soul knowing a thing about it. No, even better than that, because I remember Connie telling me there's a dinner-party on tomorrow night, so I suppose you won't have to show up till nearly nine.'

64

'But lunch? Won't they wonder where I am if I'm not at lunch.'

'Connie's lunching out. You don't suppose Clarence will notice whether you're there or not. No, the only point we haven't covered is, can you find Monty? Do you know his address?'

'He's sure to be at the Drones.'

'Then all is well. Why on earth you worry about these things, when you know you've got an expert like me behind you, I can't imagine. It's a pity about young Ronnie, though. That disposition of his to make heavy weather. Silly to be jealous. He ought to realize by this time that you love him — goodness knows why.'

'I know why.'

'I don't. Fellow's a perfect ass.'

'He's not!'

'My dear child,' said the Hon. Galahad firmly, 'if a man who doesn't know that he can trust you isn't a perfect ass, what sort of ass is he?'

# 5

In supposing that she would be able to find her former fiancé at the Drones, Sue had not erred. Telephoning there from Paddington station shortly after twelve next morning, she was rewarded almost immediately by a series of sharp, hyena-like cries at the other end of the wire. To judge from his remarks, this voice from the past was music in Monty Bodkin's ears. Nothing, he gave her to understand, could have given him more pleasure than to get in touch after two years of separation with one whom he esteemed so highly. At his suggestion, Sue had got into a taxi, and now, across a table in the restaurant of the Berkeley Hotel, she was looking at him and congratulating herself on her wisdom in having arranged this meeting. A Monty unprepared for the part he had to play at Blandings Castle would, she felt, beyond a question have crashed into poor darling Ronnie's sensibilities like a high-powered shell. Over the preliminary cocktails and right through the smoked salmon he had been a sheer foaming torrent of 'Do you remembers' and 'That reminds mes'.

It seemed to Sue that she had a difficult task before her in trying to make clear to this exuberant old friend that on his arrival at the Castle he must regard the dear old days as a sealed book and herself as a complete stranger.

Yet when a toothsome *truite bleue* had induced in him a sudden reverential silence and she was able at length to give a brief exposition of the state of affairs, she was surprised and pleased to gather from a series of understanding nods that he appeared to be following her remarks intelligently.

He finished the *truite bleue* and gave a final nod. It indicated a perfect grasp of the situation.

'My dear old soul,' he said reassuringly, 'say no more. I understand everything, understand it fully. As a matter of fact, Hugo Carmody had already tipped me off.'

'Oh have you seen Hugo?'

'I met him at the club, and he warned me about Ronnie. I had the situation well in hand. On arriving at Blandings I was planning to treat you with distant civility.'

'Then I needn't have come up at all!'

'I wouldn't say that. If Ronnie's so apt to go off the deep end at the slightest provocation, we can't be too much on the safe side. Even distant civility might have hotted him up.'

Sue considered this.

'That's true,' she agreed.

'Better to be perfect strangers.'

'Yes.' Sue gave a little frown. 'How beastly it's all going to be, though.'

'That's all right. I shan't mind.'

'I wasn't thinking about you. It seems so rotten, deceiving Ronnie.'

'You've got to get used to that. Secret of a happy and successful married life. I thought you meant that it would be rather agony you and me just giving each other a distant bow when they introduced us and then shunning one another coldly. And it does seem darned silly, what? I mean, we were very close to each other once. Can one altogether forget those happy days?'

'I can. And so must you. For goodness sake, Monty, don't let's have any of what Gally calls that touch of Auld Lang Syne.'

'No, no. Quite.'

'I don't want Ronnie driven off his head.'

'Far from it.'

'Well, do remember to be careful.'

'Oh, I will. Rely on me.'

'Thanks, Monty darling ... What's the matter?' asked Sue, as her host gave a sudden start.

A waiter had brought up a silver dish and uncovered it with the air of one doing a conjuring trick. Monty inspected it with the proper seriousness.

'Oh, nothing,' he said as the waiter retired. 'Just that 'Monty darling.' It brought back the old days.'

'For goodness sake forget the old days!'

'Oh, quite. I will. Oh, rather. Most certainly. But it made me feel how rum life was. Life *is* rummy, you know. You can't get away from that.'

'I suppose it is.'

'Take a simple instance. Here are you and I, face to face across this table, lunching together like the dickens, precisely as in the dear old days, and all the time you are contemplating getting hitched up to R. Fish, while I am heart and soul in favour of an early union with Gertrude Butterwick.'

'What!'

'Butterwick. B for blister, U for ukelele . . . '

'Yes, I heard. But do you mean you're engaged, too, Monty?'

'Well, yes and no. Not absolutely. And yet not absolutely not. I am, as it were, on appro.'

'Can't she make up her mind?'

'Oh, her mind's made up all right. Oh, yes, yes, yes, indeed there's no doubt about good old Gertrude's mind, bless her. She loves me like billy-o. But there are wheels within wheels.'

'What do you mean?'

'It's an expression. It signifies . . . well, by Jove, now you bring up the point,' said Monty frankly. 'I'm dashed if I know just what it does signify. Wheels within wheels. Why wheels? What wheels? Still, there it is. I suppose the idea is to suggest that everything's pretty averagely complicated.'

'I understand what it means, of course. But why do you say it about yourself?'

'Because there's a snag sticking up in the course of true love. A very sizeable, jagged snag. Her blighted father, to wit, J. G. Butterwick, of Butterwick, Price, and Mandelbaum, export and import merchants.'

He swallowed a roast potato emotionally. Sue was touched. She had never ceased to congratulate herself on her sagacity in breaking off her engagement to this young man, but she was very fond of him.

'Oh, Monty, I'm so sorry. Poor darling.

69

Doesn't he like you?' Monty weighed this.

'Well, I wouldn't say that exactly. On two separate occasions he has said good morning to me, and once, round about Christmas time, I received a distinct impression that he was within an ace of offering me a cigar. But he's a queer bird. Years of exporting and importing have warped his mind a bit, with the result that for some reason I can't pretend to understand he appears to look on me as a sort of waster. The first thing he did when I ankled in and told him that subject to his approval I was about to marry his daughter was to ask me how I earned my living.'

'That must have been rather a shock.'

'It was. And a still worse one was when he went on to add that unless I got a job of some kind and held it down for a solid year, to show him that I wasn't a sort of waster, those wedding bells would never ring out.'

'You poor lamb. How perfectly awful!'

'Ghastly. I reeled. I stared. I couldn't believe the fellow was serious. When I found he was, I raced off to Gertrude and told her to jam her hat on and come round to the nearest registrar's. Only to discover, Sue, that she was one of those old-fashioned girls who won't dream of doing the dirty on Father. Solid middle-class stock, you understand. Backbone of England, and all that. So, elopements being off, I had no alternative but to fall in with the man's extraordinary scheme. I got my Uncle Gregory to place me with the Mammoth Publishing Company in the capacity of assistant editor of *Tiny Tots*. And if only I could have contrived to remain an assistant editor, I should be there now. But my boss went off on a holiday, silly ass, leaving me in charge of the sheet and in a well-meant attempt to ginger the bally thing up a bit I made rather a bloomer in the Uncle Woggly department. The result being that a couple of days ago they formed a hollow square and drummed me out. And now I'm starting all over again at Blandings.'

'I see. I couldn't understand why you wanted to be Lord Emsworth's secretary. I was afraid you must have lost all your money.'

'Oh, no. I've got my money all right. And what,' demanded Monty, swinging an arm in a passionate gesture and hitting a waiter on the chest and saying 'Oh, sorry!', 'does money amount to? What *is* money? Fairy gold. That's what it is. Dead Sea fruit. Because it doesn't help me a damn towards scooping in Gertrude.'

'Is she an awfully nice girl?'

'An angel, Sue. No question about that. Quite the angel, absolutely.'

'Well, I do hope you will come out all right, Monty dear.'

'Thanks, old thing.'

'And I'm glad you didn't pine for me. I've felt guilty at times.'

'Oh, I pined. Oh, yes, certainly I *pined*. But you know how it is. One perks up and sees fresh faces. Tell me, Sue,' said Monty anxiously. 'I ought to be able to hold down that secretary job for a year, oughtn't I? I mean, people don't fire secretaries much, do they?'

'If Hugo could keep the place, I should think you ought to be able to. How are you on pigs?'

'Pigs?'

'Lord Emsworth . . . '

'Of course, yes, I remember now, Hugo told me. The old boy has gone porcine, has he not? You mean you would advise me to suck up to his pig, this what's-its-name of Blandings, to omit no word or act to conciliate it? Thanks for the tip. I'll bear it in mind.' He beamed affectionately at her across the table, and went so far as to take her hand in his. 'You've cheered me up, young Sue. You always did, I remember. You've got one of those sunny temperaments which look on the bright side and never fail to spot the blue bird. As you say, if a chap like Hugo could hold the job, it ought to be a snip for a man of my gifts, especially if I show myself pig-conscious. I anticipate a pleasant and successful year, with a wedding at the end of it. By which time, I take it, you will be an old married woman. When do you and Ronnie plan to leap off the dock?'

'As soon as ever Lord Emsworth lets him have his money. He wants to buy a partnership in a motor business.'

'Any opposish from the family?'

'Well, I don't think Lady Constance is frightfully pleased about it all.'

'Possibly it slipped out by some chance that you had been in the chorus?'

'It was mentioned.'

'Ah, that would account for it. But she's biting the bullet all right?'

'She seems resigned.'

'Then all is well.'

'I suppose so. And yet . . . Monty, do you ever get a feeling that something unpleasant is going to happen?'

'I got it two days ago, when my Lord Tilbury reached for the slack of my trousers and started to heave me out.'

'I've got it. I was saying so to Ronnie, and he told me not to be morbid.'

'Ronnie knows words like 'morbid', does he? Two syllables and everything.'

'Monty, what is Ronnie's mother really like?'

Monty rubbed his chin. 'Haven't you met her yet?'

'No. She's been over in Biarritz.'

'But is returning?'

'I suppose so.'

'Myes. Post-haste, I should imagine.

'Myes!'

'For goodness sake, don't say ' 'Myes'. You're making my flesh creep. Is she such a terror?'

Monty scratched his right cheekbone.

'Well, I'll tell you. Many people would say she was a genial soul.'

'That's what Ronnie said.'

'The jovial hunting type. Lady Di. Bluff goodwill, the jolly smile for everyone, and slabs of soup at Christmas time for the deserving villagers. But I don't know. I'm not so sure. I'll tell you this much. When I was a kid I was far more scared of her than I was of Lady Constance.'

'Why?'

'Ah, there you have me. But I was. Still, don't

73

let me take the joy out of your life. For all we know, she may at this very moment be practising 'O Perfect Love' on the harmonium. And now, I don't want to hurry you, but the sands are running out a bit. My train goes at two forty-five . . . '

'What?'

'Two-four-five, pip emma.'

'You aren't going to Blandings today . . . by the two forty-five?'

'That's right.'

'But I'm going back on the two forty-five.'

'Well, that's fine. We'll travel together.'

'But we mustn't travel together.'

'Why not? Nobody's going to see us, and we can be as distant as the dickens on arrival. Pleasant chit-chat as far as Market Blandings, and cold aloofness from there on, is the programme as I see it. It's silly to overdo this perfect stranger business.'

Sue, thinking it over, was inclined to agree with him. She had had one solitary railway journey that day, and was not indisposed for pleasant company on the way back.

'And if you think, young Susan,' said Monty, who, though chivalrous, could stand up for his rights, 'that I intend to wait on and travel by something that stops and shunts at every station, you err. It's a four hours' journey even by express. We'll just nip round to my flat and pick up my things . . . '

'And miss the train. No, thank you. I can't take any chances. I'll meet you at the station.'

'Just as you like,' said Monty agreeably. 'I was

only thinking that if you came to my flat. I could show you sixteen photographs of Gertrude.'

'You can describe them to me on the journey.'

'I will,' said Monty. 'Waiter, laddishiong.'

★ ★ ★

It was as the hands of the big clock at Paddington station were pointing to two-forty that Lady Julia Fish made her way through the crowd on the platform, her progress rendered impressive by the fact that her maid, two porters, and a boy who mistakenly supposed that he had found a customer for his oranges and nut-chocolate revolved about her like satellites around a sun.

Towards the turmoil in her immediate neighbourhood she displayed her usual good-humoured disdain. Where others ran she sauntered. Composedly she allowed one porter to open the door of an empty compartment, the other to place therein her bag, papers, novels, and magazines. She dismissed the maid, tipped the porters, and, settling herself in a corner seat, surveyed the bustle and stir without in an indulgent manner.

The ceremony of getting the two forty-five express off was now working up to a crescendo. Porters flitted to and fro. Guards shouted and poised green flags. The platform rang with the feet of belated travellers. And the train had just given a sort of shiver and began to move out of the station, when the door of the compartment was wrenched open and something that seemed

75

to have six legs shot in, tripped over her, and collapsed into the seat opposite. It was a perspiring young man of the popinjay type, whose face though twisted, was not so twisted that she was unable to recognize in him that Montague Bodkin who had once been so frequent a visitor at the home of her ancestors.

Monty had run it fine. What with hunting for a mislaid cigarette-case and getting held up in a traffic block in Praed Street, he had contrived this spectacular entry only by dint of sprinting the length of the platform at a rate of speed which he had not achieved since his university days.

But though warm and out of breath, he was still the *preux chevalier* who knew that when you have just barked the skin of a member of the other sex apologies must be made.

'It is quite all right, Mr Bodkin,' said Lady Julia as he made them. 'I am sorry I was in your way.'

Monty started violently.

'Gosh!' he exclaimed.

'I beg your pardon.'

'I mean — er — hullo, Lady Julia!'

'Hullo, Mr Bodkin.'

'Phew!' said Monty, dabbing agitatedly at his forehead with the handkerchief which so perfectly matched his tie and socks.

His distress was not caused entirely — or even to any great extent — by the reflection that he had just taken an inch of skin off the daughter of a hundred earls. That, no doubt, was regrettable, but what was really exercising his mind was the

76

thought that Sue being presumably on the train and having presumably observed his rush down the platform would be coming along at any moment to see if he got aboard all right. It seemed to him that it was going to require all his address to handle the situation which her advent would create.

'Fancy running into you,' he said dismally.

'"Over me" would be a better way of putting it. I felt like some unfortunate Hindu beneath the wheels of Juggernaut. And where are you bound for, Mr Bodkin?'

'Eh? Oh, Market Blandings.'

'You are going to stay with your uncle at Matchingham?'

'Oh, no. I'm booked for the Castle. Lord Emsworth has taken me on as his secretary.'

'But how very odd. I thought you were working with the Mammoth Publishing Company.'

'I've resigned.'

'Resigned?'

'Resigned,' said Monty firmly. He was not going to reveal his Moscow to this woman.

'What made you resign?'

'Oh, various things. There are wheels within wheels.'

'How cosy!' said Lady Julia.

Monty decided to change the subject.

'I hear everything's much about the same at Blandings.'

'Who told you that?'

'Fellow named Carmody, who has been secretarying there. He said everything was much about the same.'

'What a very unobservant young man he must be! Didn't he mention that there had been an earthquake there, an upheaval, a social cataclysm?'

'I beg your . . . What was that?'

'Prepare yourself for a shock, Mr Bodkin. Ronnie is at Blandings, and with him a chorus-girl of the name of Brown, whom he proposes to marry.'

A little uncertain as to the judicious line to take, Monty decided to be astounded.

'No!'

'I assure you.'

'A chorus-girl?'

'Named Sue Brown. You don't know her, by any chance?'

'No. Oh, no. No.'

'I thought possibly you might.'

Lady Julia looked out of the window at the flying countryside. 'Very trying for a parent. Don't you think so, Mr Bodkin?'

'Oh, most.'

'Still, I suppose it might have been worse. There is rather a consoling ring about that simple name. I mean, Sue Brown doesn't sound like a girl who will bring breach of promise actions when the thing is broken off.'

'Broken off!'

'It might so easily have been Suzanne de Brune.'

'But — er — are you thinking of breaking it off?'

'Why, of course. You seem very concerned. Or is this joy?'

'No — I — er — It just occurred to me that it might be a bit difficult. I mean, Ronnie's a pretty determined sort of chap.'

'He inherits it from his mother,' said Lady Julia. It was during the silence which followed this remark that Sue entered the compartment.

★　★　★

At the moment of her arrival Monty was staring out of the window and Lady Julia had leaned back in her seat. There was nothing, accordingly, to indicate any connexion between the two, and Sue was just about to address to her old friend a cordial word of congratulation on his abilities as a sprinter, when the sound of the opening door caused him to turn. And so blank, so icy was the stare of non-recognition which she encountered that she sank bewildered on the cushions with all the sensations of one who, after being cut by the county, walks into a brick wall.

It was not long, however, before enlightenment came. Monty was a young man who believed in taking no chances.

'Nice and green the country's looking, Lady Julia,' he observed. 'Isn't it, Lady Julia?'

His companion gave it a glance.

'Very, considering there has been no rain for such a long time.'

'I should think Ronnie must be enjoying it at Blandings, Lady Julia.'

'I beg your pardon?'

'I say,' said Monty, spacing his words carefully,

79

'that your son Ronnie must be enjoying the green of the countryside at Blandings Castle. He likes it green,' explained Monty. And with another frigid stare at Sue he leaned back and puffed his cheeks out.

There was a pause. Monty had not wrought in vain. An electric thrill seemed to pass through Sue's small body. Her heart was thumping.

'I beg your pardon,' she said breathlessly. 'Are you Lady Julia Fish?'

'I am.'

'My name's Sue Brown,' said Sue, wishing that she could have achieved a vocal delivery a little more impressive than that of a very young, startled mouse.

'Well, well, well!' said Lady Julia. 'Fancy that. Quite a coincidence, Mr Bodkin.'

'Oh, quite. Most.'

'We were just talking about you, Miss Brown.'

Sue nodded speechlessly.

'I am losing a son and gaining a daughter, and you're the daughter, eh?'

Sue continued to nod. Monty, personally, considered that she was overdoing it. She ought, he felt, to be saying something. Something bright and snappy like . . . well, he couldn't on the spur of the moment think just what, but something bright and snappy.

'Yes,' said Lady Julia, 'I recognize you. Ronnie sent me a photograph of you, you know. I thought it charming. Well, you must come over here and tell me all about yourself. We will get rid of Mr Bodkin . . . By the way, you did tell me you had not met Miss Brown?'

'Definitely not. Certainly not. Far from it. Not at all.'

'Don't speak in that tone of horrified loathing, Mr Bodkin. I'm sure Miss Brown is a very nice girl, well worthy of your acquaintance. At any rate, you've met her now. Mr Bodkin, Miss Brown.'

'How do you do?' said Monty stiffly.

'How do you do?' said Sue with aloofness.

'Mr Bodkin is coming to Blandings as my brother's secretary.'

'Fancy!' said Sue.

'And now run along and look at the green countryside, Mr Bodkin. Miss Brown and I want to have a talk about all sorts of things.'

'I'll go and have a smoke,' said Monty, inspired. 'Do,' said Lady Julia.

*   *   *

Monty Bodkin sat in his smoking-compartment, well pleased with himself. It had been a near thing, and it had taken a man of affairs to avert disaster, but he had brought it off. Another half-second and young Sue would have spilled the beans. He was, as we say, pleased with himself, and he was also pleased with Sue. She had shown a swift grasp of the situation. There had been a moment when he had feared he was being too subtle, trying the female intelligence, notoriously so greatly inferior to the male, too high. But all had been well. Good old Sue had understood those guarded hints of his, and now everything looked pretty smooth.

He closed his eyes contentedly, and dropped off into a refreshing sleep.

From this he was aroused some half an hour later by the click of the door; and, opening his eyes and blinking once or twice, was enabled to perceive Sue standing before him. 'Ah! Interview over?'

Sue nodded and sat down. Her face was grave, like that of a puzzled child. Extraordinarily pretty it made her look, felt Monty, and for an instant there stole over him a faint regret for what might have been. Then he thought of Gertrude Butterwick and was strong again.

'I say, I did that distant aloofness stuff rather well, don't you think?'

'Oh, yes.'

'And pretty shrewd of me to grapple with a tricky situation so promptly and give you that instant pointer as to how matters stood?'

'Oh, yes.'

'What do you mean, Oh, yes? It was genius.' He looked at her with some intentness. 'You seem a shade below par. Didn't the interview go off well?'

'Oh, yes.'

'Don't keep saying 'Oh, yes.' What happened?'

'Oh, we talked.'

'Of course you talked, chump. What did you say?'

'I told her about myself, and — oh, you know, all that sort of thing.'

'And wasn't she chummy?' She reflected, biting her lip.

'She was quite nice.'

'I know what that means — rotten.'

'No, she seemed perfectly friendly. Laughed a good deal and . . . well, just what you were saying. Lady Di. Bluff goodwill. But — '

'But you seemed to sense the velvet hand beneath the iron glove? No, dash it, that's not right,' said Monty, musing. 'The other way about it should be, shouldn't it? You got the impression that she was simply waiting till your back was turned to stick a knife in it?'

'A little. It's something about her eyes. She doesn't smile with them. Of course, I may be all wrong.'

Monty looked dubious. He lit a cigarette and puffed at it thoughtfully.

'No, I think you're right. I wish I didn't, but I do. I don't mind telling you that a second before you came in she was saying she was jolly well going to break the whole thing off.'

'Oh?'

'Of course,' Monty hastened to add consolingly, 'she hasn't got a dog's chance of doing it. There are few more resolute birds than Ronnie. But she'll try her damnedest. Tough eggs, that Blandings Castle female contingent. Odd that they should be so much deadlier than the male. Look at old Emsworth . . . old Gally . . . young Freddie . . . you've never met Freddie, have you? . . . All jolly good sorts. And against them you have this Julia, yonder Constance, and a whole lot more, all snakes of the first water. When you get to know that family better, you'll realize that there are dozens of aunts you've not heard of yet — far-flung aunts scattered all over England, and each the leading blister of her particular county. It's a sort of family taint. Still, as I say, old Ronnie is staunch. Nobody could talk him out of prancing up the aisle with the girl he loves.'

'No,' said Sue, her eyes dreamy.

'And now, pardon the suggestion, but wouldn't it be as well if you shoved off? Suppose she happened to come along and found us hobnobbing here like this?'

'I never thought of that.'

'Always think of everything,' said Monty paternally. He closed his eyes again. The train rattled on towards Market Blandings.

# 6

It was nearly an hour after the two forty-five had arrived at its destination that a slower shabbier train crawled in and deposited Ronnie Fish on the platform of the little station of Market Blandings. The festivities connected with his cousin George's wedding and the intricacies of a railway journey across the breadth of England had combined to prevent an earlier return.

He was tired, but happy. The glow of sentiment which warms young men in love when they watch other people getting married still lingered. Mendelssohn's well-known march was on his lips as he gave up his ticket, and it was with a perceptible effort that he checked himself from saying to the driver of the station cab, 'Wilt thou, Robinson, take this Ronald to Blandings Castle?' Even when he reached his destination and found the hands of the grandfather clock in the hall pointing to ten to eight, his exuberance did not desert him. It was his pride that he could shave, bathe, and dress, always provided that nothing went wrong with the tie, in nine and a quarter minutes.

Tonight, all was well. The black strip of *Crepe-de-Chine* assumed the perfect butterfly shape of its own volition, and at eight precisely he was standing in the combination drawing-room and picture-gallery in which Blandings

Castle was wont to assemble long before the evening meal.

He was surprised to find himself alone. And it was not long before surprise gave way to a stronger emotion. For some minutes he wandered to and fro, gazing at the portraits of his ancestors on the walls; but to a man who has just come from a long and dusty train journey ancestral portraits are a poor substitute for the old familiar juice. He pressed the bell, and presently Beach the butler appeared.

'Oh, hullo, Beach. I say, Beach, what about the cocktails?' The butler seemed surprised.

'I was planning to serve them when the guests arrived. Mr Ronald.'

'Guests? There aren't people coming to dinner, are there?'

'Yes, sir. We shall sit down twenty-four.'

'Good Lord! A binge?'

'Yes, sir.'

'I must go and put on a white tie.'

'There is plenty of time, Mr Ronald. Dinner will not be served till nine o'clock. Perhaps you would prefer me to bring you an aperitif in advance of the formal cocktails?'

'I certainly would. I'm dying by inches.'

'I will attend to the matter immediately.'

The butler of Blandings Castle was not a man who when he said. 'immediately' meant 'somewhere in the distant future'. Like a heavyweight Jinn, stirred to activity by the rubbing of a lamp, he vanished and reappeared; and it was only a few minutes later that Ronnie was blossoming like a flower in the gentle rain of summer and

86

finding himself disposed for leisurely chat.

'Twenty-four?' he said. 'Golly, we're going gay. Who's coming?'

The butler's eyes took on a glaze similar to that seen in those of policemen giving evidence.

'His lordship the Bishop of Poole, Sir Herbert and Lady Musker, Sir Gregory Parsloe-Parsloe . . .'

'What!'

'Yes, sir.'

'Who invited *him*?'

'Her ladyship, I should imagine, sir.'

'And he's coming? Well, I suppose he knows his own business,' said Ronnie dubiously. 'Better keep a close eye on Uncle Clarence, Beach. If you see him toying with a knife, remove it.'

'Very good, sir.'

'Who else?'

'Colonel and Mrs Mauleverer and daughter, the Honourable Major and Lady Augusta Lindsay-Todd and niece . . .'

'All right. You needn't go on. I get the general idea. Eighteen local nibs, plus the gang of six in residence.'

'Eight, Mr Ronald.'

'Eight?'

'His lordship, her ladyship, Mr Galahad, yourself, Miss Brown, Mr . . .' The butler's voice shook a little. ' . . . Pilbeam.'

'Exactly. Six, you old ass.'

'There is also Mr Bodkin, sir.'

'Bodkin?'

'Sir Gregory Parsloe's nephew, Mr Ronald. Mr Montague Bodkin. You may recall him as a somewhat frequent visitor to the Castle during his school days.'

'Of course I remember old Monty. But you've got muddled. You've counted him in among the resident patients, when he's really one of the outside crowd.'

'No, sir. Mr Bodkin is assuming Mr Carmody's duties as his lordship's secretary.'

'Not really?'

'Yes, sir. I understand the appointment was ratified two days ago.'

'But that's odd. What does Monty want, sweating as a secretary? He's got about fifteen thousand a year of his own.'

'Indeed, sir?'

'Well, he had. Somehow or other we've not happened to run into each other much these last two years. Do you think he's lost it?'

'Very possibly, sir. A great many people have become fiscally crippled of late.'

'Rummy,' said Ronnie.

Then speculation on this mystery was borne away on a flood of sober pride. With a pardonable feeling of smugness, Ronnie Fish realized that his soul had achieved such heights of nobility that the prospect of a Monty Bodkin buzzing about the Castle premises in daily contact with Sue was causing him no pang of apprehension or jealousy.

Not so very long ago, such a thought would have been a dagger in his bosom. It was just the Monty type of chap-tall, lissom, good-looking, and not pink — that he had always feared. And now he could contemplate his coming without a tremor. Pretty good, felt Ronnie.

'Well, come along with your eight,' he said.

'That's only seven, so far.' The butler coughed. 'I was assuming, Mr Ronald, that you were aware that her ladyship, your mother, arrived this evening on the two forty-five train.'

'What!'

'Yes, sir.'

'Good Lord!'

Beach regarded him solicitously, but did not develop the theme. He had a nice sense of the proprieties. Between himself and this young man there had existed for eighteen years a warm friendship. Ronnie as a child had played bears in his pantry. Ronnie as a boy had gone fishing with him on the lake. Ronnie as a freshman at Cambridge had borrowed five-pound notes from him to see him through to his next allowance. Ronnie, grown to man's estate, had given him many a sound tip on the races, from which his savings bank account had profited largely. He knew the last detail of Ronnie's romance, sympathized with his aims and objects, was aware that an interview of extreme delicacy faced him; and, had they been sitting in his pantry now, would not have hesitated to offer sympathy and advice.

But because this was the drawing-room, his lips were sealed. A mere professional gesture was all he could allow himself.

'Another cocktail, Mr Ronald?'

'Thanks.'

Ronnie, sipping thoughtfully, found his equanimity returning. For a moment, he could not deny it, there had been a slight sinking of the heart; but now he was telling himself that his mother had always been a cheery soul, one of the best, and that there was no earthly reason to suppose that she was likely to make any serious trouble now. True, there might be a little stiffness at first, but that would soon wear off.

'Where is she, Beach?'

'In the Garden Room, Mr Ronald.'

'I ought to go there, I suppose. And yet . . . No,' said Ronnie, on second thoughts. 'Might be a little rash, what? There she would be with her hair-brush handy, and the temptation to put me across her knee and . . . No. I think you'd better send a maid or someone to inform her that I await her here.'

'I will do so immediately, Mr Ronald.'

With a quiver of the left eyebrow intended to indicate that, had such a thing been possible to a man in his position, he would gladly have remained and lent moral support, the butler left the room. And presently the door reopened, and Lady Julia Fish came sailing in.

Ronnie straightened his tie, pulled down his waistcoat, and advanced to meet her.

★  ★  ★

The emotions of a young man on encountering his maternal parent, when in the interval since they last saw one another he has announced his betrothal to a member of the chorus, are necessarily mixed. Filial love cannot but be tempered with apprehension. On the whole, however, Ronnie was feeling reasonably debonair. He and his mother had laughed together at a good many things in their time, and he was optimistic enough to hope that with a little adroitness on his part the coming scene could be kept on the lighter plane. As he had said to Sue, Lady Julia Fish was not Lady Constance Keeble.

Nevertheless, as he kissed her, he was aware of something of the feeling which he had had in his boxing days when shaking hands with an unpleasant-looking opponent.

'Hullo, mother.'

'Well, Ronnie.'

'Here you are, what?'

'Yes.'

'Nice journey?'

'Quite.'

'Not rough, crossing over?'

'Not at all.'

'Good,' said Ronnie. 'Good.' He began to feel easier.

'Well,' he proceeded chattily, 'we got old George off all right.'

'George?'

'Cousin George. I've just been best-manning at his wedding.'

'Ah, yes. I had forgotten. It was today, was it not?'

'That's right. I only got back half an hour ago.'

'Did everything go off well?'

'Splendidly. Not a hitch.'

'Family pleased, I suppose?'

'Oh, delighted.'

'They would be, wouldn't they? Seeing that

George was marrying a girl of excellent position with ten thousand a year of her own.'

'H'r'rmph,' said Ronnie.

'Yes,' said Lady Julia, 'you'd better say 'H'r'rmph!'' There was a pause. Ronnie, who had just straightened his tie again, pulled it crooked and began straightening it once more. Lady Julia watched these manifestations of unrest with a grim blue stare. Ronnie, looking up and meeting it, diverted his gaze towards a portrait of the second Earl which hung on the wall beside him.

'Amazing beards those blokes used to wear,' he said nonchalantly.

'I wonder you can look your ancestors in the face.'

'I can't, as a matter of fact. They're an ugly crowd. The only decent one is Daredevil Dick Threepwood who married the actress.'

'You would bring up Daredevil Dick, wouldn't you?'

'That's right, mother. Let's see the old smile.'

'I'm not smiling. What you observed was a twitch of pain. Really, Ronnie, you ought to be certified.'

'Now, mother . . . '

'Ronnie,' said Lady Julia, 'if you dare to lift up your finger and say 'Tweet-tweet, shush-shush, come-come,' I'll hit you. It's no good grinning in that sickening way. It simply confirms my opinion that you are a raving lunatic, an utter imbecile, and that you ought to have been placed under restraint years ago.'

'Oh, dash it.'

'It's no good saying 'Oh, dash it'.'

'Well, I do say 'Oh, dash it.' Be reasonable. Naturally I don't expect you to start dancing round and strewing roses out of a hat, but you might preserve the decencies of debate. Highly offensive, that last crack.'

Lady Julia sighed.

'Why *do* all you young fools want to marry chorus-girls?'

'Read any good books lately, mother?' asked Ronnie, pacifically.

Lady Julia refused to be diverted.

'It's too amazing. It's a disease. It really is. Just like measles or whooping-cough. All young men apparently have to go through it.

It seems only the other day that my poor father was shipping your Uncle Galahad off to Africa to ensure a cure.'

'I'll tell you something interesting about that, mother. The girl Uncle Gally was in love with . . . '

'I was a child at the time, but I can recall it so distinctly. Father thumping tables, mother weeping, and all that rather charming, old-world atmosphere of family curses. And now it's you! Well, well, one can only thank goodness that it never seems to last long. The fever takes its course, and the patient recovers. Ronnie, my poor half-wit, you can't really be serious about this?'

'Serious!'

'But, Ronnie, really! A chorus-girl.'

'There's a lot to be said for chorus-girls.'

'Not in my presence. I couldn't bear it. It's so

*callow* of you, my dear boy. If this had happened when you were at Eton, I wouldn't have said a word. But when you're grown up and are supposed to have some sense. Look at the men who marry chorus-girls. A race apart. Young Datchet . . . That awful old Bellinger . . . '

'Ah, but you're overlooking something, my dear old parent. There are chorus-girls and chorus-girls.'

'This is your kind heart speaking.'

'And when you get one like Sue . . . '

'No, Ronnie. It's nice of you to try to cheer me up, but it can't be done. I regard the entire personnel of the ensembles of our musical comedy theatres as — if you will forgive me being Victorian for a moment — painted hussies.'

'They've got to paint.'

'Well, they needn't huss. And they needn't ensnare my son.'

'I'm not sure I like that word 'ensnare' much.'

'You probably won't much like any of the words you're going to get from me tonight. Honestly, Ronnie. I know it hurts your head to think, but try to just for a moment. It isn't simply a question of class. It's the whole thing . . . the different viewpoint . . . the different standards . . . everything. I take it that your idea when you marry is to settle down and lead a normal sort of life, and how are you going to have that with a chorus-girl? How are you going to trust a woman of that sort of upbringing, who has lived on excitement ever since she was old enough to kick her beastly legs up in front of an audience and sees nothing wrong in going off and having affairs with every man that takes her fancy? That sort of girl would be sneaking off round the corner the moment your back was turned.'

'Not Sue.'

'Yes, Sue.'

Ronnie smiled indulgently. 'Wait till you meet her!'

'I have met her, thanks.'

'What?'

'She was in the train, and introduced herself.'

'But what was she doing in the train?'

'Returning here from London.'

'I didn't know she had gone up to London.'

'So I imagine,' said Lady Julia.

Not many minutes had passed since Ronnie Fish had been urging his mother to smile. With these words she had done so, but the fulfilment of his wish brought him no pleasure. The pink of his face deepened. There had come a lightness about his mouth. He had changed his mind about the desirability of keeping the scene light.

'Do you mind if I just get this straight?' he said coldly. 'A moment ago you were talking about girls who ran off and had affairs . . . and now you tell me you have met Sue.'

'Exactly.'

'Then you . . . had Sue in mind?'

'Exactly.'

Ronnie laughed, unpleasantly.

'On the strength, apparently, of her having gone up to London for the day — to do some shopping or something, I suppose. I wouldn't call this your ripest form, mother.'

'On the strength, if you really wish to know, of seeing her and young Monty Bodkin lunching together at the Berkeley and finding them together on the train . . . '

'Monty Bodkin!'

' . . . where they had the effrontery to pretend they had never met before.'

'She was lunching with Monty?'

'Lunching with Monty and ogling Monty and holding hands with Monty! Oh, for heaven's sake, Ronnie, do use a little intelligence. Can't you see this girl is just like the rest of them? If you can't, you really must be a borderline case. Young Bodkin came here today to be your uncle's secretary. Two days ago he had some sort of employment with the Mammoth Publishing Company. He told me on the train that he had resigned. Why did he resign? And why is he coming here? Obviously because this girl wanted him here and put him up to it. And directly she hears it's settled, she takes advantage of your being away to sneak up to London and talk things over with him. If there was nothing underhand going on, why should they have pretended that they were perfect strangers? No, as you said just now, I am *not* dancing round and strewing roses out of a hat!'

She broke off. The door had opened. Lady Constance Keeble came in.

★　★　★

In the doorway Lady Constance paused. She looked from one to the other with speculation in her eyes. She was a veteran of too many fine old crusted family rows not to be able to detect a strained atmosphere when she saw one. Her sister Julia was clenching and unclenching her hands. Her nephew Ronald was staring straight before him, red-eyed. A thrill ran through Lady Constance, such as causes the war-horse to start at the sound of the bugle. It was possible, of course, that this was a private fight, but her battling instinct urged her to get into it.

But there was in Lady Constance Keeble an instinct even stronger than that of battle, and that was the one which impelled her to act as critic of the sartorial deficiencies of her nearest and dearest. Years of association with her brother Clarence, who, if you took your eye off him for a second, was apt to come down to dinner in flannel trousers and an old shooting-jacket, had made this action almost automatic with the chatelaine of Blandings.

So now, eager for the fray, it was as the critic rather than as the warrior queen that she spoke. 'My dear Ronald! That tie!'

Ronnie Fish gazed at her lingeringly. It needed, he felt, but this. Poison was running through his veins, his world was rocking, green-eyed devils were shrieking mockery in his ears, and along came blasted aunts babbling of ties. It was as if somebody had touched Othello on the arm as he poised the pillow and criticized the cut of his doublet.

'Don't you know we have a dinner-party tonight? Go and put on a white tie at once.'

Even in his misery the injustice of the thing

cut Ronnie to the quick. Did his aunt suppose him ignorant of the merest decencies of life? Naturally, if he had known before he started dressing that there was a big binge on, he would have assumed the correct costume of the English gentleman for formal occasions. But considering that he had been told only about two minutes ago . . .

'And a tail-coat.'

It was the end. If this woman's words had any meaning at all, it was that she considered him capable of wearing a white tie with a dinner-jacket. Until this moment he had been intending to speak. The thing had now passed beyond speech. Directing at Lady Constance a look which no young man ought to have directed at an aunt, he strode silently from the room.

Lady Constance stood listening to the echoes of a well-slammed door.

'Ronald seems upset,' she observed. 'It runs in the family,' said Lady Julia.

'What was the trouble?'

'I have just been telling him that he is off his head.'

'I quite agree with you.'

'And I should like now,' said Lady Julia, 'to apply the same remark to you.'

She was breathing quickly. The china-blue of her eyes had an enamelled look. It was thirty-five years since she had scratched Lady Constance's face, but she seemed so much in the vein for some such demonstration that the latter involuntarily drew back.

'Really, Julia!'

'What do you mean, Constance, by inviting that girl to Blandings?'

'I did nothing of the sort.'

'You didn't invite her?'

'Certainly not.'

'She popped up out of a trap, eh?'

Lady Constance emitted that sniff of hers which came so near to being a snort.

'She wormed her way into the place under false pretences, which amounts to the same thing. You remember that Miss Schoonmaker, the American girl you met at Biarritz and wrote to me about? You gave me the impression that you hoped there might eventually be something between her and Ronald.'

'I really can't understand what you are talking about. Why need we discuss Myra Schoon-maker?'

'I am trying to explain to you how this Brown girl comes to be at the Castle. About ten days ago I was in London, and I met Ronald in his car with a girl, and he introduced her to me as Miss Schoonmaker. I had no means of checking his statement. It never occurred to me to doubt it. I assumed that she really was Miss Schoonmaker, and naturally invited her to the Castle. She arrived, and she had not been here twenty-four hours when we discovered that she was not Miss Schoonmaker at all, but this chorus-girl of Ronald's. Presumably they had planned the thing between them in order to get her here.'

'And when you found out she was an impostor you asked her to stay on? I see.'

Lady Constance flushed brightly.

'I was compelled to allow her to stay on.'

'Why?'

'Because . . . Oh, Clarence!' said Lady Constance, with the exasperation which the sudden spectacle of the head of the family so often aroused in her. The ninth Earl had selected this tense moment to potter into the room.

'Eh?' he said.

'Go away!'

'Yes,' said Lord Emsworth, 'lovely.' As so frequently happened with him, he was in a gentle trance. He wandered to the piano, extended a long, lean finger, and stabbed absently at one of the treble notes.

The sharp, tinny sound seemed to affect his sister Constance like a pin in the leg. 'Clarence!'

'Eh?'

'Don't *do* that!'

'God bless my soul!' said Lord Emsworth querulously.

He turned from the piano, and Lady Constance was enabled to see him steadily and see him whole. The sight caused her to utter a stricken cry.

'Clarence!'

'Eh?'

'What — *what* is that thing in your shirt-front?' The ninth Earl squinted down.

'It's a paper-fastener. One of those brass things you fasten papers with. I lost my stud.'

'You must have more than one stud.'

'Here's another, up here.'

'Have you only two studs?'

100

'Three,' said Lord Emsworth, a little proudly. 'For the front of the shirt, three. Dashed inconvenient things. The heads come off. You screw them off and then you put them in and then you screw them on.'

'Well, go straight up to your room and screw on the spare one.'

It was not often that Lord Emsworth found himself in the position of being able to score a debating point against his sister Constance. The fact that he was about to do so now filled him with justifiable complacency. It seemed to lend to his manner a strange, quiet dignity.

'I can't,' he said. 'I swallowed it.'

Lady Constance was not the woman to despair for long. A short, sharp spasm of agony and she had seen the way.

'Wait here,' she said. 'Mr Bodkin is sure to have dozens of spare studs. If you dare to move till I come back . . . '

She hurried from the room.

'Connie fusses so,' said Lord Emsworth equably.

He pottered back to the piano.

'Clarence,' said Lady Julia.

'Eh?'

'Leave that piano alone. Pull yourself together. Try to concentrate. And tell me about this Miss Brown.'

'Miss who?'

'Miss Brown.'

'Never heard of her,' said Lord Emsworth brightly, striking a D flat.

'Don't gibber, Clarence. Miss Brown.'

'Oh, Miss Brown? Yes. Yes, of course. Yes. Miss Brown, to be sure. Yes. Nice girl. She's going to marry Ronald.'

'Is she? That's a debatable point.'

'Oh, yes, it's all settled. I'm giving the boy his money and he's going into the motor business, and they're going to get married.'

'I want to know how all this has happened. How is it that this chorus-girl . . . '

'You're quite right,' said Lord Emsworth cordially. 'I told Connie she was wrong, but she wouldn't believe me. A chorus-girl is quite different from a ballet-girl. Galahad assures me of this.'

'If you will kindly let me finish . . . '

'By all means, by all means. You were saying — ?'

'I was asking you how it has come about that everyone in this mad-house appears to have accepted it as quite natural and satisfactory that Ronnie should be marrying a girl like that. She seems to be an honoured guest at the Castle, and yet, apart from anything else, she came here under a false name . . . '

'Odd, that,' said Lord Emsworth. 'She told us her name was Schoolbred, and it turned out she was quite wrong. It wasn't Schoolbred at all. Silly mistake to make.'

'And when that turned out, may I ask why you didn't turn *her* out?'

'Why, we couldn't, of course.'

'Why not?'

'Well, naturally we couldn't. Galahad wouldn't have liked it.'

'Galahad?'

'That's right. Galahad.'

Lady Julia threw up her arms in a passionate gesture.

'Is everybody crazy?' she cried.

Lady Constance came hurrying back into the room.

'Clarence!'

'You all keep saying 'Clarence!'' said Lord Emsworth peevishly. 'Clarence . . . Clarence' . . . One would think I was a Pekingese or something. Well, what is it now?'

'Listen, Clarence,' said Lady Constance, speaking in a clear, even voice, 'and follow me carefully. Mr Bodkin is in the North Room. You know where the North Room is? On the first floor, down the passage to the right of the landing. You know which your right hand is? Very well. Then go immediately to the North Room, and there you will find Mr Bodkin. He has studs and will fit them into your shirt.'

'I'm dashed if I'm going to have my secretary dressing me like a nursemaid!'

'If you think that with sixteen people coming to dinner I am going to trust you to put in studs for yourself . . . '

'Oh, all right,' said Lord Emsworth. 'All right, all right, all right. Lots of fuss for nothing.'

The door closed. Lady Julia came out of the frozen coma into which her brother's words had thrown her.

'Constance!'

'Well?'

'Just before you came in, Clarence told me

103

that the reason why this Brown girl was allowed to stay on at the Castle was that Galahad wished it.'

'Yes.'

'And we must all respect Galahad's wishes, must we not? I don't suppose,' said Lady Julia, mastering her complex emotions with a strong effort, 'that there are forty million people in England who think more highly of Galahad than I do. Tell me,' she went on with strained politeness, 'If it is not troubling you too much, how exactly does he come into the thing at all? Why Galahad? Why not Beach? Or Voules? Or the boy who cleans the knives and boots? What earthly business is it of Galahad's?'

Lady Constance was not by nature a patient woman, but she could make allowances for a mother's grief.

'I know how you must be feeling, Julia, and you can't be more upset about it than I am. Galahad, unfortunately, is in a position to dictate.'

'I cannot conceive of any possible position Galahad could be in which would permit him to dictate to me, but no doubt you will explain what you mean later. What I would like to know first is why he wants to dictate. What is this girl to him that he should apparently have constituted himself a sort of guardian angel to her?'

'To explain that, I must ask you to throw your mind back.'

'Better not start me throwing things.'

'Do you remember, years ago, Galahad getting

entangled with a woman named Henderson, a music-hall singer?'

'Certainly. Well?'

'This girl is her daughter.'

Lady Julia was silent for a moment.

'I see. Galahad's daughter, too?'

'I believe not. But that explains his interest in her.'

'Possibly. Yes, no doubt it does. Sentiment is the last thing of which I would have suspected Galahad, but if the old love has lingered down the years I suppose we must accept it. All right. Very touching, no doubt. But it still leaves unexplained the mystery of why everybody here seems to be treating Galahad as if his word was law. You said he was in a position to dictate. Why?'

'I was coming to that. The whole thing, you see, turns on whether Clarence lets Ronald have his money or not. If he does, Ronald can defy us all. Without it he is helpless. And in ordinary circumstances you and I know that we could easily reason with Clarence and make him do the sensible thing and refuse to release the money . . . '

'Well?'

'Well, Galahad was clever enough to see that, too. So he made a bargain. You know those abominable Reminiscences he has been writing. He said that if Ronald was given his money he would suppress them.'

'What!'

'Suppress them. Not publish them.'

'Is *that* what you meant when you said that he

105

was in a position to dictate?'

'Yes. It is sheer blackmail, of course, but there is nothing to be done.'

Lady Julia was staring, bewildered. She flung her hands up to her carefully coiffured head, seemed to realize at the last moment that a touch would ruin it, and lowered them again.

'Am I mad?' she cried. 'Or is everybody else? You seriously mean that I am supposed to acquiesce in my son ruining his life simply in order to keep Galahad from publishing his Reminiscences?'

'But, Julia, you don't know what they're like. Think of the life Galahad led as a young man. He seems to have known everybody in England who is looked up to and respected today and to have shared the most disgraceful escapades with them. One case alone, for example — Sir Gregory Parsloe. I have not read the thing, of course, but he tells me that there is a story in Galahad's book about himself when he was a young man in London . . . something about some prawns — I don't know what . . . which would make him the laughing-stock of the county. The book is full of that kind of story, and every story about somebody who is looked on today as a model of propriety. If it is published, it will ruin the reputations of half the best people in England.'

Lady Julia laughed shortly.

'I'm afraid I don't share your reverence for the feelings of the British aristocracy, Connie. I agree that Galahad probably knows the shady secrets of two-thirds of the peerage, but I don't feel your shrinking horror at the thought of the public reading them in print. I haven't the slightest objection in the world to Galahad throwing bombshells. At any rate, whatever the effect of his literary efforts on the peace of mind of the governing classes, I certainly do not intend to buy him off at the price of having Ronnie marrying any Miss Browns.'

'You don't mean that you are going to try to stop this marriage?'

'I most certainly am.'

'But, Julia! This book of Galahad's. It will alienate every friend we've got. They will say we ought to have stopped him. You don't know . . . '

'I know this, that Galahad can publish Reminiscences till he is blue in the face, but I am not going to have my son making a fool of himself and doing something he'll regret for the rest of his life. And now, if you will excuse me, Connie, I propose to take a short stroll on the terrace in the faint hope of cooling off. I feel so incandescent that I'm apt to burst into spontaneous flame at any moment, like dry tinder.'

With which words Lady Julia Fish took her departure through the french windows. And Lady Constance, having remained for some few moments in anguished thought, moved to the fireplace and rang the bell.

Beach appeared.

'Beach,' said Lady Constance, 'please telephone at once to Sir Gregory Parsloe at Matchingham. Tell him I must see him immediately. Say it is of the utmost importance.

Ask him to hurry over so as to get here before people begin to arrive. And when he comes show him into the library.'

'Very good, m'lady.'

The butler spoke with his official calm, but inwardly he was profoundly stirred. He was not a nimble-minded man, but he could put two and two together, and it seemed to him that in some mysterious way, beyond the power of his intellect to grasp, all these alarms and excursions must be connected with the love-story of his old friend, Mr Ronald, and his new — but very highly esteemed — friend, Sue Brown.

He had left Mr Ronald with his mother. Then Lady Constance had gone in. A short while later, Mr Ronald had come out and gone rushing upstairs with all the appearance of an over-wrought soul. And now here was Lady Constance, after a conversation with Lady Julia, ringing bells and sending urgent telephone messages.

It must mean something. If Beach had been Monty Bodkin, he would have said that there were wheels within wheels. Heaving gently like a seaweed-covered sea, he withdrew to carry out his instructions.

The butler's telephone message found Sir Gregory Parsloe enjoying a restful cigarette in his bedroom. He had completed his toilet some little time before; but, being an experienced diner-out and knowing how sticky that anteprandial vigil in somebody else's drawing-room can be, he had not intended to set out for Blandings Castle for another twenty minutes or so. Like so many elderly, self-indulgent bachelors, he was inclined to shirk life's grimmer side.

But the information that Lady Constance Keeble wished to have urgent speech with him had him galloping down the stairs and lumbering into his car in what for a man of his build was practically tantamount to a trice. It must, he felt, be those infernal Reminiscences that she wanted to see him about: and, feeling nervous and apprehensive, he told the chauffeur to drive like the devil.

In the past two weeks, Sir Gregory Parsloe-Parsloe, of Matchingham Hall, seventh Baronet of his line, had run the gamut of the emotions. He had plumbed the depths of horror on learning that his old companion, the Hon. Galahad Threepwood, was planning to publish the story of his life. He had soared to dizzy heights of relief on learning that he had decided not to do so. But from that relief there had been a reaction. What, he had asked himself, was to prevent the old pest changing his mind again? And this telephone call seemed to suggest that he might have done so.

Of all the grey-haired pillars of Society who had winced and cried aloud at the news that the Hon. Galahad was about to unlock the doors of memory, it was probably Sir Gregory Parsloe who had winced most and cried loudest. His position was so particularly vulnerable. He had political ambitions, and was, indeed, on the eve of being accepted by the local Unionist committee as the party's candidate for the forthcoming by-election in the Bridgeford and

Shifley Parliamentary Division of Shropshire. And no one knew better than himself that Unionist committees look askance at men with pasts.

Small wonder, then, that Sir Gregory Parsloe writhed in his car and, clumping up the stairs of Blandings Castle to the library in Beach's wake, sank into a chair and sat gazing at Lady Constance with apprehension on every feature of his massive face. Years of good living had given Sir Gregory something of the look of a buck of the Regency days. He resembled now a Regency buck about to embark on a difficult interview with the family lawyer.

Lady Constance made no humane attempt to break the bad news gently. She was far too agitated for that. Sir Gregory got it like a pail of water in the face, and sat spluttering as if it had actually been water she had poured over him.

'What shall we do?' lamented Lady Constance. 'I know Julia so well. She is entirely self-centred. So long as she can get what she wants, other people don't count. Julia is like that, and always has been. She will stop this marriage. I don't know how, but she will do it. And if the marriage is broken off, Galahad will have no reason for suppressing his abominable book. The manuscript will go to the publishers next day. What did you say?'

Sir Gregory had not spoken. He had merely uttered a wordless sound half-way between a grunt and a groan.

'Have you nothing to suggest?' said Lady Constance.

Before the baronet could reply, if he would have replied, there was an interruption. The door of the library opened and a head inserted itself. It was a small, brilliantined head, the eyes beneath the narrow forehead furtive, the moustache below the perky nose a nasty little moustache. Having smiled weakly, it withdrew.

It was a desire for solitude that had brought P. Frobisher Pilbeam to the library. A few moments before, he had been in the drawing-room and had found its atmosphere oppressive. Solid county gentlemen and their wives had begun to arrive, and the sense of being an alien in a community where everybody seemed extraordinarily intimate with everybody else had weighed upon him, inducing red ears and a general sensation of elephantiasis about the hands and feet.

Taking advantage, therefore, of the fact that the lady with the weather-beaten face who had just asked him what pack he hunted with had had her attention diverted elsewhere, he had stolen down to the library to be alone. And the first thing he saw there was Lady Constance Keeble. So, as we say, Percy Pilbeam smiled weakly and withdrew.

The actual time covered by his appearance and disappearance was not more than two or three seconds, but it had been enough for Lady Constance Keeble to give him one of the celebrated Keeble looks. Turning from this task and lowering the raised eyebrow and uncurling the curled lip, she was astonished to observe that Sir Gregory Parsloe was staring at the closed door with the aspect of one who had just seen a beautiful vision.

What — what — what . . .

'I beg your pardon?' said Lady Constance, perplexed. 'Good heavens! Was that *Pilbeam?*' Lady Constance was shocked.

'Do you know Mr Pilbeam?' she asked in a tone which suggested that she would have expected something better than this from the seventh holder of a proud title.

Sir Gregory was not a man of the build that leaps from chairs, but he had levered himself out of the one he sat in with an animation that almost made the thing amount to a leap.

'Know him? Why, he's in the Castle because I know him! I engaged him to steal that infernal manuscript of your brother's.'

'What!'

'Certainly. A week or so ago. Emsworth called one morning with Threepwood to see me, and accused me of having stolen that dashed pig of his, and when I told him I knew nothing about it Threepwood got nasty and said he was going to make a special effort to remember all the discreditable things that had ever happened to me as a young man and put them in his book. So I ran up to London next day and went to see this fellow Pilbeam — he had acted for me before in a certain rather delicate matter — and found that Emsworth had asked him to come here to investigate the theft of his pig, and I offered him five hundred pounds if, when he was at the Castle, he would steal the manuscript.'

'Good gracious!'

'And then you told me the pig had been found and Threepwood was going to suppress the book, so I naturally assumed that the chap would have gone back to London. Why, if he's still here, the whole thing's simple. He must go ahead, as originally planned, and get hold of that manuscript and hand it over to us and we'll destroy it. Then it won't matter if this marriage you speak of takes place or not.' He paused. Animation gave place to concern. 'But suppose there are more copies than one?'

'There aren't.'

'You're sure? He may have had it typed.'

'No, I know he has not. He had never really finished the horrible thing. He keeps it in his desk and takes it out and adds bits to it.'

'Then we're all right.'

'If Mr Pilbeam can get possession of the manuscript.'

'Oh, he'll do that. You can rely on him. There isn't a smarter young fellow in London at that sort of thing. Why, he got hold of some letters of mine . . . but that is neither here nor there. I can assure you that if you engage Pilbeam to steal compromising papers, you will have them in the course of a day or two. It's what he's best at. You say Threepwood keeps the thing in a desk. Desks are nothing to Pilbeam. Those — er — those letters of mine . . . to which I alluded just now . . . those letters . . . perfectly innocent, you understand, but a wrong construction might have been placed upon one or two passages in them had they been published as the girl . . . as their recipient had threatened . . . Well, to cut a long story short, to secure them Pilbeam had to pretend to be the man come to inspect the gas meter and break into a safe. This will be child's play to him. If you will excuse me, I will go and find him at once. We must put the matter in hand without delay. What a pity he popped off like that. We could have had everything arranged by now.'

Sir Gregory hurried from the room, baying on the scent like one of his own hounds. And Lady Constance, drawing a deep breath, leaned back in her chair and closed her eyes. After all that had passed in the last twenty minutes, she felt the need to relax.

On her face, as she sat, there might have been observed not merely relief, but a sort of awed look, as of one who contemplates the inscrutable workings of Providence.

Providence, she now perceived, did not put even Pilbeams into the world without a purpose.

# 7

Sue stood leaning out over the battlements of Blandings Castle, her chin cupped in her hands. Her eyes were clouded, her mouth a thin red line of depression. A little furrow of unhappiness had carved itself in the smooth whiteness of her forehead.

It was an instinct for the high places, like that of a small, nervous cat which fears vague perils on the lower levels, that had sent her climbing to this eminence. Wandering past the great gatehouse where a channel of gravel divided the west wing of the castle from the centre block, she had espied an open door, giving on to mysterious stone steps; and, mounting these, had found herself on the roof, with all Shropshire spread beneath her.

The change of elevation had done nothing to alter her mood. It was four o'clock of a sultry, overcast, oppressive afternoon, and a sullen stillness had fallen on the world. The heat wave which for the past two weeks had been grilling England was in the uncomfortable process of working up to a thunderstorm. Shropshire, under a leaden sky, had taken on a sinister and a brooding air. The flowers in the gardens drooped forlornly. The lake was a grey smudge, and the river in the valley below a thread of sickly tarnished silver. Gone, too, was the friendly charm of the Scotch fir spinneys that dotted the park. They seemed now black and haunted and menacing, as if witches lived in crooked little cottages in the heart of them.

'Ugh!' said Sue, hating Shropshire.

Until this moment, except for a few cows with secret sorrows, there had been no living creature to mitigate the gloom of the grim prospect. It was as if life, discouraged by the weather conditions, had died out upon the earth. But as she spoke, shaking her head with the flicker of a grimace, she perceived on the path below a familiar form. It looked up, sighted her, waved, and disappeared in the direction of the gatehouse. And presently feet boomed hollowly on the stone stairs, and there came into view the slouch-hatted head of Monty Bodkin. 'Hullo, Sue. All alone?'

Monty, who seemed, like everything else, to be affected by the weather, puffed, removed his hat, fanned himself, and laid it down.

'Gosh, what a day!' he observed. 'You been up here long?'

'About an hour.'

'I've been closeted with that fellow Pilbeam in the smoking-room. Went in to fill my cigarette-case and got into conversation with him. He's been telling me all about himself. Interesting chap.'

'I think he's a worm.'

'He is a worm,' agreed Monty. 'But even worms, don't you think, are of more than passing interest when they run private inquiry agencies? Did you know he was a private detective?'

'Yes.'

'Now, there's a job I should like.'

'You would hate it, Monty. Sneaking about, spying on people.'

'But with a magnifying-glass, remember,' urged Monty. 'You don't feel that it makes a difference if you do it with a magnifying-glass? No? Well, perhaps you're right. In any case, I suppose it requires special gifts. I wouldn't know a clue if you brought me one on a skewer. I say, did you ever see such a day? I feel as if I were in a frying-pan. Still, I suppose one's as well off up here as anywhere.'

'I suppose so.'

Monty surveyed his surroundings with a sentimental eye.

'Must have been fifteen years since I was on this roof. As a kid you couldn't keep me off it. I smoked my first cigar behind that buttress. Slightly to the left is the spot where I was sick. You see that chimney-stack?'

Sue saw the chimney-stack.

'I once watched old Gally chase Ronnie twenty-seven times round that with a whangee. He had been putting tin-tacks on his chair. Ronnie had on Gally's chair, I mean, of course, not Gally on Ronnie's. Where is Ronnie by the way?'

'Lady Julia asked him to take her to Shrewsbury in his two-seater, to do some shopping.'

Sue's voice was flat, and Monty looked at her inquiringly. 'Well, why not?'

'Oh, I don't know,' said Sue. 'Only, considering that she was at Biarritz for three months and then in Paris and after that in London, it seems odd that she should wait to do her shopping till she got to Shrewsbury.'

Monty nodded sagely.

'I see what you mean. A ruse, you think? A cunning stratagem to keep him out of the way? I shouldn't wonder if you weren't right.'

Sue looked out over the grey world.

'She needn't have bothered,' she said, in a small voice. 'Ronnie seems quite capable of keeping out of my way without assistance.'

'What do you mean by that?'

'Haven't you noticed?'

'Well, I'll tell you,' said Monty apologetically. 'What with being a good deal exercised about my lord Emsworth's questionable attitude and musing in my spare time on good old Gertrude, I haven't been much in the vein for noticing things. Has he been keeping out of your way?'

'Ever since we got back.'

'Oh, rot.'

'It isn't rot.'

'A girlish fancy, child.'

'It's nothing of the kind. He's been avoiding me all the time. He'll do anything to keep from being alone with me. And if ever we do happen to be alone together he's quite different.'

'How do you mean, different?'

'Polite. Horribly, disgustingly polite. All sort of stiff and formal, as if I were a stranger. You know that way he gets when he's with someone he doesn't like.'

Monty was concerned.

'I say, this wants thinking over. I confess that

my primary scheme, on spotting you leaning over the ramparts, was to buzz up and pour out my troubles on your neck. But if this is really so, you had better do the pouring. As what's-his-name said to the stretcher-case, 'Your need is greater than mine'.'

'Are you in trouble, too?'

'Trouble?' Monty held up a warning hand. 'Listen. Don't tempt me. One more word of encouragement, and I'll be monopolizing the conversation.'

'Go on. I can wait.'

'You're sure?'

'Quite.'

Monty sighed gratefully.

'Well, it'll be a relief, I must own,' he admitted. 'Sue, old girl, I am becoming conscious of an impending doom. The future is looking black. For some reason which I am unable to fathom I don't seem to have made a hit with my employer.'

'What makes you think that?'

'Signs, Sue. Signs and portents. The old blighter bites at me. He clicks his tongue irritably. I look up and find his eyes fixed on me with an expression of loathing. You wouldn't think it possible that a man who could stick Hugo Carmody as a secretary for a matter of eleven weeks would be showing distress signs after a mere two days of me, but there it is. Why, I cannot say, but the ninth Earl obviously hates my insides.'

'Quite sure.'

'But it seems so unlike Lord Emsworth. I've

always thought him such an old dear.'

'Precisely how I had remembered him from boyhood days. He used to tip me when I went back to school — tip me lavishly and with the kindest of smiles. But no longer. Not any more. He now views me with concern and dogs my footsteps.'

'Does *what?*'

'Dogs my footsteps. Tails me up, as they say at Scotland Yard. Do you recall that hymn about 'See the hosts of Midian prowl and prowl around'? Well, that's what this extraordinary bloke does. For some strange reason of his own he has started watching me, as if he were suspecting me of nameless crimes. I'll give you an instance. Yesterday afternoon I had gone down to the pig-bin to chirrup to that pig of his in the hope of establishing cordial relations, as you advised, and as I approached the animal's lair I happened to glance round, and there he was peering out from behind a tree, his face alight with mistrust. Wouldn't you call that prowling?'

'It certainly seems like prowling.'

'It is prowling. Grade A prowling. And what, I am asking myself, will the harvest be? You may say, Oh, why worry? arguing that an Earl, on his own ground, has a perfect right to hide behind trees and glare at secretaries. But I go deeper than that. I look on the thing as a symptom, and a dangerous symptom. I contend that the Earl who hides behind trees today is an Earl who intends to apply the order of the boot tomorrow. And, my gosh, Sue, I can't afford to go getting the boot twice daily like this. If I don't stay put in some sort of job for a year, I fail to gather in Gertrude, and how am I to get another job if I lose this one? I'm not an easy man to place. I have my limitations, and I know it.'

'Poor old Monty!'

' "Poor old Monty" sums up the thing extraordinarily neatly,' agreed the haunted man. 'I'm sunk if this old bird fires me. And what makes it so particularly foul is that I haven't a notion what he's got against me. I've made a point of being so fearfully alert and obsequious and the perfect secretary generally. I've been simply fascinating. The whole thing's a mystery.'

Sue reflected.

'I'll tell you what to do. Why not get hold of Ronnie and ask him to ask Lord Emsworth tactfully . . . ' Monty shook his head.

'Not Ronnie. No. Not within the sphere of practical politics. Now, there's another mystery, Sue. Old Ronnie. Once one of my closest pals, and now frigid, aloof, distant. Says 'Oh, yes?' and 'Really?' when I speak to him, and turns away as if desirous of terminating the conversation.'

'Really?'

'And 'Oh, yes?' '

'I mean, does he really seem not to like you?'

'He's as sniffy as dammit. And I can't . . . Great Scott, Sue,' cried Monty, struck with an idea, 'you don't suppose that by any chance he Knows All?'

'That you and I were once engaged? How could he?'

'No, that's right. He couldn't, could he?'

'Nobody here can have told him, because nobody knows. Except Gally, who wouldn't breathe a word.'

'True. It only occurred to me as a rather rummy coincidence that he's upstage like this with both of us. Why, if he does not Know All, should he be keeping out of your way, as you say he's doing?'

All Sue's pent-up misery found voice. She had not intended to confide in Monty, for she was a girl whom life had trained to keep her troubles to herself. But Ronnie had gone to Shrewsbury, and the heat was making her head ache, and the sky was looking like the underside of a dead fish, and she wished she were dead, so she poured out all the poison that was in her heart.

'I'll tell you why. Because his mother has been talking to him . . . never stopped since she got here . . . talking to him and nagging at him and telling him what a fool he is to think of marrying a girl like me, when there are dozens of girls in his own set . . . Oh, yes, she has. I know it just as if I had been there. I know exactly the sort of things she would say. And all quite true, too, I suppose. 'My dear boy, a chorus-girl!' Well, so I am. You can't get away from that. Why should anyone want to marry me?'

Monty clicked his tongue. He could not subscribe to this.

'My dear old egg! Do it myself tomorrow, if not already earmarked elsewhere. I consider Ronnie dashed lucky.'

'That's sweet of you, Monty, but I'm afraid

Ronnie doesn't agree with you.'

'Oh, rot!'

'I wish I could think so.'

'Absolute rot. Ronnie's not the sort of chap to back out of marrying a girl he's asked to marry him.'

'Oh, I know that. His word is his bond. We men of honour! My poor old Monty, you don't really think I would marry a man who has stopped being fond of me, simply because he's too decent to break the engagement? If there's one person I despise in the world, it's the girl who clings to a man when she knows it's only politeness that keeps him from telling her for goodness' sake to go away and leave him in peace. If ever I really feel certain that Ronnie wants to be rid of me,' said Sue, staring dry-eyed at the menacing sky. 'I'll chuck it all up in a second, no matter how much it hurts.'

Monty shuffled uneasily.

'I think you're making too much of it all,' he said, but without conviction. 'If you boil it down, probably all that's happened is that the old chap's got a touch of liver. Enough to give anyone a touch of liver, weather like this.'

Sue did not reply. She had walked to the battlements and was looking down. Something in the aspect of her back seemed to tell Monty Bodkin that she was either crying or about to cry, and he did not know what to do for the best. The face of Gertrude Butterwick, floating between him and the sky, forbade the obvious move. A man with a Gertrude Butterwick on his books cannot lightly put his arms round other waists and murmur 'There, there!' into other ears.

He coughed and said, 'Er — well . . . '

Sue did not turn. He coughed again. Then, with a 'Well — I — er -ah . . . ' he sidled to the stairs. The clang of the closing door came to Sue's ears as she dabbed at her eyes with the tiny fragment of lace which she called a handkerchief. She was relieved that he had gone. There are moments when a girl must be alone to wrestle single-handed with her own particular devils.

This she did, bravely and thoroughly. There was in her small body the spirit of an Amazon. She fought the devils and routed the devils, till presently a final sniff told that the battle had been won. Shropshire, which had been a thing of mist, became firmer in its outlines. She put away the handkerchief and stood blinking defiantly.

She was happier now. The determination to finish everything, if she saw Ronnie wanted it finished had not weakened. It still lay rooted at the back of her mind. But hope had dawned again. She was telling herself that she understood Ronnie's odd behaviour. He was worried, poor darling, as who would not be with a woman of Lady Julia Fish's powerful personality going on at him all the time. And when a man is worried, he naturally becomes preoccupied.

The sound of a car drawing up on the other side of the house broke in upon her meditations. She hurried across the roof, her heart quickening.

She turned away, disappointed. It was not

Ronnie, back from Shrewsbury. It was only a short, stout man who had driven up in the station taxi. A short, stout, stumpy man of no importance whatever.

So thought Sue in her ignorance. The stout man, had he known that he was being thus casually dismissed as negligible, would have been not only offended, but amazed.

For this visitor to Blandings Castle, for all that he arrived without pomp, driven to his destination by charioteer Robinson in that humble conveyance, the Market Blandings station taxi, was none other than George Alexander Pyke, first Viscount Tilbury, founder and proprietor of the Mammoth Publishing Company of Tilbury House, Tilbury Street, London.

There are men of the bulldog breed who do not readily admit defeat. Crushed to earth, they rise again. To this doughty band belonged George Alexander, Viscount Tilbury. He had built up a very large fortune chiefly by the simple method of never knowing when he was beaten, and the fact that he was now ringing the doorbell of Blandings Castle proved that the ancient spirit still lingered. He had come to tackle the Hon. Galahad Threepwood in person about those Reminiscences of his, and he meant to stand no nonsense.

Many men in his position, informed that the Hon. Galahad had decided to withhold his book from publication, would have felt that there was nothing to be done about it. They would have accepted the situation as one beyond their power to change, and would have contented themselves with grieving over their monetary loss and thinking hard thoughts of the man responsible. Lord Tilbury was made of sterner stuff. He grieved — we have seen him grieving — and he thought hard thoughts: but it never occurred to him for an instant not to do something about it.

A busy man, he could not get away from his office immediately. Pressure of work had delayed the starting of the expedition-until today. But at eleven-fifteen that morning he had taken train for Market Blandings and, after establishing himself at the Emsworth Arms in that sleepy little town, had directed Robinson, of the station taxi, to take him on to the Castle.

His mood was one of stern self-confidence. The idea that he might fail in his mission did not strike him as even a remote possibility. He had only a dim recollection of the Hon. Galahad, for he had not met him for twenty-five years, and even in the old days had never been really an intimate of his, but he retained a sort of general impression of an amiable, easygoing man. Not at all the type of man to hold out against a forceful, straight from the shoulder talk such as he proposed to subject him to as soon as this door-bell was answered. Lord Tilbury had great faith in the magic of speech. Beach answered the bell.

'Is Mr Threepwood in? Mr Galahad Threepwood?'

'Yes, sir. What name shall I say?'

'Lord Tilbury.'

'Very good, m'lord. If you will step this way. I

fancy Mr Galahad is in the small library.'

The small library, however, proved empty. It contained evidence of the life literary in the shape of a paper-piled desk and a good deal of ink on the carpet and elsewhere, but it had no human occupant.

'Possibly Mr Galahad is on the lawn. He walks there sometimes,' said the butler indulgently, as one tolerant of the foibles of genius. 'If your lordship will take a seat . . . '

He withdrew, and began to descend the stairs with measured tread, but Lord Tilbury did not take a seat. He was staring, transfixed, at something that lay upon the desk. He drew closer — furtively, with a sidelong eye on the door.

Yes, his surmise had been correct. It was the manuscript of the Reminiscences that lay before him. Evidently its author had only just risen from the task of polishing it, for the ink was still wet on a paragraph where, searching like some Flaubert for the *mot juste*, he had run his pen through the word 'intodicated' and substituted it for the more colourful 'pickled to the gills'.

Lord Tilbury's eyes, always prominent, bulged a trifle farther from their sockets. His breathing quickened.

Every man who by his own unaided efforts has succeeded in wresting a great fortune from a resistant world has something of the buccaneer in him, a touch of the practical, Do-It-Now pirate of the Spanish Main. In Lord Tilbury, as a younger man, there had been quite a good deal. And while prosperity and the diminishing necessity of giving trade rivals the elbow had tended to atrophy this quality, it had not died altogether. Standing there within arm's length of the manuscript, with the coast clear and a taxi waiting at the front door, he was seriously contemplating the quick snatch and the masterful dash for the open.

And it was perhaps fortunate, for sudden activity of the kind might have proved injurious to a man of his full habit, that before he could quite screw his courage to the sticking point his ear caught the sound of approaching footsteps. He drew back like a cat from a cream-jug, and when the Hon. Galahad arrived was looking out of the window, humming a careless barcarolle.

The Hon. Galahad paused in the doorway and stuck his black-rimmed monocle in his eye. Behind the glass the eye was bright and questioning. His forehead wrinkled with mental strain as he surveyed his visitor.

'Don't tell me,' he begged. 'Let me think. I pride myself on my memory. You're fatter and you've aged a lot, but you're someone I used to know quite well at one time. In some odd way I seem to associate you with a side of beef . . . Shorty Smith? . . . Stumpy Whiting? . . . No, I've got it, by gad! Stinker Pyke!' He beamed with honest satisfaction. 'Not bad, that, considering that it must be fully twenty-five years since I saw you last. Pyke. That's who you are. And we used to call you Stinker. Well, well, how are you, Stinker?'

Lord Tilbury's face had taken on an austere pinkness. He disliked the reference to his increased bulk, and advancing years, and it is never pleasant for an elderly man of substance to be addressed by a name which even in his youth was offensive to him. He said as much.

'Well, all right. Pyke, then,' said the Hon. Galahad agreeably. 'How are you, Pyke? Good Lord, this certainly puts the clock back. The last time I saw you must have been that night at Romano's when Plug Basham started throwing bread and got a little over-excited, and one thing led to another and in about two minutes there you were on the floor, laid out cold by a dashed great side of beef and all the undertakers present making bids for the body. I can see your face now,' said the Hon. Galahad, chuckling. 'Most amusing.'

He grew more serious. His smile vanished. He shook his head sadly.

'Poor old Plug!' he sighed. 'A fellow who never knew where to stop. His only fault, poor chap.'

Lord Tilbury had not come a hundred and fourteen miles to talk about the late Major Wilfred Basham, a man who, even before the episode alluded to, had never been a favourite of his. He endeavoured to intimate this, but the Hon. Galahad when in reminiscent mood was not an easy man to divert.

'I took the whole thing up with him at the Pelican next day. I tried to reason with him. Throwing sides of beef about in restaurants wasn't done, I said. Not British. Bread, yes, I said. Sides of beef, no. I pointed out that all the trouble was caused by his fatal practice of always ordering a quart where other men began with pints. He saw it, too. 'I know, I know,' he said. 'I'm a darned fool. In fact, between you and me, Gally, I suppose I'm one of those fellows my father always warned me against. But the Bashams have always ordered quarts. It's an old Basham family custom.' Then the only way was, I said, to swear off altogether. He said he couldn't. A little something with his meals was an absolute necessity to him. So there I had to leave it. And then one day I met him again at a wedding reception at one of the hotels.'

'I . . . ' said Lord Tilbury.

'A wedding reception,' proceeded the Hon. Galahad. 'And, by a curious coincidence, there was another wedding reception going on at the same hotel, and, oddly enough, their bride was some sort of connexion of our bride. So pretty soon these two wedding parties began to mix and mingle, everybody happy and having a good time, and suddenly I felt something pluck at my elbow and there was old Plug, looking as white as a sheet. 'Yes Plug?' I said, surprised. The poor, dear fellow uttered a hollow groan. 'Gally, old man,' he said, 'lead me away old chap. The end has come. The stuff has begun to get me. I have had only the merest sip of champagne, and yet I assure you I can distinctly see two brides'.'

'I . . . ' said Lord Tilbury.

'A shock to the poor fellow, as you can readily imagine. I could have set his mind at rest, of course, but I saw that this was providential. Just the sort of jolt he had been needing. I drew him into a corner and talked to him like a Dutch uncle. And this time he gave me his solemn word that from that day onward he would never touch another drop. 'Can you do it, Plug?' I said. 'Have you the strength, the will-power?' 'Yes, Gally,' he replied bravely, 'I can. Why, dash it,' he said, 'I've got to. I can't go through the rest of my life seeing two of everything. Imagine! Two bookies you owe money to . . . Two process-servers . . . Two Stinker Pykes . . . 'Yes, old man, in that grim moment he thought of you . . . And he went off with a set, resolute look about his jaw which it did me good to see.'

'I . . . ' said Lord Tilbury.

'And about two weeks later I came on him in the Strand, and he was bubbling over with quiet happiness. 'It's all right, Gally.' he said, 'It's all right, old lad. I've done it. I've won the battle.' 'Amazing, Plug,' I said. 'Brave chap! Splendid fellow! Was it a terrific strain?' His eyes lit up. 'It was at first,' he said. 'In fact, it was so tough that I didn't think I should be able to stick it out. And then I discovered a teetotal drink that is not only palatable but positively appetising. Absinthe, they call it, and now I've got that I don't care if I never touch wine, spirits, or any other intoxicants again'.'

'I am not interested,' said Lord Tilbury, 'in your friend Basham.' The Hon. Galahad was remorseful.

'I'm sorry,' he said. 'Shouldn't have rattled on. An old failing of mine, I'm afraid. Probably you've come on some most important errand, and here have I been yarning away, wasting your time. Quite right to pull me up. Take a seat, and tell me why you've suddenly bobbed up like this after all these years, Stinker.'

'Don't call me Stinker!'

'Of course. I'm sorry. Forgot. Well, carry on, Pyke.'

'And don't call me Pyke. My name is Tilbury.'

The Hon. Galahad started. His monocle fell from his eye, and he screwed it in again thoughtfully. There was a concerned and disapproving look on his face. He shook his head gravely.

'Going about under a false name? Bad. I don't like that.'

'Cor!'

'It never pays. Honestly, it doesn't. Sooner or later you're bound to be found out, and then you get it all the hotter from the judge. I remember saying that to Stiffy Vokes in the year ninety-nine, when he was sneaking about London calling himself Orlando Maltravers in the empty hope of baffling the bookies after a bad City and Suburban. And he, unlike you, had had the elementary sense to put on a false beard. Stinker, old chap,' said the Hon. Galahad kindly, 'is it worth while? Can this do anything but postpone the inevitable end? Why not go back and face the music like a man? Or, if the thing's too bad for that, at least look in at some good theatrical costumier's and buy some blond whiskers. What is it they are after you for?'

Lord Tilbury was beginning to wonder if even a volume of Reminiscences which would rock England was worth the price he was paying.

'I call myself Tilbury,' he said between set teeth, 'because in a recent Honours List I received a peerage, and Tilbury was the title I selected.'

Light flooded in upon the Hon. Galahad's darkness. 'Oh, you're *Lord* Tilbury?'

'I am.'

'What on earth did they make you a lord for, Stinker?' asked the Hon. Galahad in frank amazement.

Lord Tilbury was telling himself that he must be strong.

'I happen to occupy a position of some slight importance in the newspaper world. I am the proprietor of a concern whose name may be familiar to you — the Mammoth Publishing Company.'

'Mammoth?'

'Mammoth.'

'Don't tell me,' said the Hon. Galahad. 'Let me think. Why, aren't the Mammoth the people I sold that book of mine to?'

'They are.'

'Stinker — I mean Pyke — I mean Tilbury,' said the Hon. Galahad regretfully, 'I'm sorry about that. Yes, by Jove, I am. I've let you down, haven't I? I see now why you've come here. You want me to reconsider. Well, I'm afraid you've had your journey for nothing, Stinker, old man. I won't let that book be published.'

'But . . . '

'No. I can't argue. I won't do it.'

'But, good heavens! . . . '

'I know, I know. But I won't. I have reasons.'

'Reasons?'

'Private and sentimental reasons.'

133

'But it's outrageous. It's unheard of. You signed the contract. You were satisfied with the terms we proposed . . . '

'It's got nothing to do with the terms.'

'And you can't pretend that you are not in a position to deliver the book. There it is on your desk, finished.' The Hon. Galahad took up the manuscript with something of the tenderness of a mother dandling her first-born. He stared at it, sighed, stared at it again, sighed once more. His heart was aching.

The more he reread it, the more of a tragedy did it seem to him that this lovely thing should not be given to the world. It was such dashed good stuff. Yes, if he did say it himself, such dashed good stuff. Faithfully and well he had toiled at his great task of erecting a lasting memorial to an epoch in London's history which, if ever an epoch did, deserved its Homer or its Gibbon, and he had done it, by George! Jolly good, ripping good stuff.

And no one would ever read the dashed thing.

'A book like this is never finished,' he said. 'I could go on adding to it for the rest of my life.'

He sighed again. Then he brightened. The suppression of his masterpiece was the price of Dolly's daughter's happiness. If it brought happiness to Dolly's daughter, there was nothing to regret, nothing to sigh about at all.

All the same, he did wish that his brother Clarence could have been of tougher fibre and better able, without assistance, to cope with the females of the family.

He put the manuscript away in a drawer.

'But it's finished,' he said, 'as far as any chance of its ever getting into print is concerned. It will never be published.'

'But . . . '

'No, Stinker, that's final. I'm sorry. Don't imagine I don't see your side of it. I know I've treated you badly, and I quite realize how justified you are in blinding and stiffing . . . '

'I am not blinding and stiffing. I flatter myself that I have — under extreme provocation — succeeded in keeping this discussion on an amicable footing. I merely say . . . '

'It's no use your saying anything, Stinker.'

'Don't call me . . . '

'I can't possibly explain the situation to you. It would take too long. But you can rest assured that nothing you can say will make the slightest difference. I won't publish.'

There was a pregnant silence. Lord Tilbury's gaze, which had fastened itself, like that of a Pekinese on coffee-sugar, upon the drawer into which he had seen the manuscript disappear, shifted to the man who stood between him and it. He stared at the Hon. Galahad wistfully, as if yearning for that side of beef which had once proved so irresistible a weapon in the hand of Plug Basham.

The fever passed. The battle-light died out of his eyes. He rose stiffly.

'In that case I will bid you good afternoon.'

'You're not going?'

'I am going.'

The Hon. Galahad was distressed.

'I wish you wouldn't take it like this. Why get

stuffy, Stinker? Sit down. Have a chat. Stay on and join us for a bite of dinner.' Lord Tilbury gulped. 'Dinner!'

A harmless word, but on his lips it somehow managed to acquire the sound of a rich Elizabethan oath — the sort of thing Ben Jonson, in his cups, might have flung at Beaumont and Fletcher.

'Dinner!' said Tilbury. 'Cor!'

There are moments in life when only sharp physical action can heal the wounded spirit. Just as a native of India, stung by a scorpion, will seek to relieve his agony by running, so now did Lord Tilbury, fresh from this scene with one who seemed to him well fitted to be classified as a human scorpion, desire to calm himself with a brisk cross-country walk. Reaching the broad front steps and seeing before him the station taxi, he was conscious of a feeling amounting almost to nausea at the thought of climbing into its mildew-scented interior and riding back to the Emsworth Arms.

He produced money, thrust it upon the surprised Robinson, mumbled unintelligently and, turning abruptly, began to stump off in a westerly direction. Robinson, having pursued him with a solid, silent, Shropshire stare till he had vanished behind a shrubbery, threw in his clutch and drove pensively homewards.

Lord Tilbury stumped on, busy with his thoughts.

At first chaotic, these began gradually to take shape. His mind returned to that project which he had conceived while standing alone in the small library. A single object seemed to be imprinted on his retina — that desk in which the Hon. Galahad had placed his manuscript.

He yearned for direct action against that desk.

Like all reformed buccaneers, he put up a good case for himself in extenuation of this resurgence of the Old Adam. To take that manuscript, he argued, would merely be to take that which was rightfully his. He had a legal claim to it. The contract had been signed and witnessed. Payment in advance had changed hands. Normally, no doubt, as between author and publisher, the author would have wrapped his work in brown paper, stuck stamps on it, and posted it. But if the eccentric fellow preferred to leave it in a desk for the publisher to come and fetch it, the thing still remained a legitimate business transaction.

And how simple the looting of that desk would be, he felt, if only he were staying in the house. From the careless, casual way in which the Hon. Galahad had put the manuscript in that drawer he had received a strong impression that he would not even bother to lock it. Anybody staying in the house . . .

Bitter remorse swept over Lord Tilbury as he strode broodingly through the heat-hushed grounds of Blandings Castle. He saw now what a mistake he had made in taking that proud, offended attitude with the Hon. Galahad. If only he had played his cards properly, taken the thing with a smile, accepted that invitation to dinner and gone on playing his cards properly, he would almost certainly before nightfall have been asked to move his belongings from the Emsworth Arms and come and stay at the Castle. And then . . .

Of all sad words of tongue or pen, the saddest are these: It might have been. Groaning in spirit, Lord Tilbury walked on. And suddenly as he walked there came to his nostrils the only scent in the world which could have diverted his mind from that which weighed it.

He had smelt a pig.

To those superficially acquainted with them, it would have seemed incredible that George, Viscount Tilbury, and Clarence, Earl of Emsworth, could have possessed a single taste in common. The souls of the two men, one would have said, lay poles apart. And yet such was the remarkable fact. Widely though their temperaments differed in every other respect, they were both pig-minded. In his little country place in Buckinghamshire, whither he was wont to retire for recuperating over the week-ends, Lord Tilbury kept pigs. He not only kept pigs, but loved and was proud of them. And anything to do with pigs, such as a grunt, a gollop, or, as in this case, a smell, touched an immediate chord in him.

So now he came out of his reverie with a start, to find that his aimless wanderings had brought him to within potato-peel throw of a handsomely appointed sty.

And in this sty stood a pig of such quality as he had never seen before.

The afternoon, as has been said, was overcast. An unwholesome blight, like a premature twilight, had fallen upon the world. But it needed more than a little poorness of visibility to hide the Empress. Sunshine would have brought out her opulent curves more starkly, perhaps, but even seen through this grey murk she was quite impressive enough to draw Lord Tilbury to her as with a lasso. He hurried forward and stood gazing breathlessly.

His initial reaction to the spectacle was a feeling of sick envy, a horrible, aching covetousness. That was the effect the first view of Empress of Blandings always had on visiting fanciers. They came, saw, gasped, and went away unhappy, discontented men, ever after to move through life bemused and yearning for they knew not what, like men kissed by goddesses in dreams. Until this moment Lord Tilbury had looked on his own Buckingham Big Boy as considerable pig. He felt now with a pang that it would be an insult to this supreme animal before him even to think of Buckingham Big Boy in her presence.

The Empress, after a single brief but courteous glance at this newcomer, had returned to the business which had been occupying her at the moment of Lord Tilbury's arrival. She pressed her nose against the lowest rail of the sty and snuffled moodily. And Lord Tilbury, looking down, saw that a portion of her afternoon meal, in the shape of an appetising potato, had been dislodged from the main *couvert* and had rolled out of bounds. It was this that was causing the silver medallist's distress and despondency. Like all prize pigs who take their career seriously, Empress of Blandings hated to miss anything that might be eaten and converted into firm flesh.

Lord Tilbury's pig-loving heart was touched. Envy left him, swept away on the tide of a nobler emotion. All that was best and humanest in him came to the surface. He clicked his tongue sympathetically. His build made it unpleasant for him to stoop, but he did not hesitate. At the cost of a momentary feeling of suffocation, he secured the potato. And he was on the point of dropping it into the Empress's upturned mouth, when there occurred a startling interruption.

Hot breath fanned his cheek. A hoarse voice in his ear said 'Ur!!' A sinewy hand closed vice-like about his wrist. Another attached itself to his collar. And, jerked violently away, he found himself looking into the accusing eyes of a tall, thin, scraggy man in overalls.

It was the time of day when most of Nature's children take the afternoon sleep. But Jas. Pirbright had not slept. His employer had instructed him to lurk, and he had been lurking ever since lunch. Sooner or later, Lord Emsworth had told him, quoting that second-sighted man, the Hon. Galahad Threepwood, there would come sneaking to the Empress's sty a mysterious stranger. And here he was, complete with poison-potato, and Pirbright had got him. The Pirbrights, like the Canadian Mounted Police, always got their man.

'Gur!' said Jas. Pirbright, which is Shropshire for 'You come along with me and I'll shut you up somewhere while I go and inform his lordship of what has occurred.'

Monty Bodkin, meanwhile, after parting from Sue on the roof, had been making his way slowly and pensively through the grounds in the direction of the Empress's headquarters. It was his intention to look in on the noble animal and try to do himself a bit of good by fraternizing with it.

He was not hurrying. The afternoon was too hot for that. Shropshire had become a Turkish bath. The sky seemed to press down like a poultice. Butterflies had ceased to flutter, and as he dragged himself along it was only the younger and more sprightly rabbits that had the energy to move out of his path.

Yet even had the air been nipping and eager, it is probable that he would still have loitered, for his mind was heavy with care. He didn't like the look of things.

No, mused Monty, he didn't like the look of things at all. Sheridan once wrote of 'a damned disinheriting countenance', and if Monty had ever read Sheridan he would have felt that he had found the perfect description for the face of the ninth Earl of Emsworth as seen across the table in the big library or peering out from behind trees. Not even in that interview with Lord Tilbury in his office at the Mammoth had he been surer that he was associating with a man who proposed very shortly to dispense with his services. The sack, it seemed to him, was hovering in the air. Almost he could hear the beating of its wings.

He came droopingly to the paddock where the Empress resided. There was a sort of potting-shed place just inside the gate, and here he halted, using its surface to ignite the match which was to light the cigarette he so sorely needed.

Yes, he felt, as he stood smoking there, if he had any power of reading faces, any skill whatever in interpreting the language of the human eye, his latest employer was on the eve of administering the bum's rush. It seemed to him that even now he could hear his voice, crying 'Get out! Get out!'

And then, as the sound persisted, he became aware that it was no dream voice that spoke, but an actual living voice; that it proceeded from the shed against which he was leaning; and that what it was saying was not 'Get out!' but 'Let me out!'

He was both startled and intrigued. For a moment, his mind toyed with the thought of spectres. Then he reflected, and very reasonably, that a ghost that had only to walk a quarter of a mile to find one of the oldest castles in England at its disposal would scarcely waste its time haunting potting-sheds. There was a small window close to where he stood. Emboldened, he put his face to it.

'Are you there?' he asked.

It was a fair question, for the interior of the shed was of an Egyptian blackness. Nevertheless, it appeared to annoy the captive. An explosive 'Cor!' came hurtling through the air, and Monty leaped a full two inches. The thing seemed incredible, but if a fellow was to trust the evidence of his senses this unseen acquaintance was none other than —

'I say,' he gasped, 'that isn't Lord Tilbury, by any chance, is it?'

'Who are you?'

'Bodkin speaking. Bodkin, M. Monty Bodkin. You remember old Monty?'

It was plain that Lord Tilbury did, for he spoke with a familiar vigour.

'Then let me out, you miserable imbecile. What are you wasting time for?'

Monty was groping at the door.

'Right-ho,' he said. 'In one moment. There's a sort of wooden gadget that needs a bit of shifting. All right. Done it. Out you pop. Upsy-daisy!'

And with these words of encouragement he removed the staple, and Lord Tilbury emerged, snorting.

'Yes, but I say — !' pleaded Monty, after a few moments, anxious, like Goethe, for more light. This was one of the weirdest and most mysterious things that he had encountered in his puff, and it was apparently his companion's intention merely to stand and snort about it.

Lord Tilbury found speech.

'It's an outrage!'

'What is?'

'I shall have the fellow severely punished.'

'What fellow?'

'I shall see Lord Emsworth about it immediately.'

'About what?'

Briefly and with emotion Lord Tilbury told his tale.

'I kept explaining to the man that if he had

any doubts as to my social standing your uncle, Sir Gregory Parsloe, who I believe lives in this neighbourhood, would vouch for me . . . '

Monty, who had been listening with a growing understanding, checking up each point in the narrative with a sagacious nod, felt compelled at this juncture to interrupt.

'My sainted aunt!' he cried. 'You say you offered the porker a spud? And then this chap grabbed you? And then you told him you were a friend of my Uncle Gregory? and now you're going to the Castle to lodge a complaint with Old Man River? Don't do it!' said Monty urgently, 'don't do it. Don't go anywhere near the Castle, or they'll have you in irons before you can say 'Eh, what?' You aren't on to the secret history of this place. There are wheels within wheels. Old Emsworth thinks Uncle Gregory is trying to assassinate his pig. You are caught in the act of giving it potatoes and announce that you are a pal of his. Why, dash it, they'll ship you off to Devil's Island without a trial.'

Lord Tilbury stared, thinking once again how much he disliked this young man.

'What are you drivelling about?'

'Not drivelling. It's quite reasonable. Look at it from their point of view. If this pig drops out of the betting, my uncle's entry will win the silver medal at the show in a canter. Can you blame this fellow Pirbright for looking a bit cross-eyed at a chap who comes creeping in and administering surreptitious potatoes and then gives Uncle Gregory as a reference? He probably

144

thought that potato contained some little-known Asiatic poison.'

'I never heard of anything so absurd.'

'Well, that's Life,' argued Monty. 'And, in any case, you can't get away from it that you're trespassing. Isn't there some law about being allowed to shoot trespassers on sight? Or is it burglars? No, I'm a liar. It's stray dogs when you catch them worrying sheep. Still, coming back to it, you *are* trespassing.'

'I am doing nothing of the kind. I have been paying a call at the Castle.'

The conversation had reached just the point towards which Monty had been hoping to direct it.

'Why? Now we're on to the thing that's been baffling me. What were you doing in these parts at all? Why have you come here? Always glad to see you, of course,' said Monty courteously.

Lord Tilbury appeared to resent this courtesy. And, indeed, it had smacked a little of the gracious seigneur making some uncouth intruder free of his estates.

'May I ask what you are doing here yourself?'

'Me?'

'If, as you say, Lord Emsworth is on such bad terms with Sir Gregory Parsloe, I should have thought that he would have objected to his nephew walking in his grounds.'

'Ah, but, you see, I'm his secretary.'

'Why should the fact you are your uncle's secretary — ?'

'Not my uncle's. Old Emsworth's. Pronouns arc the devil, aren't they? You start saying 'he'

145

and 'his' and are breezing Gally along, and you suddenly find you've got everything all mixed up. That's Life, too, if you look at it in the right way. No, I'm not my uncle's secretary. He hasn't got a secretary. I'm old Emsworth's. I secured the post within twenty-four hours of your slinging me out of *Tiny Tots*. Oh, yes, indeed,' said Monty, with airy nonchalance, 'I very soon managed to get another job. Dear me, yes. A good man isn't long getting snapped up.'

'You are Lord Emsworth's secretary?' Lord Tilbury seemed to have difficulty in assimilating the information. 'You are living at the Castle? You mean that you are actually living — residing at Blandings Castle?'

Monty, thinking swiftly, decided that that airy nonchalance of his had been a mistake. Well meant, but a blunder. The sounder policy here would be manly frankness. He believed in taking at the flood that tide in the affairs of men which, when so taken, leads on to fortune. It was imperative that he secure another situation before Lord Emsworth should apply the boot; and he could scarcely hope to find a more propitious occasion for approaching this particular employer of labour than when he had just released him from a smelly potting-shed.

He replied, accordingly, that for the nonce such was indeed the case.

'But only,' he went on candidly, 'for the nonce. I don't mind telling you that I expect a shake-up shortly. I anticipate that before long I shall find myself once more at liberty. Nothing actually said, mind you, but all the signs pointing that way. So if by any chance you are feeling that we might make a fresh start together — if you are willing to let the dead past bury its dead — if, in a word, you would consider overlooking that little unpleasantness we had and taking me back into the fold, I, on my side, can guarantee quick delivery. I should be able to report for duty almost immediately, with a heart for any fate.'

Upon most men listening to this eloquent appeal there might have crept a certain impatience. Lord Tilbury, however, listened to it as though to some grand sweet song. Like Napoleon, he had had some lucky breaks in his time, but he could not recall one luckier than this — that he should have found in this young man before him a man who at one and the same time was living at Blandings Castle and wanted favours from him. There could have been no more ideal combination.

'So you wish to return to Tilbury House?'

'Definitely.'

'You shall.'

'Good egg!'

'Provided-'

'Oh, golly! Is there a catch?'

Lord Tilbury had fallen into a frowning silence. Now that the moment had arrived for putting into words the lawless scheme that was in his mind, he found a difficulty in selecting the words into which to put it.

'Provided what?' said Monty. 'If you mean provided I exert the most watchful vigilance to prevent any more dubious matter creeping into the columns of *Tiny Tots*, have no uneasiness.

147

Since the recent painful episode, I have become a changed man and am now thoroughly attuned to the aims and ideals of *Tiny Tots*. You can restore my hand to the tiller without a qualm.'

'It has nothing to do with *Tiny Tots*.' Lord Tilbury paused again. 'There is something I wish you to do for me.'

'A pleasure. Give it a name. Even unto half of my kingdom, I mean to say.'

'I . . . That is . . . well, here is the position in a nutshell. Lord Emsworth's brother, Galahad Threepwood, has written his Reminiscences.'

'I know. I'll bet they're good, too. They would sell like hot cakes. Just the sort of book to fill a long-felt want. Grab it, is my advice.'

'That,' said Lord Tilbury, relieved at the swiftness with which the conversation had arrived at the vital issue, 'is precisely what I want to do.'

'Well, I'll tell you the procedure,' said Monty helpfully. 'You get a contract drawn up, and then you charge in on old Gally with your cheque-book . . . '

'The contract already exists. Mr Threepwood signed it some time ago, giving the Mammoth all rights to his book. He has now changed his mind and refuses to deliver the manuscript.'

'Good Lord! Why?'

'I do not know why.'

'But the silly ass will be losing a packet.'

'No doubt. His decision not to publish means also the loss of a considerable sum of money to myself. And so, I consider that, the contract having been signed, I am legally entitled to the possession of the manuscript, I — er -I intend — well, in short, I intend to take possession of it.'

'You don't mean pinch it?'

'That, crudely, is what I mean.'

'I say, you do live, don't you? But how?'

'Ah, there I would have to have the assistance of somebody who was actually in the house.'

A bizarre idea occurred to Monty.

'You aren't suggesting that you want *me* to pinch it?'

'Precisely.'

'Well, lord-love-a-duck!' said Monty. He stared in honest amazement.

'It would be the simplest of tasks,' went on Lord Tilbury insinuatingly. 'The manuscript is in the desk of a small room which I imagine is a sort of annexe to the library. The drawer in which it is placed is not, unless I am very much mistaken, locked — and even if locked it can readily be opened. You say you are anxious to return to my employment. So . . . well, think it over, my dear boy.'

Monty was plucking feebly at the lapel of his coat. This was new stuff to him. What with being invited to become a sort of Napoleon of Crime and hearing himself addressed as Lord Tilbury's dear boy, his head was swimming.

Lord Tilbury, a judge of men, was aware that there are minds which adjust themselves less readily than others to new ideas. He was well content to allow an interval of time for this to sink in.

'I can assure you that if you come to me with

that manuscript, I shall only be too delighted to restore you to your old position at Tilbury House.'

Monty's aspect became a little less like that of a village idiot who has just been struck by a thunderbolt. A certain animation crept into his eye.

'You will?'

'I will.'

'For a year certain?'

'A year?'

'It must be for a year, positively guaranteed. You may remember me speaking about those wheels.'

In spite of his anxiety to enrol this young man as his accomplice and set him to work as soon as possible, Lord Tilbury was conscious of a certain hesitation. Most employers of labour would have felt the same in his position. A year is a long time to have a Monty Bodkin on one's hands, and Lord Tilbury had been consoling himself with the reflection that, once the manuscript was in his possession, he could get rid of him in about a week.

'A year?' he said dubiously.

'Or twelve months,' said Monty, making a concession.

Lord Tilbury sighed. Apparently the thing had to be done. 'Very well.'

'You will take me on for a solid year?'

'If you make that stipulation.'

'You will be prepared to sign a letter — an agreement — a document to that effect, if I draw it up?'

'Yes.'

'Then it's a deal. Shake hands on it.'

Lord Tilbury preferred to omit this symbolic gesture.

'Kindly put the thing through as soon as possible,' he said coldly. 'I have no wish to remain indefinitely at a rustic inn.'

'Oh, I'll snap into it. What rustic inn, by the way? I ought to have your address.'

'The Emsworth Arms.'

'I know it well. Try their beer with a spot of gin in it. Warms the cockles. All right, then. Expect me there very shortly, with manuscript under arm.'

'Good-bye, then, for the present.'

'Toodle-oo till we meet again,' said Monty cordially.

He watched Lord Tilbury disappear, then resumed his walk, immersed in roseate daydreams.

This, he reflected, was a bit of all right. There were no traces in his mind now of the scruples and timidity which had given him that slightly sandbagged feeling when this proposition had first been sprung upon him. He felt bold and resolute. He intended to secure that manuscript if he had to use a meat-axe.

In the shimmering heat-mist that lay along the grass it seemed to him that he could see the lovely face of Gertrude Butterwick gazing at him with gentle encouragement, as if she were endeavouring to suggest that he could count on her support and approval in this enterprise. Almost he could have fancied that the ripple of a

151

lonely little breeze which had lost its way in the alder bushes was her silvery voice whispering, 'Go to it!'

Writers are creatures of moods. Too often the merest twiddle of the tap is enough to stop the flow of inspiration. It was so with the Hon. Galahad Threepwood. His recent unpleasant scene with that acquaintance of his youth, the erstwhile Stinker Pyke, had been brief in actual count of time, but it had left him in a frame of mind uncongenial to the resumption of his literary work. He was a kindly man, and it irked him to be disobliging even to the Stinker Pykes of this world.

To send poor Stinker off with a flea in his ear was not, of course, the same as rebuffing, say, dear old Plug Basham or good old Freddie Potts, but it was quite enough to upset a man who always liked to do the decent thing by everyone and hated to say No to the meanest of God's creatures. After Lord Tilbury's departure the Hon. Galahad allowed the manuscript of his lifework to remain in its drawer. With no heart for further polishing and pruning, he heaved a rueful sigh, selected a detective novel from his shelf, and left the room.

Having paused in the hall to ring the bell and instruct Beach, who answered it, to bring him a whisky and soda out on to the lawn, he made his way to his favourite retreat beneath the big cedar.

'Oh, and Beach,' he said when the butler arrived with clinking tray, 'sorry to trouble you, but I wonder if you'd mind leaping up to the

152

small library and fetching me my reading glasses. I forgot them. You'll find them on the desk.'

'No trouble at all, Mr Galahad,' said the butler affably. 'Is there anything else you require?'

'You haven't seen Miss Brown anywhere?'

'No, Mr Galahad. Miss Brown was taking the air on the terrace shortly after luncheon, but I have not seen her since.'

'All right, then. Just the reading glasses.'

Addressing himself to the task of restoring his ruffled nerves, the Hon. Galahad had swallowed perhaps a third of the contents of the long tumbler when he observed the butler returning.

'What on earth have you got there, Beach?' he asked, for the other seemed heavily laden for a man who had been sent to fetch a pair of tortoiseshell-rimmed spectacles. 'That's not my manuscript?'

'Yes, Mr Galahad.'

'Take it back,' said the author, with pardonable peevishness. 'I don't want it. Good Lord, I came out here to forget it.'

He broke off, mystified. A strange, pop-eyed expression had manifested itself on the butler's face, and his swelling waistcoat was beginning to quiver faintly. The Hon. Galahad watched these phenomena with interest and curiosity.

'What are you waggling your tummy at me for, Beach?'

'I am uneasy, Mr Galahad.'

'You shouldn't wear flannel vests, then, in weather like this.'

'Mentally uneasy, sir.'

'What about?'

'The safety of this book of yours, Mr Galahad.' The butler lowered his voice. 'May I inform you, sir, of what occurred a few moments ago, when I proceeded to the small library to find your glasses?'

'What?'

'Just as I was about to enter I heard movements within.'

'You did?' The Hon. Galahad clicked his tongue 'I wish to goodness people would keep out of that room. They know I use it as my private study.'

'Precisely, Mr Galahad. Nobody has any business there while you are in residence at the Castle. That is an understood thing. And it was for that reason that I immediately found myself entertaining suspicions.'

'Eh? Suspicions? How do you mean?'

'That some person was attempting to purloin the material which you have written, sir.'

'What!'

'Yes, Mr Galahad. And I was right. I paused for an instant,' said the butler impressively, 'and then flung the door open sharply and without warning. Sir, there was Mr Pilbeam standing with his hand in the open drawer.'

'Pilbeam?'

'Yes, Mr Galahad.'

'Good gad!'

'Yes, Mr Galahad.'

'What did you say?'

'Nothing, Mr Galahad. I looked.'

'What did *he* say?'

'Nothing, Mr Galahad. He smiled.'

'Smiled?'

'In a weak, guilty manner.'

'And then?'

'Still without speaking, I proceeded to the desk, secured the written material, and started to leave the room. At the door I paused and gave him a cold glance. I then withdrew.'

'Splendid, Beach!'

'Thank you, Mr Galahad.'

'You're sure he was trying to steal the thing?'

'The papers were actually in his grasp, sir.'

'He couldn't have been just looking for notepaper or something?'

A man of Beach's build could not look like Sherlock Holmes listening to fatuous theories from Doctor Watson, nor could a man of his position, conversing with a social superior, answer as Holmes would have done. The word 'Tush!' may have trembled on his lips, but it got no farther.

'No, sir,' he said briefly.

'But his motive? What possible motive could this extraordinary little perisher have for wanting to steal my book?'

A certain embarrassment seemed to grip Beach. He hesitated. 'Might I take the liberty, Mr Galahad?'

'Don't talk rot, Beach. Liberty? I never heard such nonsense. Why, we've known each other since we were kids of forty.'

'Thank you, Mr Galahad. Then, if I may speak freely, I should like to recapitulate briefly the peculiar circumstances connected with this book. In the first place, may I say that I am aware of its extreme importance as a factor in the affairs of Mr Ronald and Miss Brown?'

The Hon. Galahad gave a little jump. He had always known the butler as a man who kept his eyes open and his ears pricked up and informed himself sooner or later of most things that happened at the Castle, but he had not realized that his secret service system was quite so efficient as this.

'In order to overcome the opposition of her ladyship to the union of Mr Ronald and Miss Brown, you expressed your willingness to refrain from giving this volume of Reminiscences into the printer's hands — her ladyship being hostile to its publication owing to the fact that in her opinion its contents might give offence to many of her friends — notably Sir Gregory Parsloe. Am I not correct, Mr Galahad?'

'Quite right.'

'Your motive in making this concession being that you were apprehensive lest, without this check upon her actions, her ladyship might possibly persuade his lordship to refuse to countenance the match?'

' 'Possibly' is good. You needn't be coy, Beach. This meeting is tiled. No reporters present. We can take our hair down and tell each other our right names. What you actually mean is that my brother Clarence is as weak as water, and that if it wasn't for this book of mine there would be nothing to stop my sister Constance nagging him into a state where he would agree to forbid a dozen weddings just for the sake of peace and quiet.'

'Exactly, Mr Galahad. I would not have ventured to put the matter into precisely those words myself, but since you have done so I feel free to point out that, the circumstances being as you have outlined, it would be very agreeable to her ladyship were this manuscript to be stolen and destroyed.'

The Hon. Galahad sat up, electrified.

'Beach, you've hit it! That fellow Pilbeam was working for Connie!'

'The evidence would certainly appear to point in that direction, Mr Galahad.'

'Probably Parsloe's sitting in with them.'

'I feel convinced of it, Mr Galahad. I may mention that on the night of our last dinner-party her ladyship instructed me with considerable agitation to summon Sir Gregory to the Castle by telephone for an urgent conference. Her ladyship and Sir Gregory were closeted in the library for some little time, and then Sir Gregory emerged, obviously labouring under considerable excitement, and a few moments later I observed him talking to Mr Pilbeam very earnestly in a secluded corner of the hall.'

'Giving him his riding orders!'

'Precisely, Mr Galahad. Plotting. The significance of the incident eluded me at the time, but I am now convinced that that was what was transpiring.'

The Hon. Galahad rose.

'Beach,' he observed with emotion, 'I've said it before, and I say it again — you're worth your weight in gold. You've saved the situation. You have preserved the happiness of two young lives, Beach.'

'It is very kind of you to say so, sir.'

'I do say so. It's no use our kidding ourselves. With that manuscript out of the way, those two wouldn't have a dog's chance of getting married. I know Clarence. Capital fellow — nobody I'm fonder of in the world — but constitutionally incapable of standing up against arguing women. We must take steps immediately to ensure the safety of this manuscript, Beach.'

'I was about to suggest, Mr Galahad, that it might be advisable if in future you were to lock the drawer in which you keep it.'

The Hon. Galahad shook his head.

'That's no good. You don't suppose a determined woman like my sister Constance, aided and abetted by this ghastly little weasel of a detective, is going to be stopped by a locked drawer? No, we must think of something better than that. I've got it. You must take the thing, Beach, and keep it in some safe place. In your pantry, for instance.'

'But, Mr Galahad!'

'Now what?'

'Suppose her ladyship were to learn that the papers were in my possession and were to request me to hand them to her? It would precipitate a situation of considerable delicacy were I to meet such a demand with a flat refusal.'

'How on earth is she to know you've got it? She doesn't ever drop into your pantry for a chat, does she?'

'Certainly not, Mr Galahad,' said the butler,

158

shuddering at the horrid vision the words called up.

'And at night you could sleep with it under your pillow. No risk of Lady Constance coming to tuck you up in bed, what?'

This time Beach's emotion was such that he could merely shudder silently.

'It's the only plan,' said the Hon. Galahad with decision. 'I don't want any argument. You take this manuscript and you put it away somewhere where it'll be safe. Be a man, Beach.'

'Very good, Mr Galahad.'

'Do it now.'

'Very good, Mr Galahad.'

'And, naturally, not a word to a soul.'

'Very good, Mr Galahad.'

Beach walked slowly away across the lawn. His head was bowed, his heart heavy. It was a moment when a butler of spirit should have worn something of the gallant air of a soldier commissioned to carry dispatches through the enemy's lines. Beach did not look like that. He resembled far more nearly in his general demeanour one of those unfortunate gentlemen in railway station waiting-rooms who, having injudiciously consented at four-thirty to hold a baby for a strange woman, looks at the clock and see that it is now six-fifteen and no relief in sight.

Dusk was closing down on the forbidding day. Sue, looking out over her battlements, became conscious of an added touch of the sinister in the view beneath her. It was the hour when ghouls are abroad, and there seemed no reason why such ghouls should not decide to pay a visit to this roof on which she stood. She came to the conclusion that she had been here long enough. Eerie little noises were chuckling through the world, and somewhere in the distance an owl had begun to utter its ominous cry. She yearned for her cosy bedroom, with the lights turned on and something to read till dressing for dinner-time.

It was very dark on the stone stairs, and they rang unpleasantly under her feet. Nevertheless, though considering it probable that at any moment an icy hand would come out from nowhere and touch her face, she braved the descent.

Her relief as her groping fingers touched the comforting solidity of the door was short-lived. It gave way a moment later to the helpless panic of the human being trapped. The door was locked. She scurried back up the stairs on to the roof, where at least there was light to help her cope with this disaster.

She remembered now. Half an hour before, a footman had come up and hauled down the flag which during the day floated over Blandings Castle. He had not seen her, and it had not occurred to her to reveal her presence. But she wished now that she had done so, for, supposing the roof empty, he had evidently completed his evening ritual by locking up.

Something brushed against Sue's cheek. It was not actually a ghoul, but it was a bat, and bats are bad enough in the gloaming of a haunted day. She uttered a sharp scream — and, doing so, discovered that she had unwittingly hit upon the correct procedure for girls marooned on roofs.

She hurried to the battlements and began calling 'Hi!' — in a small, hushed voice at first, for nothing sounds sillier than the word 'Hi!' when thrown into the void with no definite objective; then more loudly. Presently, warming to her work, she was producing quite a respectable volume of sound. So respectable that Ronnie Fish, smoking moodily in the garden, became aware that there were voices in the night, and, after listening for a few moments, gathered that they proceeded from the castle roof.

He made his way to the path that skirted the walls.

'Who's that?'

'Oh, Ronnie!'

For two days and two nights grey doubts and black cares had been gnawing at the vitals of Ronald Fish. The poison had not ceased to work in his veins. For two days and two nights he had been thinking of Sue and of Monty Bodkin. Every time he thought of Sue it was agony. And every time his reluctant mind turned to the contemplation of Monty Bodkin it was anguish. But at the sound of that voice his heart gave an involuntary leap. She might have transferred her affections to Monty Bodkin, but her voice still remained the most musical sound on earth.

'Ronnie, I can't get down.'

'Are you on the roof?'

'Yes. And they've locked the door.'

'I'll get the key.'

And at long last she heard the clang of the lock, and he appeared at the head of the stairs.

His manner, she noted with distress, was still Eton, still Cambridge. Nobody could have been politer.

'Nuisance, getting locked in like that.'

'Yes.'

'Been up here long?'

'All the afternoon.'

'Nice place on a fine day.'

'I suppose so.'

'Though hot.'

'Yes.'

There was a pause. The heavy air pressed down upon them. In the garden the owl was still hooting. 'When did you get back?' asked Sue. 'About an hour ago.'

'I didn't hear you.'

'I didn't come to the front. I went straight round to the stables. Dropped mother at the Vicarage.'

'Yes?'

'She wanted to have a talk with the vicar.'

'I see.'

'You've not met the vicar, have you?'

'Not yet.'

'His name's Fosberry.'

'Oh?'

Silence fell again. Ronnie's eyes were roaming about the roof. He took a step forward, stooped, and picked up something. It was a slouch hat.

He hummed a little under his breath.

'Monty been up here with you?'

'Yes.'

Ronnie hummed another bar or two.

'Nice chap,' he said. 'Let's go down, shall we?'

# 8

If you turn to the right on leaving the main gates of Blandings Castle and follow the road for a matter of two miles, you will find yourself approaching the little town of Market Blandings. There it stands dreaming the centuries away, a jewel in a green heart of Shropshire. In all England there is no sweeter spot. Artists who come to paint its old grey houses and fishermen who angle for bream in its lazy river are united on this point. The idea that the place could possibly be rendered more pleasing to the eye is one at which they would scoff — and have scoffed many a night over the pipes and tankards at the Emsworth Arms.

And yet, on the afternoon following the events just recorded, this miracle occurred. The quiet charm of this ancient High Street was suddenly intensified by the appearance of a godlike man in a bowler hat, who came out of an old-world tobacco shop. It was Beach, the butler. With the object of disciplining his ample figure, he had walked down from the Castle to buy cigarettes. He now stood on the pavement, bracing himself to the task of walking back.

This athletic feat was not looking quite so good to him as it had done three-quarters of an hour ago in his pantry. That long two-mile hike had taxed his powers of endurance. Moreover, this was no weather for Marathons. If yesterday had been oppressive, today was a scorcher. Angry clouds were banking themselves in a copper-coloured sky. No breath of air stirred the trees. The pavement gave out almost visible waves of heat, and over everything there seemed to brood a sort of sulphurous gloom. If they were not in for a thunderstorm, and a snorter of a thunderstorm, before nightfall, Beach was very much mistaken. He removed his hat, produced a handkerchief, mopped his brow, replaced the hat, replaced the handkerchief, and said 'Woof!' Disciplining the figure is all very well, but there are limits. An urgent desire for beer swept over Beach.

He could scarcely have been more fortunately situated for the purpose of gratifying this wish. The ideal towards which the City Fathers of all English county towns strive is to provide a public-house for each individual inhabitant; and those of Market Blandings had not been supine in this matter. From where Beach stood, he could see no fewer than six such establishments. The fact that he chose the Emsworth Arms must not be taken to indicate that he had anything against the Wheatsheaf, the Waggoner's Rest, the Beetle and Wedge, the Stitch in Time, and the Jolly Cricketers. It was simply that it happened to be closest.

Nevertheless, it was a sound choice. The advice one would give to every young man starting life is, on arriving in Market Blandings on a warm afternoon, to go to the Emsworth Arms. Good stuff may be bought there, and of all the admirable hostelries in the town it possesses the largest and shadiest garden. Green and inviting, dotted about with rustic tables and snug summerhouses, it stretches all the way down to the banks of the river; so that the happy drinker, already pleasantly in need of beer, may acquire a new and deeper thirst from watching family parties toil past in row-boats. On a really sultry day a single father, labouring at the oars of a craft loaded down below the Plimsoll mark by a wife, a wife's sister, a cousin by marriage, four children, a dog, and a picnic basket, has sometimes led to such a rush of business at the Emsworth Arms that seasoned barmaids have staggered beneath the strain.

It was to one of these summerhouses that Beach now took his tankard. He generally went there when circumstances caused him to visit the Emsworth Arms, for as a man with a certain position to keep up he preferred privacy when refreshing himself. It was not as if he had been some irresponsible young second footman who could just go and squash in with the boys in the back room. This particular summerhouse was at the far end of the garden, hidden from the eye of the profane by a belt of bushes.

Thither, accordingly, Beach made his way. There was nobody in the summerhouse, but he did not enter it, having a horror of earwigs and suspecting their presence in the thatch of the roof. Instead, he dragged a wicker chair to the table which stood at the back of it, and, sinking into this, puffed and sipped and thought. And the more he thought, the less did he like what he thought about.

As a rule, when members of the Family showed their confidence in him by canvassing his assistance in any little matter, Beach was both proud and pleased. His motto was 'Service'. But he could not conceal it from himself that the Family had a tendency at times to go a little too far.

The historic case of this, of course, had been when Mr Ronald, having stolen the Empress and hidden her in a disused keeper's cottage in the west wood, had prevailed upon him to assist in feeding her. His present commission was not as fearsome an ordeal as that, but nevertheless he could not but feel that the Hon. Galahad, in appointing him the custodian of so vitally important an object as the manuscript of his book of Reminiscences, had exceeded the limits of what a man should ask a butler to do. The responsibility, he considered, was one which no butler, however desirous of giving satisfaction, should have been called upon to undertake.

The thought of all that hung upon his vigilance unnerved him. And he had been brooding on it with growing uneasiness for perhaps five minutes, when the sound of feet shuffling on wood told him that he had no longer got his favourite oasis to himself. An individual or individuals had come into the summerhouse.

'We can talk here,' said a voice, and a seat creaked as if a heavy body had lowered itself upon it.

And such was, indeed, the case. It was Lord Tilbury who had just sat down, and his was one of the heaviest bodies in Fleet Street.

When, a few minutes before, meditating in the lounge of the Emsworth Arms, he had beheld Monty Bodkin enter through the front door, Lord Tilbury's first thought had been for some quiet retreat where they could confer in solitude. He could see that the young man had much to say, and he had no desire to have him say it with half a dozen inquisitive Shropshire lads within easy earshot.

Great minds think alike. Beach, intent on an unobtrusive glass of beer, and Lord Tilbury, loath to have intimate private matters discussed in an hotel lounge, had both come to the conclusion that true solitude was best to be obtained at the bottom of the garden. Silencing his young friend, accordingly, with an imperious gesture his lordship had led the way to this remote summerhouse.

'Well,' he said, having seated himself. 'What is it?' It seemed to Beach, who had settled himself comfortably in his chair and was preparing to listen to the conversation with something of the air of a nonchalant dramatic critic watching the curtain go up, that that voice was vaguely familiar. He had a feeling that he had heard it before, but could not remember where or when. He had no difficulty, however, in recognizing the one which now spoke in answer. Monty Bodkin's vocal delivery, when his soul was at all deeply disturbed, was individual and peculiar, containing something of the tonal quality of a bleating sheep combined with a suggestion of a barking prairie wolf. 'What is it? I like that!'

Monty's soul at this moment was very deeply

disturbed. Since breakfast-time that morning, this young man, like Sir Gregory Parsloe, had run what is known as the gamut of the emotions. A pictorial record of his hopes and despairs would have looked like a fever chart.

He had begun, over the coffee and kippers, by feeling gay and buoyant. It seemed to him that Fortune — good old Fortune — had amazingly decently put him on to a red-hot thing. All he had to do, in order to ensure the year's employment which would enable him to win Gertrude Butterwick, was to nip into the small library and lift the manuscript out of the desk in which, Lord Tilbury had assured him, it reposed.

Feeling absolutely in the pink, accordingly, and nipping as planned, he had fallen, like Lucifer, from heaven to hell. The bally thing was not there. Fortune, in a word, had been pulling his leg.

And here was this old ass before him saying 'What is it?'

'Yes, I like that!' he repeated. 'That's rich! Oh, very fruity, indeed.'

Lord Tilbury, as we have said, had never been very fond of Monty. In his present peculiar mood he found himself liking him less than ever.

'What is it you wish to see me about?' he asked, with testy curtness.

'What do you think I want to see you about?' replied Monty shrilly. 'About that dashed manuscript of Gally's that you told me to pinch, of course,' he said with a bitter laugh, and Beach, having given a single shuddering start like a harpooned whale, sat rigid in his chair; his gooseberry eyes bulging; the beer frozen, as one might say, on his lips.

Nor was Lord Tilbury unmoved. No plotter likes to have his accomplices bellowing important secrets as if they were calling coals.

'Sh!'

'Oh, nobody can hear us.'

'Nevertheless, kindly do not shout. Where is the manuscript? Have you got it?'

'Of course I've not got it.'

Lord Tilbury was feeling dismally that he might have expected this. He saw now how foolish he had been to place so delicate a commission in the hands of a popinjay. Of all classes of the community, popinjays, when it comes to carrying out delicate commissions, are the most inept. Search History's pages from end to end, reflected Lord Tilbury, and you will not find one instance of a popinjay doing anything successfully except eat, sleep, and master the new dance steps.

'It's a bit thick . . . ' bellowed Monty.

'Sh!'

'It's a bit thick,' repeated Monty, sinking his voice to a conspiratorial growl. 'Raising hopes only to cast them to the ground is the way I look at it. What did you want to get me all worked up for by telling me the thing was in that desk?'

'It is not?' said Lord Tilbury, staggered.

'Not a trace of it.'

'You cannot have looked properly.'

'Looked properly!'

'Sh!'

'Of course I looked properly. I left no stone

unturned. I explored every avenue.'

'But I saw Threepwood put it there.'

'Says you.'

'Don't say 'says you'. I tell you I saw him with my own eyes place the manuscript in the top right-hand drawer of the desk.'

'Well, he must have moved it. It's not there now.'

'Then it is somewhere else.'

'I shouldn't wonder. But where?'

'You could easily have found out.'

'Oh, yeah?'

'Don't say 'Oh, yeah'.'

'Well, what can I say, dash it? First you keep yowling 'Shush' every time I open my mouth. Then you tell me not to say, 'Says you'. And now you beef at my remarking 'Oh, yeah'. I suppose what you'd really like,' said Monty, and it was plain to the listening ear that he was deeply moved, 'would be for me to buy a flannel dressing-gown and a spade and become a ruddy Trappist monk.'

This spirited outburst led to a certain amount of rather confused debate. Lord Tilbury said that he did not propose to have young popinjays taking that tone with him; while Monty, on his side, wished to be informed who Lord Tilbury was calling a popinjay. Lord Tilbury then said that Monty was a bungler, and Monty said, Well, dash it, Lord Tilbury had told him to be a burglar, and Lord Tilbury said he had not said 'burglar', he had said 'bungler', and Monty said, What did he mean, bungler, and Lord Tilbury explained that by the expression 'bungler', he had intended to signify a wretched, feckless, blundering, incompetent, imbecile. He added that an infant of six could have found the manuscript, and Monty, in a striking passage, was making a firm offer to give any bloodhound in England a shilling if it could do better than he had done, when the argument stopped as abruptly as it had started. Childish voices had begun to prattle close at hand and it was evident that one of those picnic parties from the river was approaching.

'Cor!' said Lord Tilbury, rather in the manner of the moping owl in Gray's 'Elegy' under similar provocation.

One of the childish voices spoke.

'Pa, there's someone here.'

Another followed.

'Ma, there's someone here.'

The deeper note of a male adult made itself heard.

'Emily, there's someone here.'

And then the voice of a female adult.

'Oh dear. What a shame! There's someone here.'

The conspirators appeared to be men who could take a tactful hint when they heard one. There came to Beach's ears the sound of moving bodies. And presently, from the fact that the summerhouse seemed to have become occupied by a troupe of performing elephants, he gathered that the occupation had been carried through according to plan.

He sat on for some minutes; then, hurrying to the inn, asked leave of the landlord to use his telephone in order to summon Robinson and his station taxi. His mind was made up. He would not know an easy moment until he was back in his pantry, on guard. The station taxi would run into money, for Robinson, like all monopolists, drove a hard bargain; but if it would get him to the Castle before Monty it would be half a crown well spent.

'Robinson's taxi's outside now, Mr Beach,' said the landlord, tickled by the coincidence. 'A gentleman phoned for it only two minutes ago. Going up to the Castle himself he is. Maybe he'd give you a lift. You can catch him if you run.'

Beach did not run. Even if his figure had permitted such a feat, his sense of his position would have forbidden it. But he walked quite rapidly, and was enabled to leave the front door just as Monty was bidding farewell to a short, stout man in whom he recognized the Lord Tilbury who had called at the Castle on the previous day to see Mr Galahad. So it was he who had been egging young Mr Bodkin on to bungle!

For an instant, this discovery shocked the butler so much that he could hardly speak. That Baronets like Sir Gregory Parsloe should be employing minions to steal important papers had been a severe enough blow. That Peers should stoop to the same low conduct made, the foundations of his world rock. Then came a restorative thought. This Lord Tilbury, he reminded himself, was no doubt a recent creation. One cannot expect too high a standard of ethics from the uncouth *(hoi polloi)* who crash into Birthday Honours lists.

He found speech.

'Oh, Mr Bodkin. Pardon me, sir.'

Monty turned.

'Why, hullo, Beach.'

'Would it be a liberty, sir, if I were to request permission to share this vehicle with you?'

'Rather not. Lots of room for all. What are you doing in these parts, Beach? Slaking the old thirst, eh? Drinking-bouts in the tap-room, yes?'

'I walked down from the Castle to purchase cigarettes at the tobacconist's, sir,' replied Beach with dignity. 'And as the afternoon heat proved somewhat trying . . . '

'I know, I know,' said Monty sympathetically. 'Well, leap in, my dear old stag at eve.'

At any other moment Beach would have been offended at such a mode of address and would have shown it in his manner. But just as he was about to draw himself up with a cold stare he chanced to catch sight of Lord Tilbury, who had retreated to the shadow of the inn wall.

On his marriage to the daughter of Donaldson's Dog-biscuits, of Long Island City, N.Y., and his subsequent departure for America, the Hon. Freddie Threepwood, Lord Emsworth's younger son, who had assembled in the days of his bachelorhood what was pretty generally recognized as the finest collection of mystery thrillers in Shropshire, had bequeathed his library to Beach; and the latter in his hours of leisure had been making something of a study of the literature of Crime of late.

Lord Tilbury, brooding there with folded

174

arms, reminded him of The Man With The Twisted Eyebrows in *The Casterbridge Horror*.

Shuddering strongly, Beach climbed into the cab.

When two careworn men, one of whom has just discovered that the other has criminal tendencies, take a drive together on a baking afternoon, conversation does not run trippingly. Monty was thinking out plans and schemes; and Beach, in the intervals of recoiling with horror from this desperado, was wondering why the latter had called him a stag at eve. Silence, accordingly, soon fell upon the station taxi and lasted till it drew up at the front door of the castle. Here Monty alighted, and the taxi took Beach round to the back door. As he got down and handed Robinson his fare, the butler was conscious of an unwilling respect for the fiendish cunning of the criminal mind — which, having offered you a lift in a cab, gets out first and leaves you to pay for it.

He hastened to his pantry. Reason told him that the manuscript must still be in the drawer where he had placed it, but he did not breathe easily until he had seen it with his own eyes. He took it out and, having done so, paused irresolutely. It was stuffy in the pantry and he longed to be in the open air, in that favourite seat of his near the laurel bush outside the back door. And yet he could not relax with any satisfaction there, separated from his precious charge.

There is always a way. A few moments later he perceived that all anxiety might be obviated if he took the manuscript with him. He did so. Then, reclining in his deck-chair, he lit one of the cigarettes which it had cost him such labour to procure, and gave himself up to thought.

His moonlike face was drawn and grave. The situation, he realized, was becoming too complex for comfort.

The views of butlers who have been given important papers to guard and find that there are persons on the premises who wish to steal them are always clear-cut and definite. Broadly speaking, a butler in such a position can bear up with a reasonable amount of fortitude against the menace of one gang of would-be thieves. He may not like it, but he can set his teeth and endure. Add a second gang, however, and the thing seems to pass beyond his control.

Beach's researches in the library bequeathed to him by the Hon. Freddie Threepwood had left him extremely sensitive on the subject of Gangs. In most of the volumes in that library Gangs played an important part, and he had come to fear and dislike them. And here in Blandings Castle, groping about and liable at any moment to focus their malign attention on himself, were two Gangs — the Parsloe and the Tilbury. It made a butler think a bit.

To divert his mind, he began to read the manuscript. Being of an inquisitive nature, he had always wanted to do so, and this seemed an admirable opportunity. Opening the pages at random, therefore, and finding himself in the middle of Chapter Six ('*Nightclubs of the Nineties*'), he plunged into a droll anecdote

176

about the Bishop of Bangor when an under-graduate at Oxford, and despite his cares was soon chuckling softly, like some vast kettle coming to the boil.

It was at this moment that Percy Pilbeam, who had been smoking cigarettes in the stable yard, came sauntering round the corner.

★ ★ ★

The stable yard had been a favourite haunt of Percy Pilbeam's ever since his arrival at the Castle. A keen motorcyclist, he liked talking to Voules, the chauffeur, about valves and plugs and things. And, in addition to this, he found the place soothing because it was out of the orbit of the sisters and nephews of his host. You did not meet Lady Constance Keeble there, you did not meet Lady Julia Fish there, and you did not meet Lady Julia Fish's son Ronald there; and for Percy Pilbeam that was sufficient to make any spot Paradise enough.

He was also attracted to the stable-yard because he found it a good place to think in.

He had been thinking a great deal these last two days. A self-respecting private investigator is always loath to admit that he is baffled, but baffled was just what Pilbeam had been ever since a second visit to the small library had informed him that the manuscript which he had been commissioned to remove was no longer in its desk. Like Monty, he felt at a loss.

It was all very well, he felt sourly, for that Keeble woman to say in her impatient, duchess-talking-to-a-worm way that it must be somewhere and that she was simply amazed that he had not found it. The point was that it might be anywhere. No doubt if he had a Scotland Yard search-warrant, a troupe of African witch-doctors and unlimited time at his disposal he could find it. But he hadn't.

A well-defined dislike of Lady Constance Keeble had been germinating in Percy Pilbeam since the first moment they had met. He was brooding upon that unpleasantly supercilious manner of hers as he turned the corner now. And he had just come to the conclusion, as he always came on these occasions, that what she needed was a thoroughly good ticking off, when he was suddenly jerked out of his daydreams by the sound of a huge, reverberating, explosive laugh; and looking up with a start, espied protruding over the top of a deck-chair a few feet before him an egg-shaped head which he recognized as that of Beach, the butler.

★ ★ ★

We left Beach, it will be remembered, chuckling softly. And for a few minutes soft chuckles had contented him. But in a book of the nature of the Hon. Galahad Threepwood's Reminiscences the student is sure sooner or later to come upon some high spot, some supreme expression of the writer's art which demands a more emphatic tribute. What Beach was reading now was the story of Sir Gregory Parsloe-Parsloe and the prawns.

'HA . . . HOR . . . HOO!' he roared.

Pilbeam stood spellbound. His had not been a wide experience of butlers, and he could not recall ever before having heard a butler laugh — let alone laugh in this extraordinary fashion, casting dignity to the winds and apparently without a thought for his high blood-pressure and the stability of his waistcoat buttons. As soon as the first numbing shock had passed away, an intense curiosity seized him. He drew near, marvelling. On tiptoe he stole behind the chair, agog to see what it could be that had caused this unprecedented outburst.

The next moment he found himself gazing upon the manuscript of the Hon. Galahad's Reminiscences.

He recognized it instantly. Ever since that attempt upon it which this same butler had foiled, its shape and aspect had been graven upon his memory. And even if that straggling handwriting had not been familiar to him, the two lines which he read before uttering an involuntary cry would have told him what it was that flickered before his eyes.

'Oof!' said Pilbeam unable to check himself.

Beach gave a convulsive start, turned, and, looking up, beheld within six inches of his eyes the face of the leading executive of the sinister Parsloe Gang.

'Oof!' he exclaimed in his turn, and the deck-chair, as if in sympathy, also made an oof-like sound. Then, cracking under the strain, it spread itself out upon the ground.

Even under the most favourable conditions,

the situation would have been one of embarrassment. The peculiar circumstances rendered it cataclysmic. Pilbeam, who had never seen a butler take a toss out of a deck-chair before, stood robbed of speech; while Beach, his heart palpitating dangerously, sat equally silent. He was frozen with horror. That the enemy should have succeeded in tracking him down already seemed to him to argue a cunning that transcended the human.

Rising with the manuscript clutched to the small of his back, if his back could be said to have a small, he began to retreat slowly towards the house. Continuing to recoil, he bumped into stonework, and with an infinite relief found that he was within leaping distance of the back door. With a last, lingering look, of a nature which a sensitive snake would have resented, he shot in, leaving Pilbeam staring like one in a dream.

Almost exactly at the instant when he reached the haven of his pantry, Monty Bodkin, taking a thoughtful stroll on the terrace, suddenly remembered with a start of shame and remorse that he had left Beach to pay that cab fare.

One points at Monty Bodkin with a good deal of pride. Most young men in his position would either have dismissed the matter with a careless 'What of it?' or possibly even the still more ignoble reflection that a bit of luck had put them half a crown up; or else would have made a mental note to slip the fellow the money at some vague future date. For in the matter of Debts the young man of today wavers between straight repudiation and a moratorium.

But in a lax age Monty Bodkin had his code. To him this obligation was a blot on the Bodkin escutcheon which had to be wiped off immediately.

And so it came about that Beach, panting from his recent clash with the Parsloe Gang and in his dazed condition not having heard the door open, became suddenly aware of emotional breathing in the vicinity of his left ear and discovered that the right-hand man of the Tilbury Gang had now invaded his fastness.

It was a moment which would have tried the *morale* of the hero of a Secret Service novel. It made Beach feel like a rabbit with not one stoat but a whole platoon of stoats on its track. He had been sitting, relaxed. He now rose like a rocket and, snatching up the manuscript in the old familiar manner, stood holding it to his heaving chest.

Monty, who, like Pilbeam, had reacted strongly to the wholly unforeseen discovery of the precious object in the butler's possession, was the first to recover from the shock.

'What ho!' he said. 'Afraid I startled you, what?'

Beach continued to pant.

'I came to give you the money for that cab.'

Beach, though reluctant to take even one hand off the manuscript, was not proof against half-crowns. Cautiously extending a palm, he accepted the coin, thrust it into his pocket, and restored his grasp to the papers almost in a single movement.

'Must have given you a jump. Sorry. Ought to

have blown my horn.'

There was a pause.

'I see you've got that book of Mr Galahad's there,' said Monty, with a rather overdone carelessness.

To Beach it seemed more than rather overdone. He had been manoeuvring with the open door as his objective, and he now took a shuffling step in that direction.

'Pretty good, I should imagine? Now, there's a thing,' said Monty, 'that I'd very much like to read.'

Beach had now reached the door, and the thought of having a clear way to safety behind him did something to restore his composure. That trapped feeling had left him, and in its stead had come a stern, righteous wrath. He stared at Monty, breathing heavily. A sort of glaze had come over his eyes, causing them to resemble two pools of cold gravy.

'You couldn't lend it to me, I suppose?'

'No, sir.'

'No?'

'No, sir.'

'You won't?'

'No, sir.'

There was a pause. Monty coughed. Beach, with an inward shudder, felt that he had never heard anything so roopy and so villainous. He was surprised at Monty. A nice, respectable young gentleman he had always considered him. He could only suppose that he had been getting into bad company since those early days when he had been a popular visitor at the Castle.

'I'd give a good deal to read that thing, Beach.'

'Indeed, sir?'

'Ten quid, in fact.'

'Indeed, sir?'

'Or, rather, twenty.'

'Indeed, sir?'

'And when I say twenty,' explained Monty, 'I mean, of course twenty-five.'

The sophisticated modern world has, one fears, a little lost its taste for the type of scene, so admired of an older generation, where Virtue, drawing itself up to its full height, scorns to be tempted by gold. Yet even the most hard-boiled and cynical could scarcely have failed to be thrilled had they beheld Beach now. He looked like something out of a symbolic group of statuary — Good Citizenship Refusing To Accept A Bribe From Big Business Interests In Connexion With The Contract For The New Inter-Urban Tramway System, or something of that kind. His eyes were hard, his waistcoat quivered, and when he spoke it was with a formal frigidity.

'I regret to say, sir, that I am not in a position to fall in with your wishes.'

And with a last stare, of about the same calibre as the last stare which he had directed at Percy Pilbeam, he moved in good order to the Housekeeper's Room, leaving Monty plunged in thought.

★ ★ ★

Too often, when a man of Monty Bodkin's mental powers is plunged in thought, nothing

183

happens at all. The machinery just whirs for a while, and that is the end of it. But on the present occasion this was not so. Love is the great driving force, and now it was as if Gertrude Butterwick had her dainty foot on the accelerator of his brain, whacking it up to unprecedented m.p.h. The result was that after about two minutes of intense concentration, during which he felt several times as if the top of his head were coming off, an idea suddenly shot out of the welter like a cork from the Old Faithful geyser.

It was obvious that, with Beach turning so unaccountably spiky as he had done, he could accomplish nothing further by his own efforts. He must put the matter into the hands of a competent agent. And the chap to apply to was beyond a question this bird Pilbeam.

Pilbeam, he reasoned, was a private detective. The job to be done, therefore, would be right up his street: for stealing things must surely be one of the commonplaces of a private detective's daily life. From what he could remember of his reading, they were always being called upon to steal things — compromising letters, Admiralty Plans, Maharajah's rubies, and what not. No doubt the fellow would be only too glad of the commission.

He went in search of him, and found him lying back in an armchair in the smoking-room. He had the tips of his fingers together, Monty noted approvingly. Always a good sign.

'I say, Pilbeam,' he said, 'are you in the market at the moment for a bit of stealthy stuff?'

'Pardon?'

'If so, I've got a job for you.'

'A job?'

Like Monty, Pilbeam had been thinking tensely, and what with the strain on his brain and the warmth of the weather, was not feeling so bright as he usually did.

'You *are* a detective?' said Monty anxiously. 'You weren't just pulling my leg about that, were you?'

'Certainly I am a detective. I think I have one of my cards here.'

Monty inspected the grubby piece of pasteboard, and all anxiety left him. Argus Inquiry Agency. You couldn't get round that. Secrecy and Discretion Guaranteed. Better still. A telegraphic code address, too — Pilgus, Piccy, London. Most convincing.

'Topping,' he said. 'Well, then, coming back to it, I can put business in your way.'

'You wish to make use of my professional services?'

'If you're open for a spot of work at this juncture, I do. Of course, if you're simply down here taking a well-earned rest . . . '

'Not at all. I shall be glad to render you any assistance that is in my power. Perhaps you will tell me the facts.'

Monty was a little doubtful about the procedure. He had never engaged a private detective before.

'Do you want to know my name?'

'Isn't your name Bodkin?' said Pilbeam surprised.

'Oh, yes. Rather. Definitely. Only in all the

stories I've read the chap who comes to the detective always starts off with a long yarn about what his name is and where he lives and who left him his money, and so forth. Save a lot of time if we can cut all that.'

'All I require are the facts.'

Monty hesitated again.

'It sounds so dashed silly,' he said coyly.

'I beg your pardon?'

'Well, bizarre, if you prefer the expression. Nobody could say it wasn't. Bizarre is the word that absolutely springs to the lips. It's about that book of Gally Threepwood's.'

Pilbeam gave a little jump.

'Oh?'

'Yes. You knew he had written a book?'

'Quite.'

'Well ... ' Monty giggled ' ... I suppose you'll think I'm a silly ass, but I want to get hold of it.'

Pilbeam was silent for a moment. He had not known that he had a rival in the field, and was none too pleased to hear it.

'You do think I'm a silly ass?'

'Not at all,' said Pilbeam, recovering himself. 'No doubt you have your reasons?'

It had just occurred to him that, so far from being a disconcerting piece of news, what he had heard was really tidings of great joy. He supposed, mistakenly, that Monty, who no doubt had many friends in high places, had been asked by one of them to take advantage of his being at the Castle to destroy the book. England, he knew, was full of men besides Sir

Gregory Parsloe who wanted those Reminiscences destroyed.

The situation now began to look very good to Percy Pilbeam. He had only to secure that manuscript and he would be in the delightful position of having two markets in which to sell it. Competition is the soul of Trade. The one thing a man of affairs wants, when he has come into possession of something valuable, is to have people bidding against one another for it.

'Oh, I have my reasons all right,' said Monty. 'But it's a long story. Do you mind if we just leave it at this, that there are wheels within wheels?'

'Just as you please.'

'The thing is, a certain bloke — whom I will not specify — has asked me to get hold of this manuscript — for reasons into which I need not go — and . . . well, there you are.'

'Quite,' said Pilbeam, satisfied that the position was exactly as he had supposed.

Monty proceeded with more confidence.

'Well, that's that, then. Now we get down to it. I've just found out that the chap who's got the thing is — '

'Beach,' said Pilbeam.

Monty was astounded.

'You knew that?'

'Certainly.'

'But how on earth — ?'

'Oh, well,' said Pilbeam carelessly, as one who has his methods.

Monty was now convinced that he had come to the right shop. This man was uncanny.

'Beach,' he had said. Just like that. Might have been a mind-reader.

'Yes, that's the strength of it,' he went on as soon as he had ceased marvelling. 'That's where the snag lies. Beach has got it and is hanging on to it like a limpet. He won't let me lay a finger on the thing. So the problem, as I see it . . . You don't mind me outlining the problem as I see it? . . .'

Pilbeam waved a courteous hand.

'Well, then, the problem, as I see it,' said Monty, 'is, how the hell is one to get it away from the blighter?'

'Quite.'

'That is, as you might say, the nub?'

'Quite.'

'Have you any ideas on the subject?'

'Oh, yes.'

'Such as — ?'

'Ah, well,' said Pilbeam, a little stiffly. Monty was all apologies.

'I see, I see,' he said. 'Naturally you don't want to blow the gaff prematurely. Shouldn't have asked. Sorry. But I can leave the matter in your hands with every confidence, as I believe the expression is?'

'Quite.'

'He might let you borrow the thing to read?'

'At any rate, I have no doubt that I shall find a way of getting it into my possession.'

Monty eyed him admiringly. Externally, Percy Pilbeam was not precisely his idea of a detective. Not quite enough of that cold, hawk-faced stuff, and a bit too much brilliantine on the hair. But as far as brain was concerned he was undoubtedly the goods.

'I bet you will,' he said. 'You can't run a business like yours without knowing a thing or two. I expect you've pinched things before.'

'I have occasionally been commissioned to recover papers, and so forth, of value,' said Pilbeam guardedly.

'Well, consider yourself jolly well commissioned now,' said Monty.

# 9

Safe in the Housekeeper's Room, Beach sat gazing out of the window at the lowering sky. His chest was still rising and falling like a troubled ocean.

Too hot, felt Beach, too hot. Things were becoming too hot altogether.

His whole mind was obsessed by an insistent urge to get rid of these papers, the guardianship of which had become so hazardous a matter. The chase was growing too strenuous for a man of regular habits who liked a quiet life.

Nearly everything in this world cuts both ways. A fall from a deck-chair, for instance, is — physically — a painful experience. Against its obvious drawbacks, however, must be set the fact that it does render the subject nimbler mentally. It shakes up the brain. To the circumstance of his having so recently come down with a bump on his spacious trousers-seat must be attributed the swiftness with which Beach now got an idea that seemed to him to solve everything.

He saw the way out. He would hand this manuscript over to Mr Ronald. There was its logical custodian. Mr Ronald was the person most interested in its safety. He was, moreover, a young man. And the more he mused on the whole unpleasant affair, the more firmly did Beach come to the conclusion that the foiling of the Parsloe Gang and the Tilbury Gang was young man's work.

It would be necessary, of course, to apply to the Hon. Galahad for permission to take the step. If you went behind his back and acted on your own initiative after he had given you instructions, Mr Galahad could be quite as bad as any gang. Years of association with London's toughest citizens had given him a breadth of vocabulary which was not lightly to be faced. Beach had no intention of drawing upon himself the lightnings of that Pelican-Club trained tongue. As soon as he felt sufficiently restored to move, he went in search of the Hon. Galahad and found him in the small library.

'Might I speak to you, Mr Galahad?'

'Say on, Beach.'

Clearly and well the butler told his talc. He recounted the scene at the Emsworth Arms, the subsequent invasion of his pantry by the man Bodkin, the proffered bribe. The Hon. Galahad listened with fire smouldering behind his monocle.

'The young toad!' he cried. 'Monty Bodkin. A fellow I've practically nursed in my bosom. Why, I can remember, when he was a boy at Eton, taking him aside as he was going back to school one time and urging him to put his shirt on Whistling Rufus for the Cesarewitch.'

'Indeed, sir?'

'And he notified me subsequently that, thanks to my kindly advice, he had cleaned up to the extent of eleven shillings — in addition to a bag of bananas, two strawberry ice-creams, and a three-cornered Cape of Good Hope stamp at a hundred to sixteen from a schoolmate who was making a book. And this is how he repays me!' said the Hon. Galahad, looking like King Lear. 'Isn't there such a thing as gratitude in the world?'

He expressed his disgust with a wide, passionate gesture. The butler, with his nice instinct for class distinctions, expressed his with one a little less wide and not quite so passionate. These callisthenics seemed to relieve them both, for when the conversation was resumed it was on a calmer note.

'I might have known,' said the Hon. Galahad, 'that a fellow like Stinker Pyke . . . what does he call himself now, Beach?'

'Lord Tilbury, Mr Galahad.'

'I might have known that a fellow like Lord Tilbury wouldn't give up the struggle after one rebuff. You don't make a large fortune by knuckling under to rebuffs, Beach.'

'Very true, Mr Galahad.'

'I suppose old Stinker has been up against this sort of thing before. He knows the procedure. The first thing he would do, after I had turned him down, would be to set spies and agents to work. Well, I don't see what there is to be done except employ renewed vigilance, like Clarence with his pig.'

Beach coughed.

'I was thinking, Mr Galahad, that if I were to hand the documents over to Mr Ronald . . . '

'You think that would be safer?'

'Considerably safer, sir. Now that Mr Pilbeam

is aware that they are in my possession, I am momentarily apprehensive lest her ladyship approach me with a direct request that I deliver them into her hands.'

'Beach! Are you afraid of my sister Constance?'

'Yes, sir.'

The Hon. Galahad reflected.

'Well, I see what you mean. It would be difficult for you. You couldn't very well tell her to go and put her head in a bag.'

'No, sir.'

'All right, then. Give the thing to Mr Ronald.'

'Thank you very much, Mr Galahad.'

Infinitely relieved, Beach allowed his gaze, hitherto concentrated on his companion, to travel to the window. 'Storm looks like breaking at last, sir.'

'Yes.'

The Hon. Galahad also looked out of the window. It was plain that Nature in all her awful majesty was about to let herself go. On the opposite side of the valley there shot jaggedly across the sky a flash of lightning. Thunder growled, and raindrops began to splash against the pane.

'That fool's going to get wet,' he said.

Beach followed his pointing finger. Into the scene below a figure had come, walking rapidly. His interview with Percy Pilbeam had left Monty in that exhilarated frame of mind which demands strenuous exercise. Where Lord Tilbury, on a previous occasion, had walked because his heart was heavy, Monty walked

193

because his heart was light. Pilbeam had filled him with the utmost confidence. He did not know how or when, but he felt that Pilbeam would find a way.

So now he strode briskly across the park, regardless of the fact that the weather was uncertain.

'Mr Bodkin, sir.'

'So it is, the young reptile. He'll get soaked.'

'Yes, sir.'

There was quiet satisfaction in the butler's voice. It was even possible, he was reflecting, that this young man might be struck by lightning. If so, it was all right with Beach. As far as he was concerned, Nature's awful majesty could go the limit. He only wished that Pilbeam, too, were being exposed to the fury of the elements. He viewed members of gangs in rather an Old Testament spirit, and believed in their getting treated rough.

★   ★   ★

Ronnie was in his bedroom. When the heart is aching, there are few better refuges than a country-house bedroom. A man may smoke and think there, undisturbed.

Beach, tracking him down a few minutes later, found him well disposed to the arrangement he had come to suggest. He made no difficulties about accepting custody of the manuscript. Indeed, it seemed to Beach that he was scarcely interested. Listless was the word that occurred to the butler, and he put it down to the weather. He

194

took his departure with feelings resembling those of the man who got rid of the Bottle Imp; and Ronnie, having thrown the manuscript into a drawer, resumed his seat and began thinking of Sue once more.

Sue! . . .

It wasn't that he blamed her. If she loved Monty Bodkin — well, that was that. You couldn't blame a girl for preferring one fellow to another.

All that stuff his mother had been saying about her being the typical chorus-girl fluttering from affair to affair was, of course, just a lot of pernicious bilge. Sue wasn't like that. She was as straight as they make 'em. It was simply that she had been dazzled by this blasted lissom Monty and couldn't help herself.

You were always reading about that sort of thing in novels. Girl gets engaged to bloke, thinking at the moment that he is what the doctor ordered. Then runs into second bloke and discovers in a sort of flash that she has picked the wrong one. No doubt, on that trip of hers to London she had happened to meet Monty accidentally in Piccadilly or somewhere and the thing had come on her like a thunderbolt.

It was what he had been expecting all along, of course. He had told her so himself. It stood to reason, he meant, that a terrific girl like her — a girl who practically stood alone, as you might say — was bound sooner or later to come across someone capable of cutting out a bally pink-faced midget who, except for getting a featherweight Boxing blue at Cambridge, had never done a thing to justify his existence.

Yes, that was about what it all boiled down to, felt Ronnie. He rose and went to the window. For some time now, in a subconscious sort of way, he had been dimly aware that there was something rummy going on outside.

He found himself looking out upon a changed world. The storm was now at its height. Torrents of rain were coursing down the glass. Thunder was booming, lightning flashing. A hissing, howling, roaring, devastated world. A world that seemed to fit in neatly with his stormy emotions.

Sue! . . .

Yesterday on the roof. Finding that hat and realizing that she and Monty had been up there together all the afternoon. He flattered himself that she couldn't possibly have detected anything from his manner — no, he had worn the good old mask all right -but there had been a moment, before he got hold of himself, when he had understood how those chaps you read about in the papers who run amok and slay two get that way.

Yes, reason might tell him that it was perfectly natural for Sue to be in love with Monty Bodkin, but nothing was going to make him like it.

The storm seemed to be conking out a bit. The thunder had rolled away into the distance. The lightning flashes had lost much of their zip. Even the rain showed a disposition to cheese it. What had been a Niagara was now little more than a drizzle. And suddenly, watery and faint, there gleamed on the drenched stone of the terrace, a ray of sunshine.

It grew. Blue spread over the sky. Across the valley there was a rainbow. Ronnie opened the window and a wave of cool, sweet-smelling air poured into the room.

He leaned out, sniffing. And abruptly he became aware that the heavy depression of the last two days had left him. The thunderstorm had wrought its customary miracle. He felt like a man recovered from a fever. It was as if the whole world had suddenly been purged of gloom. A magic change had come over everything.

Birds were singing in the shrubberies below, and for twopence Ronnie could have sung himself.

Why, dash it, he felt, he had been making a fat-headed fuss about absolutely nothing. He saw it all now. What had given him that extraordinary notion that Sue was in love with Monty was simply the foul weather. Of course there was nothing between them really. That lunch could easily be explained. So could that afternoon together on the roof. Everything could easily be explained in this best of all possible worlds.

And scarcely had he reached this conclusion when he perceived on the drive below him a draggled figure. It was Monty Bodkin, home from his ramble. He leaned farther out of the window, overflowing with the milk of human kindness.

'Hullo,' he said.

Monty looked up.

'Hullo.'

'You're wet.'

197

'Yes.'

'By Jove, you *are* wet!' said Ronnie. It hurt him to think that this brave new world could contain a fellow human being in such a soluble condition. 'You'd better go and change.'

'Yes.'

'Into something dry.'

Monty nodded, scattering water like a public fountain. He brushed the tangle of hair out of his eyes, and squelched on his way.

It was perhaps two minutes later that Ronnie, still aching with compassion, remembered that on the shelf above his wash-stand he had a bottle of excellent embrocation.

★  ★  ★

When once a man has reacted from a mood of abysmal depression, there is no knowing how far he will go in the opposite direction. In a normal frame of mind, Ronnie would probably have dismissed the moistness of Monty from his thoughts as soon as the other had left him. But now, in the grip of this strange feeling of universal benevolence, he felt that those few words of sympathy had not been enough. He wanted to do something practical, something constructive that would help to ward off the nasty cold in the head which this man might so easily catch as the result of his total immersion. And, as we say, he remembered that bottle of embrocation.

It was Rigg's Golden Balm, in the large (or seven-and-sixpenny) size, and he knew, not only

198

from the advertisements, which were very frank about it, but also from personal trial, that it communicated an immediate warm glow to the entire system, averting catarrh, chills, rheumatism, sciatica, stiffness of the joints, and lumbago, and in addition imparted a delightful sensation of *bien-être*, toning up and renovating the muscular tissues. And if ever a fellow stood in need of warm glows and tonings up, it was Monty.

Seizing the bottle, he hurried off on his errand of mercy. He found Monty in his room, stripped to the waist, rubbing himself vigorously with a rough towel.

'I say,' he said, 'I don't know if you know this stuff! You might like to try it. It communicates a warm glow.'

Monty, the towel draped about him like a shawl, examined the bottle with interest. He sloshed it tentatively. This consideration touched him.

'Dashed good of you.'

'Not a bit.'

'You're sure it's not for horses?'

'Horses?'

'Some of these embrocations are. You rub them well in, and then you take another look at the directions and you see 'For horses only', or words to that effect, and then you suffer the tortures of the damned for about half an hour, feeling as if you had been having a dip in vitriol.'

'Oh, no. This stuff's all right. I use it myself.'

'Then have at it!' said Monty, relieved.

He poured some of the fluid into the palm of

his hand and expanded his torso. And, as he did so, Ronnie Fish uttered a quick, sharp exclamation.

Monty looked up, surprised. His benefactor had turned a vivid vermilion and was staring at him in a marked manner.

'Eh?' he said, puzzled.

Ronnie did not speak immediately. He appeared to be engaged in swallowing some hard, jagged substance.

'On your chest,' he said at length, in a strange, toneless voice. 'Eh?'

Eton and Cambridge came to Ronnie's aid. Outwardly calm, he swallowed again, picked a piece of fluff off his left sleeve, and cleared his throat.

'There's something on your chest.'

He paused.

'It looks like 'Sue'.'

He paused again.

' 'Sue',' he said casually, 'with a heart round it.'

The hard jagged substance seemed to have transferred itself to Monty's throat. There was a brief silence while he disposed of it.

He was blaming himself. Rummy, he reflected ruefully, how when you saw a thing day after day for a couple of years or so it ceased to make any impression on what he rather fancied was called the retina. This heart-encircled 'Sue', this pink and ultramarine tribute to a long-vanished love, which in a gush of romantic fervour he had caused to be graven on his skin in the early days of their engagement, might during the last eighteen months just as well not have been there for all the notice he had taken of it. He had practically forgotten that it was still in existence.

It was a moment for quick thinking.

'Not 'Sue',' he said. ''S.U.E.' — Sarah Ursula Ebbsmith.'

'What!'

'Sarah Ursula Ebbsmith,' repeated Monty firmly. 'Girl I used to be engaged to. She died. Pneumonia. Very sad. Don't let's talk of it.'

There was a long pause. Ronnie moved to the door. His feelings were almost too deep for words, but he managed a couple. 'Well, bung-o!'

★   ★   ★

The door closed behind him.

Sue had watched the storm from the broad window-seat of the library.

Her feelings were mixed. As a spectacle she enjoyed it, for she was fond of thunderstorms. The only thing that spoiled it for her was the knowledge that Monty was out in it. She had seen him cross the terrace in an outward bound direction just as it began to break. The poor lamb, she felt, must be getting soaked.

Her first act, accordingly, when the rain stopped and that sea of blue began to spread itself over the sky, was to go out on to the balcony and scan the horizon, like Sister Ann, for signs of him. She was thus enabled to witness his return and to hear the brief exchange of remarks between him and Ronnie.

'Hullo.'

'Hullo.'

'You're wet.'

'Yes.'

'By Jove, you *are* wet. You'd better go and change.'

'Yes.'

'Into something dry.'

Considered as dialogue, not, perhaps, on the highest level. Reading it through, one sees that it lacks a certain something. But the noblest effort of a great dramatist could not have stirred Sue more. It seemed to her, as she listened, that a great weight had rolled off her heart.

It was the way Ronnie had spoken that impressed and thrilled. The kindly, considerate tone. The cheerful cordiality. For two days it had been as though some sullen changeling had taken his place; and now, if one could judge from the genial ring of his voice, the old Ronnie was back again.

She stood on the balcony, drinking in the fragrant air. It was astonishing what a change that healing storm had brought about. Shropshire, which yesterday had been so depressing a spectacle, was now an earthly Paradise. The lake glittered. The river shone. The spinneys were their friendly selves again. Rabbits were darting about in the park with all the old carefree abandon, and as far as the eye could reach there were contented cows.

She left the room, humming a little tune. Eventually, she would seek out Monty and make inquiries after his well-being, but her immediate desire was to find Ronnie.

The click of billiard-balls arrested her

attention as she came to the foot of the stairs. Gally, probably, playing a solitary hundred up; but he might be able to tell her where Ronnie was. His voice during that conversation with Monty had seemed to come from one of the passage windows.

She opened the door, and Ronnie, sprawled over the table, looked up at her.

That tattoo-mark had settled things for Ronnie. It had swept away in an instant all the gay optimism brought by the passing of the storm. With a heart like lead, he had groped his way downstairs. The open door of the billiard-room had seemed to offer a means of diverting his thoughts temporarily, and he had gone in and begun to practise sombre cannons. For even if a man is leaden-hearted there is no harm in his brushing up his near-the-cushion game a bit. Indeed, it is an intelligent thing to do, for if the girl he loves loves another his life is obviously going to be pretty much of a blank for the next fifty years or so, and he will have to fall back for solace on his ambitions. One of Ronnie's ambitions was some day to make a flukeless break of thirty.

'Hullo,' he said politely, straightening himself and standing with cue at rest. Eton and Cambridge stood at his elbow, to help him through this ordeal.

No sense of impending disaster came to Sue. To her, this man was still the sort of modern Cheeryble Brother whom she had heard chatting to Gally out of the window.

'Oh, Ronnie,' she said, 'you can't stay indoors

on an evening like this. It's simply lovely out.'

'Oh, yes?' said Eton.

'Perfectly wonderful.'

'Oh, yes?' said Cambridge.

Something seemed to stab at Sue's heart. Her eyes widened. A numbing thought had begun to frame itself. Could it be that that sunny geniality which she had so recently observed playing upon Monty Bodkin like a fountain was to be withheld from her?

But she persevered.

'Let's go for a drive in your car.'

'I don't think I will, thanks.'

'Then let's take a boat out on the lake.'

'Not for me, thanks.'

'Or the court might be dry enough for tennis by now.'

'I shouldn't think so.'

'Well, then, come for a walk.'

'Oh, for God's sake,' said Ronnie, 'let me alone!'

They stared at one another. Ronnie's eyes were hot and miserable. But they did not look hot and miserable to Sue. She read in them only the dislike, the sullen, trapped dislike of a man tied to a girl for whom he has ceased to feel any affection, so that merely to speak to her is an affliction to his nerves. She drew a deep breath, and walked to the window.

'Sorry,' said Ronnie gruffly. 'Shouldn't have said that. 'I'm glad you did,' said Sue. 'It's better to come right out with these things.'

She traced little circles with her finger on the glass. A heavy silence filled the room. 'I think we might as well chuck it, don't you?' she said. 'Just as you say,' said Ronnie. 'All right,' said Sue.

She moved to the door. He hurried forward and opened it for her. Polite to the last.

\* \* \*

Up in his bedroom, meanwhile, anointing his chest with Riggs's Golden Balm, Monty Bodkin had suddenly become amazingly cheerful.

'Tiddly-iddly-om, pom-POM,' he chanted, as blithely as any thrush in the shrubbery below. A great idea had just come to him.

It was the embrocation that had done the trick. As he stood there enjoying the immediate warm glow and the delightful sensation of *bien-être*, it was as if his brain, as well as his muscular tissues, had been toned up and renovated. This bottle of embrocation, it suddenly occurred to him, was more than a mere three or four fluid ounces of stuff that smelled like a miasmic swamp — it was a symbol. If Ronnie was taking the trouble to bring him bottles of embrocation, it must mean that all was well between them; that that odd coldness had ceased to be; that his dear old pal, in a word, was once more a dear old pal. And if a man is a dear old pal, it stands to reason that he will be delighted to do a fellow a good turn.

The good turn Monty wanted Ronnie to do for him now was to go to Beach and use his influence with that obdurate butler to persuade him to cough up that manuscript.

It was not that Monty had lost faith in

205

Pilbeam. No doubt, if given time, Pilbeam, exercising his subtle craft, would be able to secure the thing all right. But why go to all that trouble when you could take a short cut and work the wheeze quite simply without any fuss? Besides, there was the fellow's fee to be considered. These sleuths probably came pretty high, and a penny saved is a penny earned.

A room-to-room search brought him to where the Last of the Fishes was once more practising cannons. He approached him with all the happy confidence of a child entering the presence of a rich and indulgent uncle.

For Monty Bodkin was no mind-reader. He had detected no change in his friend's manner at the end of their recent interview. It had been awkward for a moment, no doubt, that business of the tattoo-mark, but he felt that his quick thinking had passed off a tricky situation pretty neatly, satisfactorily lulling all possible suspicions.

'I say, Ronnie, old lad,' he said, 'I wonder if you could spare me a moment of your valuable time?'

Ronnie laid the cue down carefully. For all that he had now resigned himself to the fact that Sue preferred this man to him, he was conscious of a well-defined desire to bat him over the head with the butt end. White-hot knives were gashing Ronnie Fish's soul, and he could not but feel a very vivid distaste for the man responsible for his raw misery.

'Well?' he said.

It seemed to Monty that his friend was a bit

206

on the chilly side, not quite the effervescing chum of the dear old embrocation days, but he carried on with only a momentary twinge of concern.

'Tell me, old man, how do you stand with Beach?'

'With Beach? How do you mean?'

'Well, does he feel pretty feudal where you're concerned? Would he, in fine, be inclined to stretch a point to oblige the young master?'

Ronnie stared bleakly. He had been prepared to be civil to this man who had wrecked his life, but he was dashed if he was going to spend the evening listening to him talking drip.

'What is all this bilge?' he demanded sourly. 'Come to the point.'

'Oh, I'm coming to the point.'

'Well, be quick.'

'I will, I will. Here, then, is the gist or nub. Beach has got something I badly want, and he refuses to disgorge. And I thought that perhaps if you went to him and did the Young Squire a bit — exerting your influence, I mean to say, and rather throwing your weight about generally — he might prove more . . . what's the word . . . begins with an A . . . amenable.'

Ronnie glowered wearily.

'I can't understand a damn thing you're talking about.'

'Well, in a nutshell, Beach has got that book of old Gally's and I can't get him to let me have it.'

'Why do you want it?'

Monty decided, as he had done when talking with Lord Tilbury by the potting-shed, that manly frankness was the only policy.

'You know all about that book?'

'Yes.'

'That Gally won't let it be published, I mean?'

'Yes.'

'And that he had signed a contract for it with the Mammoth Publishing Company?'

'No. I didn't know that.'

'Well, he did. And his backing out has rendered poor old Pop Tilbury, the boss of same, as sick as mud. Well, naturally, I mean to say, Old Tilbury had got serial rights and book rights and American rights and every other kind of rights including the Scandinavian, and you know what a packet there is in any literary effort, that really dishes the dirt about the blue-gored. I should say, taking it one way and another, he stands to lose in the neighbourhood of twenty thousand quid if Gally sticks to his resolve not to publish. And so, to cut a long story s., old man, this Tilbury is so anxious to get hold of the manuscript that he states specifically that if I can snitch it from him he will take me back into his employment — from which, as I dare say you know, I was recently booted out.'

'I thought you resigned.'

Monty smiled sadly.

'That may be the story going the round of the clubs,' he said, 'but as a matter of actual fact I was booted out. There was a spot of technical trouble which wouldn't interest you and into which I will not go. Suffice it to say that we did not see eye to eye as regarded the conduct of the Uncle Woggly to his Chicks department, and my

208

services were dispensed with. So now you get the run of the scenario. The thing is a straight issue. Let me grab this MS. and turn it in to the Big Chief, and I start working again at Tilbury House.'

'What do you want to do that for?'

'It's imperative. I must have a job.'

'I should have thought that you would have been happy enough here.'

'Ah, but I'm liable to get the sack here at any moment.'

'Too bad.'

'Quite bad enough,' agreed Monty. 'But it'll be all right if you can induce Beach to give up that manuscript, I shall then secure a long-term contract with old Tilbury and be in a posish to marry the girl I love.'

A strong convulsion shook Ronnie Fish. This, he considered, was pretty raw. A nice thing, taking a fellow's girl away from him and then coming to him to ask him to help him marry her. He had credited the other with more delicacy.

'You will, eh?' he said, after a pause to master his emotion.

'Positively. It's all fixed up.'

'Who is she?' asked Ronnie sardonically. 'Sarah Ursula Ebbsmith?'

'Eh? Oh, ah,' said Monty hastily. He had forgotten for the moment. 'No, not poor dear Sarah. Oh, no, no, no. She's dead. Tuberculosis. Very sad.'

'You told me it was pneumonia.'

'No, tuberculosis.'

'I see.'

'This is a new one. Girl named Gertrude Butterwick.'

Misunderstandings being always unfortunate, it was a pity, firstly, that Monty should have paused for a reverent second before uttering that sacred name and, secondly, that the girl of his dreams should have possessed a name which, one has to admit, sounded a little thin. In certain moods, a man whose mind is biased simply does not believe that there is such a name as Gertrude Butterwick. To Ronnie, noting that second's hesitation, it was just one this man had made up on the spur of the moment, even he not having the face to tell Sue's fiancé, as he supposed him still to be, that he wanted his assistance in taking Sue from him.

'Gertrude Butterwick, eh?'

'That's right.'

'Fond of her?'

'My dear chap!'

'And I suppose she's crazy about you?'

'Oh, deeply enamoured.' Ronnie felt suddenly listless. What, he asked himself, did it matter, anyway? What did anything matter now?

Every man is tempted at times by the great gesture. This temptation had just come overwhelmingly upon Ronnie Fish. From the other's words he had become confirmed in his suspicion that somehow or other Monty since their last meeting must have lost all his money. Otherwise, why should jobs at Tilbury House be of such importance to him?

Unless he got that job at Tilbury House, he would not be able to marry Sue. And unless he,

Ronnie Fish, helped him, he would not get it.

The Sidney Carton spirit descended upon Ronnie — with this difference, that where Sidney, if one remembers correctly, was rather pleased about the whole thing he himself felt bitter and defiant.

Monty had taken Sue from him. Sue had gone to Monty without a pang. All right, then. All jolly right. He would show them he didn't care. He would let them see the stuff Fishes were made of.

'Listen,' he said. 'There's no need to worry about Beach. He hasn't got that manuscript.'

'Oh, yes, he has. I saw him reading . . . '

'He gave it to me,' said Ronnie. He picked up his cue and shaped at the spot ball. 'You'll find it in the chest of drawers in my room. Take the damned thing if you want it.'

Monty gasped. No Israelite caught in a sudden manna-shower in mid-desert could have felt a greater mixture of surprise and gratification.

'My dear old man!' he began effusively.

Ronnie did not speak. He was practising cannons.

# 10

The passing of the storm had left the Hon. Galahad Threepwood at rather a loose end. He was not quite sure where he wanted to go or what he wanted to do. His favourite lawn, he knew, would be too wet to walk on, his favourite deck-chair too wet to sit in. The whole world out of doors, in fact, for all that the sun was shining so brightly, was much too moist and dripping to attract a man with his feline dislike of dampness.

After Beach had left him, he had remained for a while in the small library. Then, tiring of that, he had wandered aimlessly about the house, winding as many clocks as he could find. He was, and always had been, a great clock-winder. Eventually, he had drifted to the hall, and was now lounging on a settee there in the hope that, if he lounged long enough, somebody would come along with whom he might chat till it was time to dress for dinner. He always found this part of the evening a little depressing.

Up to the present, he had had no luck. Monty Bodkin had come downstairs, but after Beach's revelations he had no wish to do anything but glower sternly at Monty. Without attempting to draw him into conversation, though he had just remembered a thirty-year-old Limerick which he would have liked to recite to someone, he watched him go into the billiard-room, where the opening door showed a glimpse of Ronnie practising cannons. Presently, he had come out again and gone upstairs, followed as before by that stern eye.

'Young toad!' muttered the Hon. Galahad severely. He was shocked at Monty, and disappointed in him. He wished he had never given him that tip on the Cesarewitch.

Soon after this, Pilbeam had appeared, smiled weakly, and gone into the smoking-room. Here, again, there was nothing for the Hon. Galahad to work on. He had no desire to tell Limericks to Pilbeam. Apart from the fact that the fellow was conspiring with his sister Constance to steal his manuscript, he did not like the detective. Brought up in a sterner school of hairdressing, he disapproved of these modern young men who went about with their fungoid growth in sticky ridges.

It began to look to him as if in the matter of society he had but two choices open. Clarence, who would have appreciated that Limerick once he could have been induced to bring his mind to bear upon it, was presumably down at the sty making eyes at that pig of his; and Sue, the person he really wanted to talk to, seemed to have disappeared off the face of the earth. As far as he could see, he was reduced to the alternatives of going into the billiard-room and joining Ronnie, and of stepping up to the drawing-room and having a word with his sister Constance, who at this hour would no doubt be taking tea there. He was just about to adopt this second course, for he rather wanted a straight talk with Constance about that Pilbeam matter, when Sue came in from the garden.

Immediately, the idea of tackling Connie left him. He could do that at his leisure, and he was in the mood now for something pleasanter than a brother-and-sister dog-fight. Sue's bright personality was just the tonic he needed at this lowering point in the day's progress. He would be unable to tell her the Limerick, it not being that sort of Limerick, but at any rate they could talk of this and that.

He called to her, and she came over to where he sat. It was dim in the hall, but it struck him that she was not looking quite herself. The elasticity seemed to have gone out of her walk, that jaunty suppleness which he had always admired so in Dolly. But possibly this was merely his imagination. He was always inclined to read a fictitious sombreness into things when the shadows began to creep over the world and it was still too early for a cocktail.

'Well, young woman.'

'Hullo, Gally.'

'What have you been doing with yourself?'

'I was walking on the terrace.'

'Get your feet wet?'

'I don't think so. Perhaps I had better go up and change my shoes, though.'

The Hon. Galahad would have none of this. He pulled her down on to the settee beside him.

'Amuse me,' he said. 'I'm bored.'

'Poor Gally. I'm sorry.'

'This,' said the Hon. Galahad, 'is the hour of the day that searches a man out. It makes him examine his soul. And I don't want to examine

214

my soul. I expect the thing looks like an old boot. So, as I say, amuse me, child. Sing to me. Dance before me. Ask me riddles.'

'I'm afraid . . . '

The Hon. Galahad gave her a sharp glance through his monocle. It was as he had suspected. This girl was not festive. 'Anything the matter?'

'Oh, no.'

'Sure?'

'Quite.'

'Cigarette?'

'No, thanks.'

'Shall I turn on the radio? There may be a lecture on Newts.'

'No, don't.'

'There *is* something the matter?'

'There isn't, really.'

The Hon. Galahad frowned. Then a possible solution occurred to him.

'I suppose it's the heat.'

'It was hot, wasn't it. It's better now.'

'You're under the weather.'

'I am a little.'

'Thunderstorms often upset people. Are you afraid of thunder?'

'Oh, no.'

'Lots of girls are. I knew one once who, whenever there was a thunderstorm, used to fling her arms round the neck of the nearest man, hugging and kissing him till it was all over. Purely nervous reaction, of course, but you should have seen the young fellows flocking round as soon as the sky began to get a little overcast. Gladys, her name was. Gladys Twistleton. Beautiful girl with large, melting eyes. Married a fellow in the Blues called Harringay. I'm told that the way he used to clear the drawing-room during the early years of their married life at the first suspicion of a rumble was a sight to be seen and remembered.'

The Hon. Galahad had brightened. Like all confirmed raconteurs, he took on new life when the anecdotes started to come.

★   ★   ★

The Hon. Galahad swelled like a little turkey-cock. His monocle was now a perfect searchlight.

'Just off be damned!' he snorted. 'You sit down and listen to me. Just off, indeed! You can go off when I've finished talking to you, and not before.'

Ronnie abandoned the snooker theory. Plainly it did not cover the facts. His moroseness had become tinged with bewilderment. It was many years since he had beheld his good-natured relative in a mood like this. It seemed to bring back the tang of the brave old days of chimney-stacks and whangees. He could think of nothing in his recent conduct that could have caused so impressive an upheaval.

'Now, then,' said the Hon. Galahad, 'what's all this?'

'That's just what I was going to ask,' said Ronnie. 'What *is* all this?'

'Don't pretend you don't know.'

'But I don't know.'

'It's no good taking that attitude.' The Hon.

Galahad jerked his thumb at the door. 'I've just been talking to young Sue out there.'

A thin coating of ice seemed to creep over Ronald Fish. 'Oh, yes?' he said politely.

'She's crying.'

'Oh, yes?' said Ronnie, still politely, but with those white-hot knives at work on his soul again. His mind was divided against itself. Part of it was pointing out passionately that it was ghastly to think of Sue in tears. The other part was raising its eyebrows and shooting its cuffs and observing with a sneer that it was blowed if it could see what *she* had to cry about.

'Crying, I tell you! Crying her dashed eyes out!'

'Oh, yes?'

The Hon. Galahad Threepwood was himself an Old Etonian, and in his time had frequently had occasion to employ the Eton manner to the undoing of his fellow-men. There were grey-haired bookies and elderly card-sharps going about London to this day, who still felt an occasional twinge, as of an old wound, when they recalled the agony of seeing him stare at them as Ronnie was staring and of hearing him say 'Oh, yes?' as Ronnie was saying it now. But this did not make his nephew's attitude any the easier for him to endure. The whole point of the Eton manner, as of a shotgun, is that you have to be at the right end of it.

He brought his fist down on the billiard-table with a thump.

'So you're not interested, eh? You don't care? Well, let me tell you,' said the Hon. Galahad, once more maltreating the billiard-table, 'that I do care. That girl's mother was the only woman I ever loved, and I don't propose to have her daughter's happiness ruined by any sawn-off young half-portion with a face like a strawberry ice who takes the notion into his beastly turnip of a head to play fast and loose with her. Understand that!'

There were so many ramifications to this insult that Ronnie was compelled to take them in rotation.

'I can't help it if my face is like a strawberry ice,' he said, electing to begin with that one.

'It ought to be much more like a strawberry ice. You ought to be blushing yourself sick.'

'And when,' said Ronnie, feeling on safe ground here, 'you talk about sawn-off half-portions, may I point out that I'm about an inch taller than you are?'

'Rot!' said the Hon. Galahad, stung.

'I am.'

'You're certainly not.'

'Measure you against the wall,' insisted Ronnie.

'I'll do nothing of the sort. And what the devil,' demanded the Hon. Galahad, suddenly aware that the main issue of debate was becoming shelved, 'has that got to do with it? You may be a giraffe, for all I care. The point I am endeavouring to make is that you are breaking this girl's heart, and I'm not going to have it. She tells me your engagement is off.'

'Quite right.'

Once more the Hon. Galahad smote the green

cloth. 'You'll smash that table,' said Ronnie.

There flashed into the Hon. Galahad's mind the story of how old Beefy Muspratt, with some assistance, actually had smashed a billiard-table in the year ninety-eight; and such is the urge to the raconteur's ruling passion that he almost stopped to tell it. Then he recovered himself.

'Curse the table!' he cried. 'I didn't come here to talk about tables. I came to tell you that, if you care to know what a calm, unprejudiced observer thinks of you, you're an infernal young snob . . . and a hound . . . '

'What!'

' . . . and a worm,' went on the Hon. Galahad, as pink himself now as any pink-faced nephew. 'Do you think I can't see what's happened? If you want to know, Sue told me herself. Told me in so many words, out there in the hall just now. You're such a wambling, spineless, invertebrate jellyfish that you've let your mother talk you into breaking off this engagement. You've allowed her to persuade you that that poor child isn't good enough for you.'

'What!'

'As if Dolly Henderson's daughter wasn't good enough for the finest man in the kingdom — let alone a . . . '

On the brink of becoming a little personal again, the Hon. Galahad found himself interrupted. This time it was Ronnie who had thumped the table.

'Don't talk such absolute dashed nonsense!' thundered Ronnie. 'You don't suppose I broke off the engagement, do you? Sue broke it off herself.'

'Yes, because she could see that you wanted to get out of it and, being the splendid girl she is, wasn't going to cheapen herself by hanging on to a man who was obviously dying to be rid of her.'

'Hike that! Dying to be rid of her! I . . . I . . . Why, damn it!'

'You aren't telling me you're still fond of her?'

'What do you mean, still? And what do you mean, fond of her? Fond of her! My God!' The Hon. Galahad was astounded.

'Then what on earth have you been going about for these last few days like a spavined frog? Treating her as if . . . '

His manner softened. He began to see daylight. He could not lay his hand gently on his nephew's shoulder, for they were at opposite sides of a regulation-sized billiard-table. But he infused a gentle hand-laying into his voice.

'I see it all! You were worrying about something else; is that it? Or was it the heat? Anyhow, for some reason you allowed yourself to be odd in your manner. My dear boy, when you get to my age you'll know better than to take chances like that. Never be odd in your manner with a woman. Don't you realize that, even under the best of conditions, there's practically nothing that won't make a sensitive, highly strung girl break off her engagement? If she doesn't like her new hat . . . or if her stocking starts a ladder . . . or if she comes down late to breakfast and finds all the scrambled eggs are finished. It's like servants giving notice. I had a man back in the nineties — Spatchett, his name was — who used to give me notice every time he backed a horse that didn't finish in the first three. Why, he gave me notice once purely and simply because his wife's sister had had a baby. I never paid any attention to it. I knew it was just a form of emotional expression. Where you or I would have lit a cigarette, Spatchett gave notice. And it's the same with women. No doubt Sue saw you brooding and assumed that love was dead. Well, this has certainly eased my mind, Ronnie, my dear boy. I'll go and explain things to her at once.'

'Half a minute, Uncle Gally.'

'Eh?'

Pausing half-way to the door, the Hon. Galahad saw that a peculiar expression had come into his nephew's face. An expression a little like that of a young Hindu fakir who, having settled himself on his first bed of spikes, is beginning to wish that he had chosen one of the easier religions.

'I'm afraid it isn't quite so simple as that,' said Ronnie.

The Hon. Galahad drew in the slack of his monocle, which in the recent excitement had fallen from his eye. He screwed the thing into place, and surveyed his nephew inquiringly.

'What do you mean?'

'You've got it all wrong. Sue doesn't love me.'

'Nonsense!'

'It isn't nonsense. She's in love with Monty Bodkin.'

'What!'

'It's all settled between them that they're going to get married.'

'I never heard such . . . '

'Oh, it's perfectly true,' said Ronnie, his mouth twisting. 'I'm not blaming her. Nobody's fault. Just one of those things. Still, there it is. She's crazy about him. She went up to London to meet him the moment I was out of the place, just because she couldn't keep away from him. She got him to apply for Hugo's job as Uncle Clarence's secretary, just because she was so keen to have him here.

She was up on the roof with him all yesterday afternoon. And . . . ' Ronnie had to pause for a moment here to control his voice ' . . . he's got her name tattooed on his chest, with a heart round it.'

'You don't mean that?'

'I saw it myself.'

'Well, I'm dashed! Hurts like sin, that sort of thing. I haven't heard of anybody having a girl's name tattooed on him since the year ninety-nine, when Jack Bellamy-Johnstone . . . '

Ronnie held up a restraining hand.

'Not now, uncle, if you don't mind.'

'Most amusing story,' said the Hon. Galahad, wistfully.

'Later on, what?'

'Well, yes, perhaps you're right,' admitted the Hon. Galahad. 'I suppose you're not in the mood for stories. It was simply that poor old Jack fell in love with a girl named Esmeralda Parkinson-Willoughby and had the whole thing tattooed on his wishbone, and the wounds had scarcely healed when they quarrelled and he got engaged to another girl called May Todd. So if he had only waited . . . However, as you say, that is neither here nor there. Ronnie, my dear boy,' said the Hon. Galahad, 'this beats me. I had always looked on you as a pretty average sort of young poop, but never, never would I have imagined that you could have allowed yourself to believe all that drivel . . . '

'Drivel!'

'Perfect drivel. You've got hold of the wrong end of the stick entirely. Suppose Sue did go to London . . . '

'There's no supposition about it. My mother saw her and Monty lunching together at the Berkeley.'

'She would. Dashed Nosey Parker. Sorry, my boy. Forgot she was your mother. Still, she was my sister before you were ever born or thought of, and I hope a man can call his own sister a Nosey Parker. What did she tell you?'

'She said . . . '

'All right. Never mind. I can guess. No doubt she's been filling you up with all sorts of stories. Well, now you can hear the truth. Young Sue had nothing whatever to do with Monty Bodkin coming here. The first she heard of his having been taken on as Clarence's secretary was from me, and the news absolutely bowled her over. I can see her now, looking at me like a dying duck and saying here was a nice bit of fruit-box because she had once, when a mere child, been engaged to the fellow . . . '

'What!'

'Certainly. Years ago. Before she ever met you. Only lasted a week or two, as far as I can gather, and she was glad to get out of it. But there the fact was. She had been engaged to him, and he was coming here, and if he wasn't tipped off to keep the thing dark he would be sure to say something tactless about the old days, and that would upset you, because you were such a blasted jealous halfwit, always ready to make heavy weather about nothing. She asked me what she ought to do. I gave her the only possible advice. I told her to rush up to London before you got back, get hold of Monty, and tell him to keep his mouth shut. Which she did. That is how she came to be in London that day, and that is why she was lunching with him. So there you are. The whole thing, you observe, done from start to finish in the kindliest spirit of altruism, with no other motive than to preserve your peace of mind. Perhaps this will be a lesson to you in future not to give way to jealousy, which I have always said and always shall say is one of the dashed silliest . . . '

Ronnie was staring, perplexed in the extreme.

'Is this true?'

'Of course it's true. If you can't see by this time that Sue is a girl in a million — pure gold — and that you've been treating her abominably . . . '

'But she was up on the roof with him.'

The childishness of this seemed to nettle the Hon. Galahad. He uttered a sound which was rather like Lord Tilbury's 'Cor!'

'Why shouldn't she be up on the roof with

224

him? Must people be in love with one another just because they are up on roofs together? I was up on that roof with you once, but if you thought I was in love with you you must have been singularly obtuse. It's been a grief to me for years that you were so nippy round that chimney-stack. Sue in love with young Bodkin, indeed! Why, Monty Bodkin is engaged himself. She told me so. To a girl named Gertrude Butterwick. Butterwick,' said the Hon. Galahad musingly. 'I used to know several Butterwicks. I wonder if she would be any relation to old Legs Butterwick, who used to paint his face with red spots to make duns who called at his rooms think he'd got smallpox.'

A shuddering groan burst from the lips of Ronnie Fish. 'Oh, gosh, what a fool I've made of myself!'

'You have.'

'I'm a hound and a cad.'

'You are.'

'I ought to be kicked.'

'You ought.'

'Of all the . . . '

'Hold it,' urged the Hon. Galahad. 'Don't waste all this on me. Tell it to Sue. I'll fetch her.'

He darted from the room, to return a moment later, dragging the girl behind him.

'Now!' he said authoritatively. 'Do your stuff. Tie yourself in knots at her feet, and ask her to kick you in the face. Grovel before her on your wretched stomach. Roll about the floor and bark. And while you're doing it I'll be stepping up to the drawing-room and having a word with your mother and my sister Constance.'

A stern, resolute look came into the Hon. Galahad's face.

'I'll spoil their tea and shrimps!' he said.

In the drawing-room, however, when he arrived there after taking the stairs three at a time in that juvenile way of his which gout-crippled contemporaries so resented, he found only his sister Julia. She was seated in an armchair, smoking a cigarette and reading an illustrated weekly paper. The tea which he had hoped to spoil was in the process of being cleared away by Beach and a footman.

She looked contented, and she was feeling contented. Ronnie's growing gloom during the past two days had not escaped her. In a mood to be genial to everybody, even to one on whom she had always looked as the Family Blot, she welcomed the Hon. Galahad with a pleasant nod.

'You're late, if you've come for tea,' she said.

'Tea!' snorted the Hon. Galahad.

He stood fuming until the door closed.

'Now, then, Julia,' he said, 'I want a word with you.'

Lady Julia raised her shapely eyebrows.

'My dear Galahad! This is very menacing and ominous. Is something the matter?'

'You know what's the matter. Where's Connie?'

'Gone to answer the telephone, I believe.'

'Well, you'll do to start with.'

'Galahad, really!'

'Put down that paper.'

226

'Oh, very well.'

The Hon. Galahad strode to the hearthrug and stood with his back to the empty fireplace. Racial instinct made him feel more authoritative in that position. He frowned forbiddingly.

'Julia, you make me sick.'

'Indeed? Why is that?'

'What the devil do you mean by trying to poison young Ronnie's mind against Sue Brown?'

'Really, Galahad!'

'Do you deny that that is what you have been doing ever since you got here?'

'I may have pointed out to him once or twice the inadvisability of marrying a girl who appears to be in love with another man. If this be treason, make the most of it. Surely it's a tenable theory?'

'You think she's in love with young Bodkin?'

'Apparently.'

'If you will step down to the billiard-room,' said the Hon. Galahad, 'I think you may possibly alter your opinion.' Something of Lady Julia's self-confidence left her. 'What do you mean?'

'Touching,' said the Hon. Galahad unctuously. 'That's what it was. Touching. It nearly made me cry. I never saw a more united couple. All their doubts and misunderstandings cleared away . . . '

'What!'

'Locked in each other's arms, weeping on each other's chests . . . you ought to go down and have a look, Julia. You'll be in plenty of time. It's evidently going to be one of those non-stop performances. Well, anyway, that's the first thing I came up here to tell you. You have been taking a lot of trouble to ruin this girl's happiness these last few days, and now you are getting official intimation that you haven't succeeded. They are all right, those two. Sweethearts still is the term.'

The Hon. Galahad spread his coat-tails to the invisible blaze and resumed.

'The other thing I came to say is that there must be no more of this nonsense. If you have objections to young Ronnie marrying Sue, don't mention them to him. It worries him and makes him moody, and that worries Sue and makes her unhappy, and that worries me and spoils my day. You understand?'

Lady Julia was shaken, but she had not lost her spirit.

'I'm afraid you must make up your mind to having your days spoiled, Galahad.'

'You don't mean that even after this you intend to keep making a pest of yourself?'

'You put these things so badly. What you are trying to say, I imagine is, do I still intend to give my child a mother's advice? Certainly I do. A boy's best friend is his mother, don't you sometimes think? Ronnie, handicapped by being virtually half-witted, may not have seen fit to take my advice as yet; but if in the old days you ever had a moment to spare from your life-work of being thrown out of shady night-clubs and were able to look in at the Adelphi Theatre, you may remember the expression 'the time will come!''

The Hon. Galahad stared at this indomitable

woman with something that was almost admiration. 'Well, I'm dashed!'

'Are you?'

'You always were a tough nut, Julia.'

'Thank you.'

'Always. Even as a child. It used to interest me in those days to watch you gradually dawning on the latest governess. I could have read her thoughts in her face, poor devil. First, she would meet Connie and you could almost hear her saying to herself, 'Hullo! A vicious specimen this one.' And then you would come along, all wide, innocent blue eyes and flaxen curls, and she would feel a great wave of relief and fling her arms round you; thinking, 'Well, here's one that's all right, thank God!' Little knowing that she had just come up against the stoniest-hearted, beastliest-natured, and generally most poisonous young human rattlesnake in all Shropshire.'

Lady Julia seemed genuinely pleased at this tribute. She laughed musically.

'You are silly, Galahad.'

The Hon. Galahad adjusted his monocle.

'So your hat is still in the ring, eh?'

'Still there, my dear.'

'But what have you got against young Sue?'

'I don't like chorus-girls as daughters-in-law.'

'But, great heavens above, Julia, surely you can see that Sue isn't the sort of girl you mean when you say 'chorus-girls' in that beastly sniffy way?'

'You can't expect me to classify and tabulate chorus-girls. I haven't your experience. They're all chorus-girls to me.'

'There are moments, Julia,' said the Hon. Galahad meditatively, 'when I should like to drown you in a bucket.'

'A butt of malmsey would have been more in your line, I should have thought.'

'Your attitude about young Sue infuriates me. Can't you see the girl's a nice girl . . . a sweet girl . . . and a lady, if it comes to that.'

'Tell me, Gally,' said Lady Julia, 'just as a matter of interest, *is* she your daughter?' The Hon. Galahad bristled.

'She is not. Her father was a man in the Irish Guards, named Cotterleigh. He and Dolly were married when I was in South Africa.'

He stood for a moment, his mind in the past.

'Fellow told me about it quite casually one day when I was having a drink in a Johannesburg bar,' he said with a far-off look in his eyes. 'I see that girl Dolly Henderson who used to be at the Tivoli has got married,' he said. Out of a blue sky . . . '

Lady Julia took up her paper.

'Well, if you have no further observations of interest to make . . . '

The Hon. Galahad came back to the present. 'Oh, I have.'

'Please hurry, then.'

'I have something to say which I fancy will interest you very much.'

'That will make a nice change.'

The Hon. Galahad paused a moment. His sister took advantage of the fact to interject a question. 'It isn't by any chance that, if this marriage of Ronnie's is stopped, you will publish those Reminiscences of yours, is it?'

'It is.'

Lady Julia gave another of her jolly laughs.

'My dear man, I had all that days ago from Constance. And my flesh didn't even creep a bit. It seems to agitate Connie tremendously but speaking for myself I haven't the slightest objection to you publishing a dozen books of Reminiscences. It will be nice to think of you making some money at last, and as for the writhings of the nobility and gentry . . . '

'Julia,' said the Hon. Galahad, 'one moment.'

He eyed her intently. She returned his gaze with an air of faintly bored inquiry.

'Well?'

'You are the relict of the late Major-General Sir Miles Fish, C.B.E., late of the Brigade of Guards.'

'I have never denied it.'

'Let us speak for awhile,' said the Hon. Galahad gently, 'of the late Major-General Sir Miles Fish.'

Slowly a look of horror crept into Lady Julia's blue eyes. Slowly she rose from the chair in which she had been reclining. A hideous suspicion had come into her mind.

'When Miles Fish married you,' said the Hon. Galahad, 'he was a respectable — even a stodgily respectable — Colonel. I remember your saying the first time you met him that you thought him slow. Believe me, Julia, when I knew dear old Fishy Fish as a young subaltern, while you were still poisoning governesses' lives at Blandings Castle, he was quite the reverse of slow. His jolly

231

rapidity was the talk of London.'

She stared at him, aghast. Her whole outlook on life, as one might say, had been revolutionized. Hitherto, her attitude towards the famous Reminiscences had been, as it were, airy . . . detached . . . academic is perhaps the word one wants. The thought of the consternation which they would spread among her friends had amused her. But then she had naturally supposed that this man would have exercised a decent reticence about the pasts of his own flesh and blood.

'Galahad! You haven't . . . ?'

The historian was pointing a finger at her, like some finger of doom.

'Who rode a bicycle down Piccadilly in sky-blue underclothing in the late summer of '97?'

'Galahad!'

'Who, returning to his rooms in the early morning of New Year's Day, 1902, mistook the cost-scuttle for a mad dog and tried to shoot it with the fire-tongs?'

'Galahad!'

'Who . . . '

He broke off. Lady Constance had come into the room.

'Ah, Connie,' he said genially. 'I've just been having a chat with Julia. Get her to tell you all about it. I must be going down and seeing how the young folks are getting on.'

He paused at the door.

'Supplementary material,' he said, focusing his monocle on Lady Julia, 'will be found in

232

Chapters Three, Eleven, Sixteen, Seventeen, and Twenty-one, especially Chapter Twenty-one.'

With a final beam, he passed jauntily from the room and began to descend the stairs.

★ ★ ★

In the billiard-room, the scene which he had rightly described as touching was still in progress. He wished he could take a snapshot of it to show to his sister Julia.

'That's right, my boy,' he said cordially. 'Capital!'

Ronnie detached himself and began to straighten his tie. He had not heard the door open.

'Oh, hullo, Uncle Gally,' he said. 'You here?'

Sue ran to the Hon. Galahad and kissed him.

'I shouldn't,' said the gratified but cautious man. 'He'll be getting jealous of me next.'

'There is no need,' said Ronnie with dignity, 'to rub it in.'

'Well, I won't, then. Merely contenting myself with remarking that of all the young poops I ever met . . . '

'He is not a poop!' said Sue.

'My dear,' insisted the Hon. Galahad, 'I was brought up among poops. I spent my formative years among poops. I have been a member of clubs which consisted exclusively of poops. You will allow me to recognize a poop when I see one. Moreover, we won't argue the point. What I want to talk about now is that manuscript of mine.' A wordless cry broke from Ronnie's lips.

'Poop or no poop,' proceeded the Hon. Galahad, 'he has got to guard that manuscript with his life. Because if ever there were two women who would descend to the level of the beasts of the field to lay their hooks on it . . .'

'Uncle Gally!'

'Ronnie, darling,' cried Sue, 'What is it?'

She might well have asked. The young man's eyes were fixed in a ghastly stare. His usually immaculate hair was disordered where he had thrust a fevered hand through it. Even his waistcoat seemed ruffled.

' . . . they are your mother and Lady Constance,' proceeded the Hon. Galahad, who was never an easy man to interrupt. 'And here's something that will surprise you. Young Monty Bodkin is after the thing, too. Young Bodkin has turned out to be an A1 snake in the grass, I'm sorry to say. He's under orders from the man who runs the firm that was going to publish my book to pinch it and take it to him — Lord Tilbury. I used to know him years ago as Stinker Pyke. Why they ever made young Stinker a peer . . .'

'Uncle Gally!'

A little testily the Hon. Galahad allowed the stream of his eloquence to be diverted at last. 'Well, what is it?'

A sort of frozen calm, the calm of utter despair, had come upon Ronnie Fish.

'Monty Bodkin was in here just now,' he said. 'He wanted that manuscript. I told him where it was. And he went off to get it.'

# 11

No joy in the world is ever quite perfect. *Surgit*, as the old Roman said, *oliquid amari*. Monty Bodkin, having removed the manuscript from Ronnie's chest of drawers and gloated over it and taken it to his room and, after gloating over it again, deposited it in a safe place there, found his ecstasy a little dimmed by the thought of the awkward interview with Percy Pilbeam which now faced him. He was a young man who shrank from embarrassing scenes, and it seemed to him that this one threatened to be extremely embarrassing. Pilbeam, he realized, would have every excuse for being as sore as a gumboil.

Look at the thing squarely, he meant to say. A private detective has his feelings. He resents being made a silly ass of. If you commission him to do something, and then buzz off and do it yourself, pique inevitably supervenes. Suppose Sherlock Holmes, for instance, had sweated himself to the bone to recover the Naval Plans or something, and then the Admiralty authorities had come along and observed casually, 'Oh, I say, you know those Naval Plans, old man? Well, don't bother about them. We've just gone and snitched them ourselves.' Pretty sick the poor old human bloodhound would have felt, no doubt. And pretty sick in similar circumstances Monty anticipated that Percy Pilbeam was going to feel. He did not like the job of breaking the news at all.

However, it had to be done. He found the proprietor of the Argus (Pilgus, Piccy, London) in the smoking-room, massaging his moustache, and with some trepidation proceeded to edge into the agenda.

'Oh, there you are, Pilbeam. I say . . . '

The investigator looked up. It increased Monty's feeling of guilt to note that he had evidently been thinking frightfully hard. He had a sort of boiled look. 'Ah, Bodkin, I was just coming to find you. I have been thinking . . . '

Monty's tender heart bled for the fellow, but he supposed it was kindest to let him have it on the chin without preamble.

'I know you have, my poor old sleuth,' he said. 'I can see it in your eye. Well, I've got a bit of bad news for you, I'm afraid. What I came to tell you was to switch off the brain-power. Stop scheming. Put the mind back into neutral. I'm taking you off the case.'

'Eh?'

'I'm sorry, but there it is. You see, what with one thing and another, I've been and got that manuscript myself.'

'What!'

'Yes.'

There was a long pause.

'Well, that's fine,' said Pilbeam. 'I hope you have hidden it carefully?'

'Oh, yes. It's shoved away under the bed in my room. Right up against the wall.'

'Well, that's fine,' said Pilbeam.

His attitude occasioned Monty much relief.

He had braced himself up to endure reproaches, to wince beneath recriminations. It seemed to him extraordinarily decent of the man to take it like this. He was dashed, indeed, if he could remember ever having met anyone who, under such provocation, had been so extraordinarily decent.

'What are you going to do with it?' asked Pilbeam. 'I'm taking it down to the Emsworth Arms to a fellow of the name of Tilbury.'

'Not Lord Tilbury?'

'That's right,' said Mont', surprised. 'Do you know him?'

'Before I opened the Argus, I was editor of *Society Spices* 'No, really? Fancy that. Before he booted me out, I was assistant editor of *Tiny Tots*. It seems to bring us very close together what?'

'But why does Lord Tilbury want it?'

'Well, you see, he has a contract with Gally for the book, and when Gally refused to publish he saw himself losing the dickens of a lot of money. Naturally he wants it.'

'I see. He ought to give you a pretty big reward.'

'Oh, I'm not asking him for money. I've got lots of money. What I want is a job. He promised to take me back on *Tiny Tots* if I would get the thing for him.'

'You are leaving here, then?'

Monty chuckled amusedly.

'You bet I'm leaving here. I expect the sack any moment. I'd have got it yesterday, all right,' said Monty, with another chuckle, 'if old

Emsworth had happened to come along when I was working on the door of that potting-shed.'

'What was that?'

'Rather amusing. I found old Tilbury locked up in a species of shed yesterday afternoon. Apparently he had been caught in conversation with that pig of the old boy's, offering it potatoes and so forth, and was suspected of trying to poison the animal. So they shut him up in this shed, and I came along and let him out. Just imagine how quick I should be leaving if Emsworth knew that I was the chap who flung wide the gates.'

'My word, yes!' said Pilbeam, laughing genially.

'He'd throw me out in a second.'

'He certainly would.'

'Rummy, his attitude about that pig,' said Monty musingly. 'A few years ago, he used to be crazy about pumpkins. I suppose, if you really face the facts, he's the sort of chap who has to be practically off his rocker about something. Yesterday, pumpkins. Today, pigs. Tomorrow, rabbits. This time next year, roosters or rhododendrons.'

'I suppose so,' said Pilbeam. 'And when are you thinking of taking this manuscript to Lord Tilbury?'

'Right away.'

'I wouldn't do that,' said Pilbeam, shaking his head. 'No, I don't think I would advise you to do that. You want to wait till everybody's dressing for dinner. Suppose you were to run into Threepwood.'

'I never thought of that.'

'Or Lady Constance.'

'Lady Constance?'

'I happen to know that she is trying to get that manuscript. She wants to destroy it.'

'I say! You certainly find things out, don't you?'

'Oh, one keeps one's ears open.'

'I suppose you've got to, if you're a detective. Well, I do seem properly trapped in the den of the Secret Nine, what? I'd better not make a move till dressing for dinner time, as you say. I'm glad you gave me that tip. Thanks.'

'Don't mention it,' said Pilbeam.

He rose.

'You off?' said Monty.

'Yes. I've just remembered there is something I want to speak to Lord Emsworth about. You don't know where he is, do you?'

'Sorry, no. The ninth doesn't confide in me much.'

'I suppose he's in the pigsty.'

'You can tell him by his hat,' said Monty automatically. 'Yes, I imagine he would be. Anything special you wanted to see him about?'

'Just something he asked me to find out for him.'

'In your professional capacity, do you mean? Pilgus, Piccy, London?'

'Yes.'

'Is he employing your services, then?'

'Oh, yes. That's why I'm here.'

'I see,' said Monty.

This made him feel much easier in his mind. If

Pilbeam was drawing a nice bit of cash from old Simon Legree, it put a different complexion on everything. Naturally, in that case, he wouldn't so much mind being done out of the Bodkin fee.

Still, he did feel that the fellow had behaved most extraordinarily decently.

★　★　★

Lord Emsworth was not actually in the pigsty, but he was quite near it. It took more than a thunderstorm to drive him from the Empress's side. A vague idea that he was getting a little wet had caused him to take shelter in the potting-shed during the worst of the downpour, but he was now out and about again. When Pilbeam arrived, he was standing by the rails in earnest conversation with Pirbright. He welcomed the detective warmly.

'You're just the man I was wanting to see, my dear Pilbeam,' he said. 'Pirbright and I have been discussing the question of moving the Empress to a new sty. I say Yes, Pirbright says No. One sees his point, of course. I quite see your point, my dear Pirbright. Pirbright's point,' explained Lord Emsworth, 'is that she is used to this sty and moving her to a strange one might upset her and put her off her feed.'

'Quite,' said Pilbeam, profoundly uninterested.

'On the other hand,' proceeded Lord Emsworth, 'we know that there is this sinister cabal against her well-being. Attempts have already been made to nobble her, as I believe the term is. They may be made again. And my view is that this sty here is in far too lonely and remote a spot for safety. God bless my soul,' said Lord Emsworth, deeply moved, 'in a place like this, a quarter of a mile away from anywhere, Parsloe could walk in during the night and do her a mischief without so much as taking the cigar out of his mouth. Where I was thinking of moving her, Pirbright would be within call at any moment. It's near his cottage. At the slightest sign of anything wrong, he could jump out of bed and hurry to the rescue.'

It was possibly this very thought that had induced the pig-man to say 'Nur' as earnestly as he had done. He was a man who liked to get his sleep. He shook his head now, and a rather bleak look came into his gnarled face.

'Well, there is the position, my dear Pilbeam. What do you advise?'

It seemed to the detective that the sooner he gave his decision the sooner the unprofitable discussion would be ended. He was completely indifferent about the whole thing. Officially at the castle to help guard the Empress, his heart had never been in that noble task. Pigs bored him.

'I'd move her,' he said.

'You really feel that?'

'Quite.'

A mild triumph shone from Lord Emsworth's pince-nez.

'There you have an expert opinion, Pirbright,' he said. 'Mr Pilbeam knows. If Mr Pilbeam says

Move her, she must certainly be moved. Do it as soon as possible.'

'Yur, m'lord,' said the pig-man despondently.

'And now, Lord Emsworth,' said Pilbeam, 'can I have a word with you?'

'Certainly, my dear fellow, certainly. But before you do so I have something very important to tell you. I want to hear what you make of it. Let me mention that first, and then you can tell me whatever it is that you have come to talk about. You won't forget whatever it is that you have come to talk about?'

'Oh, no.'

'I frequently do. I intend to tell somebody something, and something happens to prevent my doing so immediately, and when I am able to tell it to them I find I have forgotten it. My sister Constance has often been very vehement about it. I recollect her once comparing my mind to a sieve. I thought it rather clever. She meant that it was full of holes, you understand, as I believe sieves are. That was on the occasion when — '

Pilbeam had not had the pleasure of the ninth Earl's acquaintance long, but he had had it long enough to know that, unless firmly braked, he was capable of trickling on like this indefinitely.

'What was it you wished to tell me, Lord Emsworth?' he said.

'Eh? Ah, yes, quite so, my dear fellow. You want to hear that very important fact that I was going to put before you. Well, I would like you to throw your mind back, my dear Pilbeam, to yesterday. Yesterday evening. I wonder if you remember my mentioning to you the extraordinary mystery of that man getting out of the potting-shed?'

'Certainly.'

'The facts — '

'I know.'

'The facts — '

'I remember them.'

'The facts,' proceeded Lord Emsworth evenly, 'are as follows. In pursuance of my instructions, Pirbright was lurking near this sty yesterday afternoon, and what should he see but a ruffianly-looking fellow trying to poison my pig with a potato. He crept up and caught him in the act, and then shut him in that shed over there, intending to come back after he had informed me of the matter and hale him to justice. I should mention that, after placing the fellow in the shed, he carefully secured the door with a stout wooden staple.'

'Quite. I . . . '

'It seemed out of the question that he could effect an escape — I am speaking of the fellow, not of Pirbright — and you may imagine his astonishment, therefore — I am speaking of Pirbright, not of the fellow — when, on returning, he discovered that that is just what had occurred. The door of the shed was open, and he — I am once more speaking of the fellow — was gone. He had completely disappeared, my dear Pilbeam. And here is the very significant thing I wanted to tell you. Just before you came up I got Pirbright to shut me in the shed and secure the door with the staple, and I found it impossible — quite impossible, my dear fellow, to release myself from within. I tried and tried and tried, but no, I couldn't do it. Now, what does that suggest to you, Pilbeam?' asked Lord Emsworth, peering over his pince-nez. 'Somebody must have let him out.'

'Exactly. Undoubtedly, Beyond a question. Who it was of course, we shall never know.'

'I have found out who it was.'

Lord Emsworth was staggered. He had always known in a nebulous sort of way that detectives were gifted beyond the ordinary with the power to pierce the inscrutable, but this was the first time he had actually watched them at it.

'You have found out who it was?' he gasped.

'I have.'

'Pirbright, Mr Pilbeam has found out who it was.'

'Ur, m'lord.'

'Already! Isn't that amazing, Pirbright?'

'Yur, m'lord.'

'I wouldn't have thought it could have been done in the time. Would you, Pirbright?'

'Nur, m'lord.'

'Well, well, well!' said Lord Emsworth. 'That is the most extraordinary . . . Ah, I knew there was something I wanted to ask you . . . Who was it?'

'Bodkin.'

'Bodkin!'

'Your secretary, young Bodkin,' said Pilbeam.

'I knew it!' Lord Emsworth shook a fist skywards, and his voice, as always in moments of emotion, became high and reedy. 'I knew it! I suspected the fellow all along. I was convinced that he was an accomplice of Parsloe's. I'll dismiss him,' cried Lord Emsworth, almost achieving an A in alt. 'He shall go at the end of the month.'

'It would be safer to get him off the place at once.'

'Of course it would, my dear fellow. You are quite right. He shall be turned out immediately. Where is he? I must see him. I will go to him instantly.'

'Better let me send him to you out here. More dignified. Don't go to him. Let him come to you.'

'I see what you mean.'

'You wait here, and I'll go and tell him you wish to see him.'

'My dear fellow, I don't want to put you to all that trouble.'

'No trouble,' Pilbeam assured him. 'A pleasure.'

★ ★ ★

It is one of the distinguishing characteristics of your man of the world that he can keep his poise even under the most trying of conditions. Beyond a sort of whistling gasp and a sharp 'God give me strength!' the Hon. Galahad Threepwood displayed no emotion at Ronnie's sensational announcement.

He did, however, gaze at his nephew as if the latter had been a defaulting bookmaker.

'Are you crazy?' he said.

It was a question which Ronnie found difficult to answer. Even to himself, as he now told it, the story of that great gesture of his sounded more than a little imbecile. The best, indeed, that you could really say of the great gesture, he could not help feeling, was that, like so many rash acts, it had seemed a good idea at the time. He was bright scarlet and had had occasion to straighten his tie not once but many times before he reached the end of the tale. And not even the fact that Sue, with womanly sympathy, put her arm through his and kissed him was able to bring real consolation. To his inflamed senses that kiss seemed so exactly the sort of kiss a mother might have given her idiot child.

'You see what I mean, I mean to say,' he concluded lamely. 'I thought Sue had finished with me, so there didn't seem any point in holding on to the thing any longer, and Monty said he wanted it, and so . . . well, there you are.'

'You can't blame the poor angel,' said Sue.

'I can,' said the Hon. Galahad. He moved to the fire-place and pressed the bell. 'It would surprise you how easily I could blame the poor angel. And if there was time I would. But we haven't a moment to waste. We must get hold of young Monty without a second's delay and choke the thing out of him. We'll have no nonsense. I am an elderly man, past my prime, but I am willing and ready to sit on his head while you, Ronnie, kick him in the ribs. We'll soon make him — Ah, Beach.'

The door had opened.

'You rang, Mr Galahad?'

'I want to see Mr Bodkin, Beach. At once.'

'Mr Bodkin has left, sir.'

'Left!' cried the Hon. Galahad.

'Left!' shouted Ronnie.

'Left!' squeaked Sue.

'It is possible that he may still be in his bedchamber, packing the last of his effects,' said the butler, 'but I was instructed some little while ago that he was leaving the Castle immediately. There has been trouble, sir, between Mr Bodkin and his lordship. I am unable to inform you as to what precisely eventuated, but . . . '

A cry like that of a tiger leaping on its prey interrupted him. Through the open door the Hon. Galahad had espied a lissom form crossing the hall. He was outside in a flash, confronting it.

'You, there! You bloodstained Bodkin!'

'Oh, hullo.'

The Hon. Galahad, as his opening words had perhaps sufficiently indicated, had not come for any mere exchange of courtesies.

'Never mind the 'Oh, hullo.' I want that manuscript of mine, young Bodkin, and I want it at once, so make it slippy, you sheep-faced young exile from Hell. If it's on your person, disgorge it. If it's in your suitcase, unpack it. And Ronnie here and I will be standing over you while you do it.'

There was an infinite sadness in Monty Bodkin's gaze. He looked like a male Mona Lisa.

'I haven't got your bally manuscript.'

'Don't lie to me, young Bodkin.'

'I'm not lying. Pilbeam's got it.'

'Pilbeam!'

Monty's voice trembled with intense feeling.

'I told the foul, double-crossing little blister where it was, like a silly chump, and he went off and squealed to Lord Emsworth about my letting old Tilbury out of the potting-shed, and Lord Emsworth sent for me and fired me, and while I was out of the way, being fired, he nipped up to my room and sneaked the thing.'

'Where is he? Where is this Pilbeam?'

'Ah,' said Monty, 'I'd like to know myself. Well, good-bye, all. I'm off to the Emsworth Arms.'

He strode sombrely out of the front door and down the steps. A cough sounded behind the Hon. Galahad.

'Would there be anything further, sir?'

The Hon. Galahad drew a deep breath.

'No thank you, Beach,' he said. 'I think that perhaps this will be enough to be getting on with.'

# 12

At the moment when Monty Bodkin and the Hon. Galahad Threepwood, two minds with but a single thought, were wondering where he was and wishing they could have a word with him, Percy Pilbeam, the manuscript under his arm, had just emerged furtively from the back of the Castle. He did not wish to have anything to do with front doors. Directly he had crawled out from under Monty's bed, dragging his treasure trove after him, he had dusted his fingers and made for the servants' staircase. This had led him through twisting by-ways to a vast echoing stone passage, and from that to the back door was but a step. He had not encountered so much as a housemaid.

In his bearing, as he hurried along the path that skirted the kitchen garden — in the oily smirk beneath his repellent moustache, in the jaunty tilt of his snub nose, even in the terraced sweep of the brilliantine swamps of his corrugated hair — there was the look of a man who is congratulating himself on a neat bit of work. Brains, reflected Percy Pilbeam — that was what you needed in this life. Brains and the ability to seize your opportunity when it was offered to you.

He had a long walk before him. It was his intention, in order to avoid meeting any interested party, to make a wide circle round the outskirts of Lord Emsworth's domain and strike the road to Market Blandings near Matchingham. There, no doubt, he would be able to get a lift to the Emsworth Arms. Then, having seen Lord Tilbury and arrived at some satisfactory financial arrangement with him, he proposed to take the next train to London. He had his whole plan of campaign neatly mapped out.

The one thing he had not allowed for was a sudden change in the weather. When he had left the Castle, the sun had been shining; but now it was blotted out by a dark rack of clouds. Apparently some minor storm, late for the big event, had come hurrying up and intended to hold a private demonstration of its own. There was a tentative rumble over the hills, and a raindrop splashed on his face. Before he had reached the end of the kitchen garden, quite a respectable deluge was falling.

Pilbeam, like the Hon. Galahad, hated getting wet. He looked about him for shelter, and perceived standing by itself in a small paddock not far away a squat building of red brick and timber. A man not used to country life, he had no idea what it was supposed to be, but it had a stout tiled roof beneath which he could keep dry, so he hastened thither, arriving just in time, for a moment later the world had become a shower-bath. He retreated farther into his nook and sat down on some straw.

In such a situation, the only method of passing the time is to think. Pilbeam thought. And as he did so he began to revise that scheme of his of taking the manuscript straight to Lord Tilbury.

It was a scheme which he had adopted as seeming to be the only one open to him. He would vastly have preferred his original idea of holding an auction sale, with Lord Tilbury and Lady Constance Keeble raising each other's bids; but until now the fatal objection to that course had seemed to him to be that there was no safe place where he could store the goods till the auction sale was over.

A visitor at a country house with something to hide is a good deal restricted in his choice of caches. He is, indeed, more or less driven back to his bedroom. And a bedroom, as had been proved in the case of Monty Bodkin, is very far from being a safe-deposit. From the inception of their acquaintance, Pilbeam had been greatly impressed by Lady Constance's strong personality. A woman of action, he considered, if ever there was one. If she knew that he had the manuscript and deduced that it was hidden in his bedroom, he could see her acting very swiftly. She would have the thing in her hands in half an hour.

But suppose he were to hide it in some such place as that in which he was now sitting. Things would be very different then.

He glanced round the dim interior, and felt that he was on the right track. This building was a deserted building. It did not appear to be used for anything. Presumably no one ever came here. And even if someone did happen to wander in, it would be a simple matter to hide the manuscript . . . under this straw, for instance.

He rose and thrust the papers under the straw.

He eyed the straw appraisingly. It had as innocent look as any straw he had ever seen.

A shaft of sunlight played in the doorway. The brief storm was over. Well content, Percy Pilbeam came out and started to walk back to the Castle.

Beach met him in the hall.

'Her ladyship is expressing a desire to see you, sir,' said Beach, regarding him with restrained horror and loathing. The recent exchange of remarks between Monty Bodkin and the Hon. Galahad in his presence had confirmed the butler in his view that of all the human serpents that ever wriggled their way into a respectable castle this private investigator was the worst. Knowing what the manuscript of the Reminiscences meant to Mr Ronald and his betrothed, Beach, had he been younger and slimmer and in better condition and not a butler, could — for two pins — have taken Percy Pilbeam's unpleasant neck in his hands and twisted it into a lover's knot.

His physique and his circumstances being as they were, he merely delivered the message he had been instructed to deliver. As far as any hostile demonstration was concerned, he had to be content with letting his lip curl.

Percy Pilbeam, however, was feeling far too pleased with himself to be daunted by butlers' curling lips. On the present occasion, moreover, he was not aware that the other's lip *was* curling. He had noted the facial spasm, but attributed it to a tickling nose.

'Lady Constance?'

'Yes, sir. Her ladyship is in the drawing-room, awaiting you.'

What the proprietor of Rigg's Golden Balm embrocation would have described as the delightful sensation of *bien-être* began to leave Pilbeam. He stood there looking thoughtful. He twisted his moustache uneasily.

Now that the moment had actually arrived for confronting Lady Constance Keeble and informing her that he was proposing to double-cross her and hold her up and extract large sums of money from her, he felt unpleasantly weak about the knees.

'H'm!' said Percy Pilbeam.

And then suddenly he remembered that nature in her infinite wisdom has provided a sovereign specific against these Lady Constance Keebles.

'Well, then, I'll tell you what,' he said, inspired. 'Bring me a large bottle of champagne, and I'll look into the matter.'

Beach withdrew to execute the commission. His demeanour, as he passed from the hall, was downcast. There in a nutshell, he was feeling, you had the tragedy of a butler's life. His not to reason why; his not to discriminate between the deserving and the undeserving; his but to go and bring bottles of champagne to marcelled-haired snakes to whom he would greatly have preferred to supply straight cyanide.

The eternal conflict between duty and personal inclination, with duty, because one was a conscientious worker and took one's profession reverently, winning hands down.

Her sister Julia's report of her conversation with the Hon. Galahad, retailed to her immediately, upon the latter's departure, had strengthened Lady Constance Keeble's already firm view that something had got to be done without any more of what she forcefully described as dilly-dallying.

The fact that it was now three days since the task of securing the manuscript had been placed in Percy Pilbeam's hands and that he had to all appearances accomplished absolutely nothing seemed to her to argue dilly-dallying of the worst kind, if not actual shilly-shallying. She could not understand why Sir Gregory Parsloe seemed to entertain so high an opinion of this young man's abilities. So far as she had been able to ascertain, they were non-existent, and she said as much to Lady Julia, who agreed with her.

It was, therefore, to no warm-hearted assembly of personal admirers that Pilbeam some quarter of an hour later proceeded to betake himself. If his specific had acted a little less rapidly, he might have been frozen to the bone by the cold wave of aristocratic disapproval which poured over him as he entered the drawing-room. As it was, the sight of Lady Constance, staring haughtily from a high-backed chair like Cleopatra about to get down to brass tacks with an Ethiopian slave, merely entertained him. He thought she looked quaint. He was feeling just the slightest bit dizzy, but extraordinarily debonair. If Lady Constance at that moment had proposed a little part-singing, he would have fallen in with the suggestion eagerly.

'You want to see me, Beach says,' he observed, slurring the honoured name a little.

'Sit down, Mr Pilbeam.'

The detective was glad to do so. Spiritually, he was at the peak of his form, but as regards his legs there appeared to be some slight engine trouble.

'Now then, Mr Pilbeam, about that book.'

'Quite,' said Pilbeam, smiling benignly. This, he was feeling, was just the sort of thing he enjoyed — a cosy chat on current literature with cultured women. He was about to say so, when his eye, wandering to the wall, caught that of the fourth Countess — Emilia Jane, 1747-1815 — and so humorous did her aspect seem to him that he lay back in his chair, laughing immoderately.

'Mr Pilbeam!'

Before the detective had time to explain that his mirth had been caused by the fact that the fourth Countess looked exactly like Buster Keaton, Lady Constance had gone on speaking. She spoke well and vigorously.

'I cannot understand, Mr Pilbeam, what you have been doing all this time. You know perfectly well the vital importance of getting my brother's book into our hands. The whole thing has been clearly explained to you both by Sir Gregory Parsloe and myself. And yet you appear to have done nothing whatever about it. Sir Gregory told me you were enterprising. You seem to me to have about as much enterprise as a . . .'

She paused to search her mind for fauna of an admittedly unenterprising outlook on life, and

Lady Julia, who had been listening with approval, supplied the word 'slug'. The agitation which Lady Julia Fish had betrayed in the presence of her brother Galahad had passed. She had become her cool, sardonic self again. She was watching Pilbeam with a brightly interested eye, trying to diagnose the strangeness which she sensed in his manner.

'Exactly,' said Lady Constance, welcoming the suggestion. 'As much enterprise as a slug.'

'Less,' said Lady Julia.

'Yes, less,' agreed Lady Constance.

'Much less,' said Lady Julia. 'I've seen some quite nippy slugs.'

Pilbeam's amiability waned a little. He frowned. His mind was not at its clearest, but it seemed to him that a derogatory remark had been passed.

The Pilbeams had always been a clan to stand up for themselves.

Treat them right and, if it suited their convenience, they would treat you right. But try to come it over them, and they could be very terrible. It was a Pilbeam — Ernest William of Mon Abri, Kitchener Road, East Dulwich — who sued his next-door neighbour, George Dobson, of The Elms, for throwing snails over the fence into his back garden. Another Pilbeam — Claude — once refused to give up his hat and umbrella at the Hornibrook Natural History Museum, Sydenham Hill. P. Frobisher was no unworthy kin of these sturdy fighters.

'Did you call me a slug?' he asked sternly.

'In a purely Pickwickian sense,' said Lady Julia.

'Ah,' said Pilbeam, his affability returning. 'That's different.'

Lady Constance resumed the speech for the prosecution.

'You have had three whole days in which to do something, and you have not even found out where the manuscript is.'

Pilbeam smiled roguishly.

'Oh, haven't I?'

'Well, have you?'

'Yes, I have.'

'Then why in the name of goodness, Mr Pilbeam,' said Lady Constance, 'did you not tell us? And why don't you do something about it? Where is it. then? You said it was not in my brother's desk. Did he give it to somebody else?'

'He gave it to Beash.'

'Beash?' Lady Constance seemed at a loss. 'Beash?'

'Reading between the lines,' said Lady Julia, 'I think he means Beach.'

Lady Constance uttered an exclamation which was almost a battle cry. This was better than she had hoped. She felt a complete confidence in her ability to impose her will upon the domestic staff.

'Beach?' Her eyes lit up. 'I will see Beach at once.' Pilbeam chuckled heartily.

'You may see him,' he said, 'but a fat lot of good that's going to do you. A fat, fat, fat lot of good.' Lady Julia had completed her diagnosis.

'Forgive the personal question, Mr Pilbeam,'

she said, 'but are you slightly intoxicated?'

'Yes,' said Pilbeam sunnily.

'I thought so.'

Lady Constance was less intrigued by the detective's physical condition than the mystical obscurity of his speech. 'What do you mean?'

'A little blotto,' explained Pilbeam. 'I've just had a bollerer champagne, and, what's more, I had it on an empty stomach.'

'Are you interested in Mr Pilbeam's stomach, Constance?'

'I am not.'

'Nor I,' said Lady Julia. 'Let us waive your stomach, Mr Pilbeam, and get back to the point. Why will it do us a fat lot of good seeing Beach?'

'Because he hasn't got it.'

'You seemed to suggest that he had.'

'So he had. But he hasn't. He gave it to Ronnie.'

'My son, do you mean?'

'That's right. I always think of him as Ronnie.'

'How sweet of you.'

'He tried to break my neck once,' said Pilbeam, throwing out the information for what it was worth.

'And of course that forms a bond, doesn't it?' said Lady Julia sympathetically. 'So now Ronnie has the manuscript?'

'No, he hasn't.'

'But you said he had.'

'I said he had, and he had, but he hasn't. He gave it to Bonty Modkin.'

'Oh, the man's impossible,' cried Lady

Constance. Pilbeam looked about him, but could see no man. Some mistake, probably.

'What is the good of wasting any more time on a person in his condition? Can't you see he's just maundering?'

'Wait a minute, Connie. I may be wrong, but I think something will soon emerge from the fumes. Everybody seems to have been handing Galahad's great work to somebody else. A little patient inquiry, and he may discover to whom Mr Bodkin handed it.'

Pilbeam laughed a ringing laugh.

''Handed it' is good. Oh, very good, indeed. Considering that I had to crawl under his bed to get it.'

'What!'

'Gave my head a nasty bump, too, on the woodwork.'

'Do you mean to say, Mr Pilbeam, that all this time we've been talking *you* have got my brother's manuscript?'

'I told you something would emerge, Connie.'

'Yes, Connie,' said Pilbeam, 'I have.'

'Then why in the name of goodness could you not have said so from the first? Where is it?'

'Ah, that's telling,' said Pilbeam, wagging a playful finger.

'Mr Pilbeam,' said Lady Constance, with all the Cleopatrine haughtiness at her command, 'I insist on knowing what you have done with it. Kindly let us have no more of this nonsense.'

She could not have taken a more unfortunate attitude. The detective's resemblance to a roguish, if slightly inebriated, pixie vanished and in its place came pique, mortification, resentment, anger and defiance. His beady little eyes hardened, and from them there peeped out the fighting spirit of that Albert Edward Pilbeam who once refused to pay a fine and did seven days in Brixton jail for failing to abate a smoky chimney.

'Oh?' he said. 'Oh? It's like that, is it? Let me tell you, Connie, that I don't like your tone. Insist, indeed! A nice way to talk. I've got that manuscript hidden away somewhere where you won't find it let me inform you. And it's going to stay there till I take it to Tilbury . . . '

'What *is* he talking about?' asked Lady Constance despairingly. Tilbury to her suggested merely a small town in Essex. She had a vague recollection that Queen Elizabeth had once held a review there or something.

But Lady Julia, with her special knowledge of Tilburies, had become suddenly grave.

'Wait,' she said. 'This is beginning to look a little sticky. I wouldn't take it to Lord Tilbury, Mr Pilbeam, really I wouldn't. I'm sure, if we only talk it over sensibly, we can come to some arrangement.'

Pilbeam, who had risen and was now tacking uncertainly towards the door waved a hand and clutched at a table to restore his balance.

'Too late,' he said. 'Too late for that. Been insulted. Don't like Connie's tone. I was going to sit and let you bid against each other, but too late, too late, too late, because I've been insulted. No further discussion. Tilbury gets it. He's waiting for it at the Emsworth Arms. Well, good-by-ee,' said Percy Pilbeam, and was gone.

Lady Constance turned to her sister for enlightenment. 'But I don't understand, Julia. What did he mean! Who is this Lord Tilbury?'

'Only the proprietor of the publishing concern with whom Gally signed his contract, my angel. Nothing more than that.'

'You mean,' cried Lady Constance, aghast, 'that if the manuscript gets into his hands, he will publish it?'

'That's it.'

'I won't allow him to. I'll get an injunction.'

'How can you? He'll stand on the contract.'

'Do you mean, then, that nothing can be done?'

'All I can suggest is that you telephone to Sir Gregory Parsloe and get him over. Tell him to come to dinner. He seems to have some influence with that little fiend. He may be able to talk him round. Though I doubt it. He's in a nasty mood. I rather wish sometimes, Connie,' said Lady Julia meditatively, 'that you were, a little less of the *grande dame*. It's wonderful to watch you in action, I admit — one seems to hear the bugles blowing for the Crusades and the tramp of the mailed feet of a hundred steel-clad ancestors — but there's no getting away from it that you do put people's backs up a bit.'

★ ★ ★

Down at the Emsworth Arms, a servitor informed Lord Tilbury that he was wanted on the telephone. He walked to the instrument broodingly. The Bodkin popinjay, he presumed, that broken reed on which he had foolishly supposed that it would be possible to lean. He prepared to be a little terse with Monty.

Ever since his interview with Monty in the garden of the Emsworth Arms, Lord Tilbury had found his thoughts turning wistfully to the one man of his acquaintance who could have been relied upon to put through this commission of his. During the years when P. Frobisher Pilbeam had worked on his staff as editor of *Society Spice* Lord Tilbury had never actually asked him to steal anything, but he had no doubt at all that, if adequately paid, Percy would have sprung to the task. And now that he had blossomed out as a private investigator it was probable that he would spring to it with an even greater readiness. All that afternoon Lord Tilbury had been wondering whether the solution of the whole thing would not be to send Pilbeam a wire, telling him to come at once.

What deterred him was the reflection that it would be impossible to get him into the Castle. You cannot insert private inquiry agents in country-houses as if you were slipping ferrets down a rabbit-hole. This it was that had made him abandon the roseate dream. And it was the fact that he had been compelled to abandon it that lent additional asperity to his manner as he now took up the receiver.

'Yes?' he said curtly. 'Well?'

A rollicking voice nearly cracked his eardrum. 'Hullo, there, Tilbury! This is Pilbeam.'

Lord Tilbury's eyes seemed to shoot out

suddenly, like a snail's. This was the most amazing coincidence he had ever experienced. More a miracle, he felt with some awe, than a mere coincidence.

'Speaking from Blandings Castle, Tilbury.'

'What!'

The receiver shook in Lord Tilbury's hands. Was this what was known as the direct answer to prayer? Or — taking the gloomier view — was he undergoing some aural hallucination?

'Speaking from Blandings Castle, Tilbury,' repeated the voice. 'You don't mind me calling you Tilbury, do you, Tilbury?' it added solicitously. 'I'm a bit tight.'

'Pilbeam!' Lord Tilbury's voice shook. 'Did I really understand you to say that you were speaking from Blandings Castle?'

'Quite.'

A man capable of building up the Mammoth Publishing Company is not a man who wastes time in unnecessary questions. Others might have asked Pilbeam how he had got there, but not Lord Tilbury. He could do all that later.

'Pilbeam,' he said, 'this is providential! Kindly come to me here as soon as possible. There is something I wish you to do for me. Most urgent.'

'A commission?'

'Yes, a commission.'

'And what,' inquired the voice, playfully, yet with a certain metallic note, 'is there in it for me?'

Lord Tilbury thought rapidly.

'A hundred pounds.'

A hideous noise sent his head jerking back. It was apparently a derisive laugh. When it was repeated more softly a moment later, he recognized it as such.

'Two hundred, Pilbeam.'

'Listen, Tilbury. I know what it is you want me to do. Oh, yes, I know. Something to do with a certain book . . . '

'Yes, yes.'

'Then let me tell you, Tilbury, that I've been offered five hundred in another quarter, and can easily work it up to the level thousand. But, seeing it's you, I won't sting you for more than that. Think on your feet, Tilbury. One thousand is the figure.'

Lord Tilbury thought on his feet. There were few men in England whom the prospect of parting with a thousand pounds afflicted with a greater sensation of nausea, but he could speculate in order to accumulate. And in the present case, what was a mere thousand? A sprat to catch a whale.

'Very well.'

'It's a deal?'

'Yes. I agree.'

'Right!' said the voice, with renewed cheeriness. 'Be in after dinner tonight. I'll bring the thing down with me.'

'What!'

'I say I'll bring the you-know-what to you after dinner tonight. And now a river-whatever-it-is, Tilbury, old cock. *An revoir*, Tilbury. I'm feeling rather funny, and I think I'll get a bit of sleep. Ay tank I go home, Tilbury. Pip-pip!'

There was a click at the other end of the wire. Pilbeam had hung up.

*  *  *

Fingers tried the handle of Pilbeam's bedroom door. A fist banged on the panel. The detective looked up frowningly from the bed on which he lay. He had been on the point of sinking into a troubled doze.

'Who's that?'

'Open this door and I'll show you who it is.'

'Is that old Gally?'

'Damn your impudence!'

'What do you want?'

'A little talk with you, young man.' 'Go away, old Gally,' said Pilbeam. 'Don't want any little talks. Trying to get to sleep, old Gally. Tell 'em I shan't be down to dinner. Feeling funny.'

'You'll feel funnier if I can get in.'

'Ah, but you can't get in,' Pilbeam pointed out.

And, laughing softly to himself at the wit and cleverness of the retort, he sank back on the pillows and closed his eyes again. The handle rattled once more. The door creaked as a weight was pressed against it. Then there was silence, broken shortly by a rhythmic snoring.

Percy Pilbeam slept.

# 13

Darkness had fallen on Blandings Castle, the soft, caressing darkness that closes in like a velvet curtain at the end of a summer day. Now slept the crimson petal and the white. Owls hooted in the shadows. Bushes rustled as the small creatures of the night went about their mysterious business. The scent of the wet earth mingled with the fragrance of stock and of wallflower. Bats wheeled against the starlit sky, and moths blundered in and out of the shaft of golden light that shone from the window of the dining-room. It was the hour when men forget their troubles about the friendly board.

But troubles like those now weighing upon the inmates of Blandings Castle are not to be purged by meat and drink. The soup had come and gone. The fish had come and gone. The entree had come and was going. But still there hung over the table a foglike pall of gloom. Of all those silent diners, not one but had his hidden care. Even Lord Emsworth, who was not easily depressed, found his meal entirely spoiled by the fact that it was being shared by Sir Gregory Parsloe-Parsloe.

As for Sir Gregory himself, the news communicated to him over the telephone by Lady Constance Keeble an hour before had been enough to ruin a dozen dinners. His might have been, as his whilom playmate, the Hon.

266

Galahad Threepwood, had made so abundantly clear in Chapters Four, Seven, Eleven, Eighteen, and Twenty-four of his immortal work, a frivolous youth, but in his late fifties he was taking life extremely seriously. Very earnest was his wish to represent the Unionist party as their Member for Bridgeford and Shifley Parliamentary Division of Shropshire: and if Pilbeam fulfilled his threat of taking that infernal manuscript to Lord Tilbury, his chances of doing so would be simply *nil*. He knew that local committee. Once let the story of the prawns appear in print, and they would drop him like a hot brick.

He had come tonight to reason with Pilbeam, to plead with Pilbeam, to appeal to Pilbeam's better feelings, if such existed. And, dash it, there was no Pilbeam to be reasoned with, to be pleaded with, or to be appealed to.

Where *was* the dam' feller?

The same question was torturing Lady Constance. Where was Pilbeam? Could he have gone straight to Lord Tilbury after taking his zigzag departure from the drawing-room?

It was Lord Emsworth who put the question into words. For some moments he had been staring down the table over the top of his crooked pince-nez in a puzzled manner like that of a cat trying to run over the muster-roll of its kittens.

'Beach!'

'M'lord?' said that careworn man hollowly. Foxes were gnawing at Beach's vitals, too.

'Beach, I can't see Mr Pilbeam. Can you see

Mr Pilbeam, Beach? He doesn't seem to be here.'

'Mr Pilbeam is in his bedchamber, m'lord. He informed the footman who knocked at the door with his hot water that he would not be among those present at dinner, m'lord, owing to a headache.'

The Hon. Galahad endorsed this.

'I knocked at his door just before the dressing gong went, and he said he wanted to go to sleep.'

'You didn't go in?'

'No.'

'You should have gone in, Galahad. The poor fellow may be feeling unwell.'

'Not so unwell as he would have felt if I could have got in.'

'You think you would have made his headache worse?'

'A good deal worse,' said the Hon. Galahad, taking a salted almond and giving it a hard look through his monocle.

The news that Pilbeam was on a bed of sickness acted on three members of the party rather as the recent rain had acted on the parched earth. Lady Constance seemed to expand like a refreshed flower. Lady Julia did the same. Sir Gregory Parsloe, in addition to expanding, gave such a sharp sigh of relief that he blew a candle out. Three pairs of eyes exchanged glances. There was the same message of cheer in each of them. If Pilbeam had not taken the irrevocable step, those eyes said, all might yet be well.

'God bless my soul,' said Lord Emsworth

solicitously, 'I hope he isn't really bad. These infernal thunderstorms are enough to give anyone a headache. I had a slight headache myself before dinner. I'll run up and see the poor chap as soon as we've finished here. My goodness, I don't want Pilbeam on the sick list now, of all times,' said Lord Emsworth, with a glance at Sir Gregory so full of meaning that the latter, who was lifting his wine-glass to his lips, shied like a startled horse and spilled half its contents.

'Why now, particularly?' asked Lady Julia.

'Never mind,' said Lord Emsworth darkly.

'I only asked,' said Lady Julia, 'because I, personally, consider that all times are good times for Mr Pilbeam to have headaches. Not to mention botts, glanders, quartan ague, frog in the throat and the Black Death.'

A soft, sibilant sound, like gas escaping from a pipe, came from the shadows by the sideboard. It was Beach expressing, as far as butlerine etiquette would pernht him to express, his adhesion to this sentiment.

Lord Emsworth, on the other hand, showed annoyance.

'I wish you wouldn't say such things, Julia.'

'On the spur of the moment I couldn't think of anything worse.'

'Don't you like Pilbeam?'

'My dear Clarence, don't be fantastic. Nobody *likes* Mr Pilbeam. There are people who do not actually put poison in his soup, but that is as far as you can go.'

'I disagree with you,' said Lord Emsworth

warmly. 'I regard him as a capital fellow, capital. And most useful, let me tell you. Attempts are being made,' said Lord Emsworth, once more sniping Sir Gregory with a penetrating eye, 'by certain parties whom I will not name, to injure my pig. Pilbeam is helping me thwart them. Thanks to his advice, I have now put my pig where the parties to whom I allude will not find it quite so easy to get at her. Let me tell you that I think very highly of Pilbeam. I've a good mind to send him up half a bottle of champagne.'

'Making the perfect example of carrying coals to Newcastle.'

'Eh?'

'Oh, nothing. 'Twas but a passing jest.'

'Champagne is good for headaches,' argued Lord Emsworth. 'It might make all the difference to Pilbeam.'

'Are we to spend the whole of dinner talking of Mr Pilbeam and his headache?' demanded Lady Constance imperiously. 'I am sick and tired of Mr Pilbeam. And I don't want to hear any more of that pig of yours, Clarence. For goodness sake let us discuss some reasonable topic'

This bright invitation having had the not unnatural effect of killing the conversation completely, dinner proceeded in an unbroken silence. Only once did one of the revellers venture a remark. As Beach and his assistants removed the plates which had contained fruit salad and substituted others designed for dessert, Lady Julia raised her glass.

'To the body upstairs — I hope,' she said.

Percy Pilbeam, however, was not actually dead. At the precise moment of Lady Julia's toast, almost as if he were answering a cue, he sat up on his bed and stared muzzily about him. The fact that the room was now in darkness made it difficult for him to find his bearings immediately, and for perhaps half a minute he sat wondering where he was. Then memory returned, and with it an opening-and-shutting sensation in the region of the temples which made him regret that he had gone on sleeping. Even if he had had the Black Death to which Lady Julia had so feelingly alluded, he could not have felt very much worse.

There are heads which are proof against over-indulgence in champagne. That of the Hon. Galahad Threepwood is one that springs to the mind. Pilbeam's, however, did not belong to this favoured class. For a while he sat there, wincing at each fresh wave of agony; then, levering himself up, he switched on the light and hobbled to the wash-stand, where he proceeded to drink deeply out of the water-jug. This done, he filled the basin and started to give himself first-aid treatment.

Presently, a little restored, he returned to the bed and sat down again. Endeavouring to recall the events which had led up to the tragedy, he found that he could do so only sketchily. One fact alone stood out clearly in his recollection — to wit, that in some way which he could not quite remember he had been insulted by Lady Constance Keeble. A great bitterness against Lady Constance began to burgeon within Percy

271

Pilbeam, and it was not long before he reached the decision that, cost what it might, she must be scored off. There would be no auction sale. As soon as he felt physically capable of moving, he would take that manuscript to Lord Tilbury at the Emsworth Arms.

At this point in his meditations the house was blown up by a bomb. Or, what amounted to much the same thing as far as the effect on the nervous system was concerned, there was a knock at the door.

'May I come in, my dear fellow?'

Pilbeam recognized the voice. He could not be rude to his only friend at Blandings Castle. He swallowed his heart again, and unlocked the door.

'Ah! Sitting up, I see. Feeling a little better, eh? We all missed you at dinner,' said Lord Emsworth, beginning to potter about the room as he pottered about all rooms which he honoured with his presence. 'We wondered what had become of you. My sister Julia, if I remember rightly, speculated as to the possibility of your having got the Black Death. What put the idea into her head, I can't imagine. Absurd, of course. People don't get the Black Death nowadays. I've never heard of anyone getting the Black Death. In fact,' said Lord Emsworth, with a burst of confidence, dropping into the fireplace the hair-brush which he had been attempting to balance on the comb, 'I don't believe I know what the Black Death *is*.'

A sense of being in hell stole over Percy Pilbeam. What with the clatter of that brush, which had set his head aching again, and his host's conversation, which threatened to make it ache still more, he was sore beset.

'No doubt all that has happened,' proceeded Lord Emsworth, moving the soap-dish a little to the left, the water-bottle a little to the right, a chair a little nearer the door, and another chair a little nearer the window, 'is that that thunder-storm gave you a headache. And I was wondering, my dear fellow, if a breath of fresh air might not do you good. Fresh air is often good for headaches. I am on my way to have a look at the Empress, and it crossed my mind that you might care to come with me. It is a beautiful night. There is a lovely moon, and I have an electric torch.'

Here, Lord Emsworth, pausing from tapping the mirror with a buttonhook, produced from his pocket the torch in question and sent a dazzling ray shooting into his companion's inflamed eyes.

The action decided Pilbeam. To remain longer in the confined space of a bedroom with this man would be to subject his sanity to too severe a test. He said he would be delighted to come and take a look at the Empress.

★ ★ ★

Out on the gravel drive he began to feel a little better. As Lord Emsworth had said, it was a beautiful night. Pilbeam was essentially a creature of the city, with urban tastes, but even he could appreciate the sweet serenity of the grounds of Blandings Castle under that gracious moon. So restored did he feel by the time they had gone a hundred yards or so that he even ventured on a remark.

'Aren't we,' he asked, 'going the wrong way?'

'What's that, my dear fellow?' said Lord Emsworth, wrenching his mind from the torch, which he was flashing on and off like a child with a new toy. 'What did you say?'

'Don't you get to the sty by crossing the terrace?'

'Ah, but you've forgotten, my dear Pilbeam. Acting on your advice, we moved her to the new one just before dinner. You recollect advising us to move her from her old sty?'

'Of course. Quite. Yes, I remember.'

'Pirbright didn't like it. I could tell that by the strange noises he made at the back of his throat. He has some idea that she will feel restless and unhappy away from her old home. But I was particularly careful to wait and see that she was comfortably settled in, and I could detect no signs of restlessness whatever. She proceeded to eat her evening meal with every indication of enjoyment.'

'Good,' said Pilbeam, feeling distrait.

'Eh?'

'I said 'Good'.'

'Oh, 'Good'? Yes, quite so. Yes, very good. I feel most pleased about it. As I pointed out to Pirbright, the risk of leaving her in her old quarters was far too great to be taken. Why, my dear Pilbeam, do you know that my sister Constance had actually invited that man Parsloe to dinner tonight? Oh, yes, there he was, at dinner with us. No doubt he had persuaded her to invite him, thinking that, having got into the place he would be able to find an opportunity during the evening of slipping away and going down to the sty and doing the poor animal a mischief. A nice surprise he's going to get when he finds the sty empty. He won't know what to make of it. He'll be nonplussed.'

Here Lord Emsworth paused to chuckle. Pilbeam, though not amused, contrived to emit on his side something that might have passed as a mirthful echo.

'This new sty,' proceeded Lord Emsworth, having switched the torch on and off six times, 'is an altogether more suitable place. As a matter of fact, I had it built specially for the Empress in the spring, but owing to Pirbright's obstinacy I never moved her there. I don't know if you know these Shropshire fellows at all, Pilbeam, but they can be as obstinate as Scotsmen. I have a Scots head gardener, Angus McAllister, and he is intensely obstinate. Like a mule. I must tell you some time about the trouble I had with him regarding hollyhocks. But Pirbright can be fully as stubborn when he gets an idea into his head. I reasoned with him. I said, 'Pirbright, this sty is a new sty, with all the latest improvements. It is up to date, in keeping with the trend of modern thought, and, what is more — and this I consider very important — it adjoins the kitchen gar-den . . .''

He broke off. A sound beside him in the darkness had touched his kindly heart.

'Is your head hurting you again, my dear fellow?'

But the bubbling cry which had proceeded from Percy Pilbeam had not been caused by pain in the head.

'The kitchen garden?' he gasped.

'Yes. And that is most convenient, you see, because Pirbright's cottage is so close. No doubt you have seen the place if you have ever strolled round by the kitchen garden. It is made of stout red brick and timber, with a good tiled roof . . . In fact,' said Lord Emsworth, flashing his torch, 'here it is. And there,' he went on with satisfaction, 'is the Empress, still feeding away without a care in the world. I told Pirbright he was all wrong.'

The Empress might have been without a care in the world, but Percy Pilbeam was very far from sharing that ideal state. He leaned on the rail of the sty and groaned in spirit.

In the light of the electric torch, Empress of Blandings made a singularly attractive, even a fascinating, picture. She had her noble head well down and with a rending, golluping sound was tucking into a late supper. Her curly little tail wiggled incessantly, and ever and anon a sort of sensuous quiver would pass along her Zeppelin-like body. But Percy Pilbeam was in no frame of mind to admire the rare and the beautiful. He was trying to adjust himself to this utterly unforeseen disaster.

He had only himself to blame — that was what made it all the more bitter. If he had not so casually given his casting vote in favour of

276

shifting this infernal pig to new quarters, he would not now have been faced by a problem which every moment seemed to become more difficult of solution.

For Pilbeam was afraid of pigs. He seemed to remember having read somewhere that if you go into a pig's sty and the pig doesn't know you it comes for you like a tiger and chews you to ribbons. Greedy though he was for Lord Tilbury's gold, something told him that never, no matter how glittering the reward, would he be able to bring himself to go into that sty in quest of the manuscript, guarded as it now was by this ravening beast. The Prodigal Son might have mixed with these animals on a clubby basis, but Percy Pilbeam knew himself to be incapable of imitating him.

How long he would have stood there, savouring the bitterness of defeat, one cannot say. Left to himself, probably quite a considerable time. But his reverie had scarcely begun when it was shattered by a cry at his elbow.

'God bless my soul!'

It seemed to Pilbeam for an instant that he had come unstuck. He clutched the rail, quivering in every limb.

'What on earth's the matter?' he demanded, far more brusquely than a guest should have done of his host.

An agitation almost equal to his own was causing the torch to wobble in Lord Emsworth's hands.

'God bless my soul, what's that she's eating? Pirbright! Pirbright! Can you see what she's eating, Pilbeam, my dear fellow? Pirbright! Pirbright! Can it be *paper*?'

With a febrile swoop Lord Emsworth bent through the rails. He came up again, breathing heavily. The light of the torch came and went like a heliograph upon something which he held in his hand.

Galloping feet sounded in the night.

'Pirbright!'

'Yur, m'lord?

'Pirbright, have you been giving the Empress paper?'

'No, m'lord.'

'Well, that's what she's eating. Great chunks of it.'

'Ur, m'lord?' said the pig-man, marvelling.

'I assure you, yes. Paper. Look! Well, God bless my soul,' cried Lord Emsworth, at last steadying the torch, 'I'm dashed if it isn't that book of my brother Galahad's!'

# 14

At about the moment when Lord Emsworth had knocked at Percy Pilbeam's door to inquire after his health and make his kindly suggestion of a breath of fresh air, his sister Lady Constance Keeble, his sister Lady Julia Fish, and his neighbour and guest Sir Gregory Parsloe-Parsloe were gathered together in the drawing-room, talking things over and endeavouring to come to some agreement as to the best method of handling the situation which had arisen.

The tone of the meeting had been a little stormy from the very outset. Owing to the suddenness of his summons to the Castle and the difficulty of explaining things over the telephone, all that Sir Gregory had known till now was the bare fact that Pilbeam had obtained possession of the manuscript and was proposing to deliver it to Lord Tilbury. Informed over the coffee cups by Lady Julia that the whole disaster was to be attributed to her sister Constance's tactless handling of the fellow, he had drawn his breath in sharply, gazed at Lady Constance in a reproachful manner, and started clicking his tongue.

Any knowledgeable person could have guessed what would happen after that. No woman of spirit can sit calmly and have a man click his tongue at her. No hostess, on the other hand, can be openly rude to a guest. Seeking an outlet for her emotions, Lady Constance had begun to quarrel with Lady Julia. And as Lady Julia, always fond of a family row, had borne her end of the encounter briskly, before he knew where he was Sir Gregory became aware that he had sown the wind and was reaping the whirlwind.

We mention these things to explain why it happened that there was a certain delay before G.H.Q. took the obvious step of trying to establish communication with Percy Pilbeam. More than a quarter of an hour had elapsed before Sir Gregory was able to still the tumult of battle with these arresting words:

'But, I say, dash it all, don't you think we ought to see the feller?'

They acted like magic. Angry passions were chained. Good things about to be said were corked up and stored away for use on some future occasion. The bell was rung for Beach. Beach was dispatched to Pilbeam's room with instructions to desire him to be so good as to step down to the drawing-room for a moment. And the end of it all was that Beach returned and announced that Mr Pilbeam was not there.

Consternation reigned.

'Not there?' cried Lady Constance.

'Not *there!*' cried Lady Julia.

'But he must be there,' protested Sir Gregory. 'Fellow goes to his room with a headache to lie down and have a sleep,' he proceeded, arguing closely. 'Stands to reason he must be there.'

'You can't have knocked loudly enough, Beach,' said Lady Constance.

'Go up and knock again,' said Lady Julia.

'Hit the dashed door a good hard bang,' said Sir Gregory.

Beach's demeanour was respectful but unsympathetic.

'Receiving no response to my knocking, m'lady, I took the liberty of entering the room. It was empty.'

'Empty?'

'Empty!'

'You mean,' said Sir Gregory, who liked to get these things straight, 'there wasn't anybody *in* the room?' Beach inclined his head.

'The bedchamber was unoccupied,' he assented.

'He may be in the smoking-room,' suggested Lady Constance.

'Or the billiard-room,' said Lady Julia.

'Having a bath,' cried Sir Gregory, inspired. 'Fellow with a headache might quite easily go and have a bath. Do his headache good.'

'I visited the smoking-room and the billiard-room, m'lady. The door of the bathroom on Mr Pilbeam's floor was open, revealing emptiness within. I am inclined to think, m'lady,' said Beach 'that the gentleman has gone for a walk.'

The awful words produced a throbbing silence. Only too well could these three visualize the direction in which, if he had taken a walk, Percy Pilbeam would have taken it.

'Thank you, Beach,' said Lady Constance dully.

The butler bowed and withdrew. The silence continued unbroken. Sir Gregory walked heavily to the window and stood looking out into the night. It almost seemed to him that across that starry sky he could see written in letters of flame the story of the prawns.

Lady Constance gave a shuddering sigh.

'We shan't have a friend left!'

Lady Julia lit a cigarette.

'Poor old Miles! Bang goes *his* reputation!'

Sir Gregory turned from the window.

'Those Local Committee chaps will give the nomination to old Billing now, I suppose.' His Regency-buck face twisted with injured wrath. 'Why the devil need the feller have been in such a hurry? Why couldn't he at least have let me *talk* to him? I brought my cheque-book with me specially. He knows I'd have given him five hundred pounds. I'll bet he won't get that from this Tilbury of his. I've met Tilbury. I've heard stories about him. Mean man. Tight with his money. Pilbeam'll be lucky if he gets a couple of hundred out of him.'

'A pity you put his back up like that, Connie,' said Lady Julia suavely. 'I don't suppose now he cares about the money so much. What he wants is to be nasty.'

'What I think a pity,' retorted Lady Constance, with the splendid Keeble spirit, 'is that Sir Gregory ever mentioned the matter to a man like this Pilbeam. He might have known that he was not to be trusted.'

'Exactly,' said Lady Julia. 'An insane thing to do.'

This unexpected alliance disconcerted Sir Gregory Parsloe. He spluttered.

'Well, I had had dealings with the fellow

282

before on a . . . on a private matter, and had found him alert and enterprising. I just went and engaged him naturally, as you would engage anyone to do something. It never occurred to me that he wasn't to be trusted.'

'Not even after you saw that moustache?' said Lady Julia. 'Well, there's just one gleam of comfort in this business, Connie'

We shall now be able to talk to Clarence and put a stop to any nonsense of his giving Ronnie his money.'

'That's true,' said Lady Constance, brightening a little.

As she spoke, the door opened and Percy Pilbeam came in.

Everybody, as the poet so well says, is loved by someone, and it is to be supposed, therefore, that somewhere in the world there were faces that lit up when even Percy Pilbeam entered the room. But never, not even by his mother, if he had a mother, nor by some warm-hearted aunt, if he had a warm-hearted aunt, could he have been more rapturously received than he was received now by Lady Constance Keeble, by Lady Julia Fish, and by Sir Gregory Parsloe-Parsloe, Bart, of Matchingham Hall, Salop. Santa Claus himself would have had a less enthusiastic welcome.

'Mr Pilbeam!'

'Mr *Pilbeam?*'

'Pilbeam, my *dear* chap!'

'Come in, Mr Pilbeam!'

'Sit down, Mr Pilbeam!'

'Pilbeam, my dear fellow, a chair.'

'How is your headache, Mr Pilbeam?'

'Are you feeling better, Mr Pilbeam?'

'Pilbeam, old man, I have a cigar here which I think you will appreciate.'

The investigator looked from one to the other with growing bewilderment. Though an investigator, he could not deduce what had caused this exuberance. He had come to the room expecting a sticky ten minutes, and had forced himself to face it because business was business and, now that that ghastly pig had transferred almost the entire manuscript of the Hon. Galahad's Reminiscences to its loathsome inside, it was from the group before him alone that he could anticipate anything in the nature of a cash settlement.

'Thanks,' he said, accepting the chair.

'Thanks,' he said, taking the cigar.

'Thanks,' he said, in response to the inquiries after his health. 'No, it isn't so bad now.'

'That's good,' said Sir Gregory heartily.

'Splendid,' said Lady Constance.

'Capital,' said Lady Julia.

These paeans of joy concluded, there occurred that momentary hush which always comes over any gathering or assembly when business is about to be discussed. Pilbeam's eyes were flickering warily from face to face. He had got to do some expert bluffing, and was bracing himself to the task.

'I came about — that thing,' he said, at length.

'Exactly, exactly, exactly,' cried Sir Gregory. 'You've been thinking it over and . . . '

'I'm afraid I was a little abrupt, Mr Pilbeam,'

said Lady Constance winningly, 'when we had our last little talk. I was feeling rather upset. The weather, I suppose.'

'You did say you had your cheque-book with you, Sir Gregory?' said Lady Julia.

'Certainly, certainly. Here it is.'

There came into Pilbeam's eyes the gleam which always came into them when he saw cheque-books.

'Well, I've done it,' he said, in what he tried to make a cheery, big-hearted manner.

'Done it?' cried Lady Constance, appalled. The words conveyed to her a meaning different from that intended by their speaker. 'You don't mean you have taken . . . ?'

'You wanted that manuscript destroyed, didn't you?' said Pilbeam. 'Well, I've done it.'

'What?'

'I've destroyed it. Torn it up. As a matter of fact, I've burned it. So . . . ' said Pilbeam, and cut his remarks off short on the word, filling out the hiatus with a meaning glance at the cheque-book. He licked his lips nervously as he did so. He was well aware that the conference had now arrived at what Monty Bodkin would have called the nub.

The committee of three evidently felt the same. There was another silence — an awkward silence this time, pulsing with embarrassment and doubt. It is always so embarrassing for well-bred people to tell a fellow human being that they do not believe him. Moreover, any intimation on the part of these particular well-bred people that they thought this man was lying to them would most certainly wound that sensitiveness of his which it was so dangerous to wound.

On the other hand, could they pay out large sums of money to a man with a moustache like that, purely on the off-chance that he might for once be telling the truth? The committee paused on the horns of a dilemma.

'Ha h'r'm'ph!' said Sir Gregory, rather neatly summing up the sentiment of the meeting.

Percy Pilbeam displayed an unforeseen amiability in this delicate situation.

'Of course, I don't expect you to take my word for it,' he said. 'Naturally you want some sort of proof. Well, here's a bit of the thing which I saved to show you. The rest is a pile of ashes.'

From his breast pocket he produced a tattered fragment of paper and handed it to Sir Gregory. Sir Gregory, after wincing with some violence, for by an odd chance the fragment happened to deal with the story of the prawns, passed it to Lady Constance. Lady Constance looked at it, and gave it to Lady Julia. The tension relaxed.

'It is not quite what we intended,' said Lady Constance. 'Naturally we expected you to bring the manuscript to us, so that we could destroy it with our own hands. Still . . . '

'Comes to the same thing,' argued Pilbeam.

'Yes, I suppose it does not really matter.'

Glances flitted to and fro like butterflies. Sir Gregory looked at Lady Constance, seeking guidance. Lady Constance silently consulted Lady Julia. Lady Julia gave a quick nod. Sir Gregory having noted it and looked at Lady

Constance again and received a nod from her, went to the writing-table and became busy with pen and ink.

Chattiness ensued. Something of the atmosphere of a Board Room at the conclusion of an important meeting had crept into the air.

'I am sure we are all very much obliged to you,' said Lady Constance.

'But tell me, Mr Pilbeam,' said Lady Julia, 'What caused this sudden change of heart?'

'Pardon?'

'Well, when you left us before dinner, you seemed so determined to . . . '

'Oh, Clarence!' cried Lady Constance, with the exasperation which the head of the family's entry into a room so often caused her. He would, she felt, choose this moment to come in and potter.

But for once in his life Lord Emsworth was in no pottering mood. The tempestuous manner of his irruption should have told Lady Constance that. His demeanour and the tone of his remarks now enabled her to perceive it. Quite plainly, something had occurred to stir him out of his usual dreamy calm.

'Who moves my books?' he demanded fiercely.

'What books?'

'I keep a little book of telephone numbers on the table in the library, and it's gone. Ha,' said Lord Emsworth. 'Beach would know.'

He leaped to the fireplace and pressed the bell.

'You'll break your neck if you go springing about like that on this parquet floor,' observed

Lady Julia languidly. 'Why skip ye so, ye high hills?'

Lord Emsworth returned to the centre of the room. He was glaring in what his sister Constance considered an extremely uppish manner. He seemed to her to have got quite above himself.

'Do go away, Clarence,' she said. 'We are talking about something important.'

'And so am I talking about something important. Once and for all, I insist on having my personal belongings respected. I will not have my things moved. My little book of telephone numbers has gone. I suppose you've got it, Connie. Took it to look up some number or other and couldn't be bothered to put it back. Tchah!' said Lord Emsworth.

'I have not got your wretched little book,' said Lady Constance wearily. 'What do you want it for?'

'I want to ring up that fellow.'

'What fellow?'

'That fellow what's-his-name. The vet. It's a matter of life and death. And I've forgotten his number.'

'What do you want the vet. for?' asked Lady Julia. 'Are you ill?' Lord Emsworth stared.

'What do I want the vet. for? When the Empress has been eating that paper?'

'What paper does the Empress take in?' said Lady Julia. 'I've often wondered. Something sound and conservative. I suppose. Probably the *Morning Post*.'

'What *are* you talking about, Clarence?' said Lady Constance.

'Why, about the Empress eating that book of Galahad's, of course. Hasn't Pilbeam told you?'

'What!'

'Certainly. Went to her sty just now and found her finishing the last chapters. How the thing got there is more than I can tell you. Ink and paper! Probably poisonous. Ha, Beach!'

'M'lord?'

'Beach, what is that vet.'s telephone number? You know what I mean. The telephone number of what's-his-name, the vet.'

'Matchingham 2–2–1, m'lord.'

'Then get him quickly and put him through to the library. Tell him my pig has just eaten the complete manuscript of my brother Galahad's Reminiscences.'

And, so saying, Lord Emsworth made a dart for the door. Finding Beach in the way, he sprang nimbly to the right. The butler also moved to the right. Lord Emsworth dashed to the left. So did Beach. From above the mantelpiece the portrait of the sixth Earl looked down approvingly on these rhythmical manoeuvres. He, too, had been fond of the minuet in his day.

'Beach!' cried Lord Emsworth, passionate appeal in his voice.

'M'lord?'

'Stand still, man. You aren't a jumping bean.'

'I beg your lordship's pardon. I miscalculated the direction in which your lordship was intending to proceed.'

This delay at such a time had robbed Lord Emsworth of the last vestiges of prudence and self-control. On the polished floor of the drawing-room only a professional acrobat could have executed without disaster the bound which he now gave. There was a slithering crash, and he came to a halt against a china-cabinet, rubbing his left ankle.

'I told you you would come a purler,' said Lady Julia, with the satisfaction of a Cassandra, one of whose prophecies has at last been fulfilled. 'Hurt yourself?'

'I think I've twisted my ankle. Beach, help me to the library.'

'Very good, m'lord.'

'Ronnie has some embrocation, I believe,' said Lady Julia.

'I don't want embrocation,' snarled the wounded man, as he hopped from the room on the butler's supporting arm. 'I want a doctor. Beach, as soon as you've got the vet., get a doctor.'

'Very good, m'lord.'

The door closed. And, as it did so, Lady Constance, her lips set and her eyes gleaming with a fierce light, walked to where Sir Gregory stood gaping, took the cheque from his fingers, and tore it across.

A passionate cry rang through the room. It came from the lips of Percy Pilbeam. 'Hi!'

Lady Constance gave him one of the Keeble looks.

'Surely, Mr Pilbeam, you do not expect to be paid for having done nothing? Your instructions were to deliver the manuscript to myself or to Sir Gregory. You have not done so. The agreement is, therefore, null and void.'

'Spoken like a man, Connie,' said Lady Julia, with approval.

The investigator was staring helplessly.

'But the thing's destroyed.'

'Not by you.'

'Certainly not,' said Sir Gregory, with animation. He could follow an argument as well as the next man. 'Not by you at all. Eaten by that pig.'

'Just an Act of God,' put in Lady Julia.

'Exactly,' agreed Sir Gregory. 'A very good way of putting it. Act of God. No obligation on our part to pay you a penny.'

'But . . .'

'I am sorry, Mr Pilbeam,' said Lady Constance, becoming queenly. 'I see no reason to discuss the matter further.'

'Especially,' said Lady Julia, 'as we have a very urgent matter to discuss with Clarence, Connie.'

'Why, of course. I was forgetting that.'

'I wasn't,' said Lady Julia. 'You will forgive us for leaving you, Sir Gregory?'

Sir Gregory Parsloe was looking like a Regency buck who has just won a fortune on the turn of a card at Wattier's.

'By all means, Lady Julia. Certainly. As a matter of fact, I think I'll be getting along.'

'I'll order your car.'

'Don't bother,' said Sir Gregory. 'Don't need a car. Going to walk. The relief of knowing that that infernal book isn't hanging over my head any longer . . . phew! I think I'll walk ten miles.'

His eye fell on the tattered fragment of paper

on the table. He gathered it up, tore it in half, and put the pieces in his pocket. Then, with the contented air of a man out of whose life stories of prawns have gone for ever, he strode briskly to the door.

Percy Pilbeam continued to sit where he was, looking like a devastated area.

# 15

While these events were in progress at Blandings Castle, there sat in the coffee-room of the Emsworth Arms in Market Blandings a young man eating turbot. It was the second course of a belated dinner which he was making under the reproachful eye of a large, pale, spotted waiter who had hoped to be off duty half an hour ago.

The first thing anyone entering the coffee-room would have noticed, apart from the ozone-like smell of cold beef, beer, pickles, cabbage, gravy soup, boiled potatoes and very old cheese which characterizes coffee-rooms all England over, would have been this young man's extraordinary gloom. He seemed to have looked on life and seen its hollowness. And so he had. Monty Bodkin — for this decayed wreck was he — was in the depths. It is fortunate that the quality of country hotel turbot is such that you do not notice much difference when it turns to ashes in your mouth, for this is what Monty's turbot was doing now.

He had never, he realized, been exactly what you might call sanguine when making his way to the Emsworth Arms to plead with Lord Tilbury to act like a sportsman and a gentleman. All the ruling of the form-book, he knew, was against him. And yet he had nursed, despite the whisperings of Reason, a sort of thin, sickly hope. This hope the proprietor of the Mammoth had slain dead within five minutes of his arrival.

When Monty had claimed consideration on the ground that it was through no fault of his own that he was not charging in, manuscript in hand, Lord Tilbury had remained mute and stony. When he had gone on to point out that Pilbeam could not have got the thing but for him, Lord Tilbury had uttered a sharp, sneering snort. And when, as happened a little farther on in the scene, Monty had called his former employer a fat, double-crossing wart-hog, the latter had terminated the interview by walking away with his hands under his coat-tails.

So Monty dined broodingly, his heart bowed down with weight of woe. Silence reigned in the coffee-room, broken only by the breathing of the waiter, a man who would have done well to put himself in the hands of some good tonsil specialist.

Optimist though he was by nature, Monty Bodkin could not conceal it from himself that the future looked black. Unless the senior partner of Butterwick Mandelbaum and Price relented — a hundred to one shot — or Gertrude Butterwick jettisoned her sturdy middle-class prejudices and decided to defy her father's wishes — call this one eighty-eight to three — that wedded bliss of which he had dreamed could never be his. It was an unpleasant thought for a man to have to face, and one well calculated to turn to ashes the finest portion of turbot ever boiled, let alone the rather obscene-looking mixture of bones and eyeballs and black mackintosh which the chef of the

Emsworth Arms had allotted to him.

Roast mutton succeeded the turbot and became ashes in its turn, as did the potatoes and brussels sprouts which accompanied it. The tapioca pudding, owing to an accident in the kitchen, was mostly ashes already. Monty gave it one look, then flung down his napkin with a Byronic gesture and, declining the waiter's half-hearted suggestion of a glass of port and a bit of Stilton, dragged himself downstairs and out into the garden.

Pacing the wet grass, he found his mind turning to thoughts of revenge. He was a kindly and good-tempered young man as a general rule, but conduct like that of Percy Pilbeam and Lord Tilbury seemed to him simply to clamour for reprisals. And it embittered him still further to discover at the end of ten minutes that he was totally without ideas on the subject. For all he could do about it, he was regretfully forced to conclude, these wicked men were apparently going to prosper like a couple of bay trees.

In these circumstances there was only one thing that could heal the spirit, viz. to go in and write a long, loving letter of appeal to Gertrude Butterwick, urging her to follow the dictates of her heart and come and spring round with him to the registrar's or Gretna Green or somewhere. With this end in view, he proceeded to the writing-room, where he hoped to be able to devote himself to the task in solitude.

The writing-room of the Emsworth Arms, as of most English rural hotels, was a small, stuffy, melancholy apartment, badly-lit and very much in need of new wallpaper. But it was not its meagre dimensions nor its closeness nor its dimness nor the shabbiness of its walls that depressed Monty as he entered. What gave him that grey feeling was the sight of Lord Tilbury seated in one of the two rickety armchairs.

Lord Tilbury was smoking an excellent cigar, and until that moment had been feeling quietly happy. His interview with Bodkin M. before dinner had relieved his mind of a rather sinister doubt which had been weighing on it. Until Monty had informed him of what had occurred, he had been oppressed by a speculation as to whether the voice which had spoken to him on the telephone had been the voice of Pilbeam or merely that of the alcoholic refreshment of which Pilbeam was so admittedly full. Had he, in short, really got the manuscript? Or had his statement to that effect been the mere inebriated babbling of an investigator who had just been investigating Lord Emsworth's cellar? Monty had made it clear that the former and more agreeable theory was the correct one, and Lord Tilbury was now awaiting the detective's arrival in a frame of mind that blended well with an excellent cigar.

The intrusion of a young man of whom he hoped he had seen the last ruffled his placid mood.

'I have nothing more to say,' he observed irritably. 'I have told you my decision, and I see nothing to be gained by further discussion.'

Monty raised his eyebrows coldly.

'I have no desire to speak to you, my good

man,' he said loftily. 'I came in here to write a letter.'

'Then go and write it somewhere else. I am expecting a visitor.'

It had been Monty's intention to ignore the fellow and carry on with the job in hand without deigning to bestow another look on him. But having gone to the desk and discovered that it contained no notepaper, no pen, not a single envelope, and in the inkpot only about a quarter of an inch of curious sediment that looked like black honey, he changed his mind.

He toyed for an instant with the idea of taking one of the magazines which lay on the table and sitting down in the other armchair and spoiling the old blighter's evening; but as those magazines were last-year copies of the *Hotel Keepers Register* and *Licensed Victuallers Gazette* he abandoned the project. With a quiet look of scorn and a meaning sniff he left the room and wandered out into the garden again.

And barely had he strolled down to the river and smoked two cigarettes and thrown a bit of stick at a water-rat and strolled back and thrown another bit of stick at a noise in the bushes, when the significance of Lord Tilbury's concluding remark suddenly flashed upon him.

If Lord Tilbury was expecting a visitor, that visitor obviously must be Pilbeam. And if Pilbeam was coming to the Emsworth Arms to see Lord Tilbury, equally obviously he must be bringing the manuscript with him.

Very well, then, where did one go from there? One went, he perceived, straight to this arresting conclusion — that there the two blisters would be in that writing-room with the manuscript between them, thus offering a perfect sitter of a chance to any man of enterprise who cared to dash in and be a little rough.

A bright confidence filled Monty Bodkin. He felt himself capable of taking on ten Tilburies and a dozen Pilbeams. All he had to do was bide his time and then rush in and snatch the thing. And when he had got it and was dangling it before his eyes, would Lord Tilbury take a slightly different attitude? Would he adopt a somewhat different tone? Would he be likely to reopen the whole matter, approaching it from another angle? The answer was definitely in the affirmative.

But first to spy out the land. He remembered that the window of the writing-room had been open a few inches at the bottom. He tiptoed across the grass with infinite caution. And just as he had reached his objective a voice spoke inside the room.

'You hid it? But are you sure it is safe?'

Monty leaned against the wall, holding his breath. He felt like the owner of a home-made radio who has accidentally got San Francisco.

\* \* \*

The Pilbeam who had borrowed Voule's motor-bicycle and ridden down to the Emsworth Arms and now faced Lord Tilbury in the writing-room of that hostelry was a very different Pilbeam from the gay telephoner of before dinner. The telephoning Pilbeam had been a man who gave free rein to a jovial exuberance, knowing himself to be sitting on top of the world. The writing-room Pilbeam was a taut and anxious gambler, staking his all on one last throw.

After that painful scene in the drawing-room, it had taken the detective perhaps ten minutes to realize that, though all seemed lost, there did still remain just one chance of saving the day. If he were salesman enough to dispose of that manuscript to Lord Tilbury, sight unseen, without being compelled to mention that it was no longer — except in a greatly transmuted state inside Empress of Blandings — in existence, all would be well.

There might possibly be a little coldness on the other's side next time they met, for Lord Tilbury, he knew, was one of those men who rather readily take umbrage on discovering that they have paid a thousand pounds for nothing, but he was used to people being cold to him and could put up with that.

So here he was, making his last throw.

'You hid it?' said Lord Tilbury, after the detective in a brief opening speech had explained that he had not come to deliver the goods in person. 'But are you sure it is quite safe?'

'Oh, quite.'

'But why did you not bring it with you?'

'Too risky. You don't know what that house is like. There's Lady Constance after the thing and Gally Threepwood after the thing and Ronnie Fish and . . . well, as I said to Monty Bodkin this afternoon, a fellow trying to smuggle that manuscript out of the place is rather like a chap in a detective story trapped in the den of the Secret Nine.'

A little gasp of indignation forced itself from Monty's outraged lips. This, he felt, was just that little bit that is too much. He had been modestly proud of that crack about the Secret Nine. Not content with pinching his manuscripts, this dastardly detective was pinching his nifties. It was enough to make a fellow chafe and, Monty chafed a good deal.

'I see,' said Lord Tilbury. 'Yes, I see what you mean. But if you hid it in your bedroom . . . '

'I didn't.'

'Then where?'

The crucial moment had arrived, and Pilbeam braced himself to cope with it.

'Ah!' he said. 'I think, perhaps, before I tell you that, we had better just get the business end of the thing settled, eh? If you have your cheque-book handy..

'But, my dear Pilbeam, surely you do not expect me to pay before . . . ?'

'Quite,' said the detective, and held his breath. His stake was on the board and the wheel had begun to spin.

It seemed to Monty that Lord Tilbury also must be holding his breath, for there followed a long silence. When he did speak, his tone was that of a man who has been wounded.

'Well, really, Pilbeam! I think you might trust me.'

' "Trust nobody" is the Pilbeam family motto,'

replied the detective with a return of what might be called his telephone manner.

'But how am I to know . . . ?'

'*You've* got to trust *me*,' said Pilbeam brightly. 'Of course,' he went on, 'if you don't like that way of doing business, well, in that case, I suppose the deal falls through. No hard feelings on either side. I simply go back to the Castle and take the matter up with Sir Gregory Parsloe and Lady Constance. They want that manuscript just as much as you do, though, of course, their reasons aren't the same as yours. They want to destroy it. Parsloe's original offer was five hundred pounds, but I shall have no difficulty in making him improve on that . . . '

'Five hundred pounds is a great deal of money,' said Lord Tilbury, as if he were having a tooth out.

'It's not nearly as much as a thousand,' replied Pilbeam, as if he were a light-hearted dentist. 'And you agreed to that on the telephone.'

'Yes, but then I assumed that you would be bringing . . . '

'Well, take it or leave it, Tilbury, take it or leave it,' said the detective, and from the little crackling splutter which followed the words Monty deduced that he was doing what we are so strongly advised to do when we wish to appear nonchalant, lighting a cigarette. 'Good!' he said a moment later. 'I think you're wise. Make it open, if you don't mind.'

There was a pause. The heavy breathing that came through the window could only be that of a parsimonious man occupied in writing a cheque for a thousand pounds. It is a type of breathing which it is impossible to mistake, though in some respects it closely resembles the sound of a strong man's death agony.

'There!'

'Thanks.'

'And now — ?'

'Well, I'll tell you,' said Pilbeam. 'It's like this. I didn't dare hide the thing in the house, so I put it carefully away in a disused pigsty near the kitchen garden. Wait. If you'll lend me your fountain pen, I'll draw you a map. See, here's the wall of the kitchen garden. You go along it, and on your left you will see this sty in a little paddock. You can't mistake it. It's the only building there. You go in and under the straw, where I'm putting this cross, is the manuscript. That's clear?'

'Quite clear.'

'You think you will be able to find it all right?'

'Perfectly easily.' — 'Good. Well, now, there's just one other thing. The merest trifle, but you want to be prepared for it. I said this pigsty was disused, and when I put the manuscript in it so it was. But since then they've gone and shifted that pig of Lord Emsworth's there, the animal they call the Empress of Blandings.'

'What?'

'I thought I had better mention it, as otherwise it might have given you a surprise when you got there.'

The momentary spasm of justifiable indignation which had attacked Lord Tilbury on hearing this piece of information left him. In its place came, oddly enough, a distinct relief. In some curious way the statement had removed from his mind a doubt which had been lingering there. It made Pilbeam's story seem circumstantial.

'That is quite all right,' he said as cheerfully as could be expected of a man of his views on parting with money so soon after the writing of a thousand-pound cheque. 'That will cause no difficulty.'

'You think you can cope with this pig?'

'Certainly. I am not afraid of pigs. Pigs like me.'

At these words, Monty found his respect for a breed of animal which he had always rather admired waning a good deal. No animal of the right sort, he felt, could like Lord Tilbury.

'Then that's fine,' said Pilbeam. 'I'd start at once if I were you. Are you going to walk?'

'Yes.'

'You'll need a torch.'

'No doubt I can borrow one from the landlord of this inn.'

'Good. Then everything's all right.'

There came to Monty's ears the sound of the opening and closing of a door. Lord Tilbury had apparently left to begin the business of the night. For a moment Monty thought that Pilbeam must have left, too, but after a brief silence there came through the window a muttered oath, and, peeping in, he saw that the detective was leaning over the writing-desk. The ejaculation had presumably been occasioned by his discovery that there was no paper, no envelope, no pen, and only what a dreamer could have described as ink.

And such, indeed, was the case. Percy Pilbeam was a man who believed in prompt action. He intended to dispatch that cheque to his bank without delay.

He rang the bell.

'I want some ink,' Monty heard him say. 'And a pen and some paper and an envelope.'

He had placed the cheque on the desk before making the discovery of its lack of stationery. He now picked it up and stood looking at it lovingly.

He was well pleased with himself. It was a far, far better thing that he had done than he had ever done, felt Pilbeam. He wondered how many men there were who would have snatched victory out of defeat like that. He reached for his unpleasant moustache and gave it a complacent tug.

And, as he did so, over his shoulder there came groping a hand. The cheque was twitched from his grasp. And, turning, he perceived Monty Bodkin.

'Hell!' cried Pilbeam, aghast.

Monty did not reply. Actions speak louder than words. With a severe look, he tore the cheque in two pieces, then in four, then in eight, then in sixteen, then in thirty-two. Then, finding himself unable to bring the score up to sixty-four, he moved to the fireplace and, still with that austere expression on his face, dropped them in the grate like a shower of confetti.

After that first anguished cry Pilbeam had not spoken. He stood watching the tragedy with a frozen stare. It seemed to him that he had spent most of his later life looking at people tearing up cheques made out to himself. For one brief instant the battling spirit of the Pilbeams urged him to attack this man with tooth and claw, but the impulse faded. The Pilbeams might be brave, but they were not rash. Monty was some eight inches taller than himself, some twenty pounds heavier, and in addition to this had a nasty look in his eye.

He accepted the ruling of Destiny. In silence he watched Monty leave the room. The door closed. Percy Pilbeam was alone with his thoughts.

★　★　★

Monty strolled into the lounge of the Emsworth Arms. It was empty, but presently Lord Tilbury appeared, hatted, booted, and ready for the long trail. Monty eyed him sardonically. He proposed very shortly to put a stick of dynamite under this Lord Tilbury.

'Going out?' he said.

'I am taking a walk, yes.'

'God bless you!' said Monty.

He followed Lord Tilbury with his eye. Shortly he was going to follow him in actual fact. But that could wait. He knew that he could give that stout, stumpy man five minutes' start and still be at the tryst before him. And in the meantime there was grim work to be done.

He went to the telephone and rang up Blandings Castle.

'I want to speak to Lord Emsworth,' he said,

in one of those gruff assumed voices that sound like a bull-frog with catarrh.

'I will put you through to his lordship,' replied the more melodious voice of Beach.

'Do so,' said Monty, sinking an octave. 'The matter is urgent.'

# 16

Lord Emsworth had taken his twisted ankle to
the library and was lying with it on one of the
leather-covered settees. The doctor had come
and gone, leaving instructions for the application
of hot fomentations and announcing that the
patient was out of danger. And as the pain had
now entirely disappeared it might have been
supposed that the ninth Earl's mind would have
been at rest.

This, however, was far from being the case.
Not only was he anxiously awaiting the
veterinary surgeon's report on the paper-filled
Empress, which was enough to agitate any man
ill accustomed to bear up calmly under suspense,
but to add to his mental discomfort, his two
sisters, the Lady Constance Keeble and the Lady
Julia Fish, had gathered about his sick-bed and
were driving him half mad with some nonsense
about his nephew Ronald's money.

However, for some time he had been adopting
the statesmanlike policy of saying 'Eh?'
'Yes?'
'Oh, ah?' and 'God bless my soul' at fairly
regular intervals, and this had given him leisure
to devote his mind to the things that really
mattered.

Paper . . . Ink . . . Wasn't ink a highly corrosive
acid or something? And could even the stoutest
pig thrive on corrosive acids? Thus Lord

Emsworth when his thoughts took a gloomy trend.

But there were optimistic gleams among the grey. He recalled the time when the Empress, mistaking his carelessly dropped cigar for something on the bill of fare, had swallowed it with every indication of enjoyment and had been none the worse next day. Also Pirbright's Sunday hat. There was another case that seemed to make for hopefulness. True, she had consumed only a mouthful or two of that, but to remain in excellent health and spirits after eating even a portion of the sort of hat that Pirbright wore on Sundays argued a constitution well above the average. Reviewing these alimentary feats of the past, Lord Emsworth was able to endure. But he wished that Beach would return and put an end to this awful suspense. The butler had been dispatched with the vet. to the sty to bring back his report, and should have been here long ago. Lord Emsworth found himself yearning for Beach's society as poets of a former age used to yearn for that of gazelles and Arab steeds.

It was at this tense moment in the affairs of the master of Blandings that Monty's telephone call came through.

'Lord Emsworth?' said a deep, odd voice.

'Lord Emsworth speaking.'

'I have reason to believe, Lord Emsworth . . . '

'Wait!' cried the ninth Earl. 'Wait a moment. Hold the line.' He turned. 'Well, Beach, well?'

'The veterinary surgeon reports, m'lord, that there is no occasion for alarm.'

'She's all right?'

'Quite, m'lord. No occasion for anxiety whatsoever.'

A deep sigh of relief shook Lord Emsworth.

'Eh?' said the voice at the other end of the wire, not knowing quite what to make of it.

'Oh, excuse me. I was just speaking to my butler about my pig. Extremely sorry to have kept you waiting, but it was most urgent. You were saying — ?'

'I have reason to believe, Lord Emsworth, that an attack is to be made upon your pig tonight.'

Lord Emsworth uttered a sharp, gargling sound.

'What!'

'Yes.'

'You don't mean that?'

'Yes.'

'Oh, do hurry, Clarence,' said Lady Constance, who wished to get on with the business of the evening. 'Who is it? Tell him to ring up later.'

Lord Emsworth waved her down imperiously, and continued to bark into the telephone's mouthpiece like a sea-lion. 'Tonight?'

'Yes.'

'What time tonight?'

'Any time now.'

'What!'

'Oh, Clarence, do stop saying 'What' and ring off.'

'Yes, almost immediately.'

'Are you sure?'

'Yes.'

'God bless my soul! What a ghastly thing! Well, I am infinitely obliged to you, my dear fellow

. . . By the way, who are you?'

'A Well-wisher.'

'What?'

'Oh, *Clar-ence?*

'A Well-wisher.'

'Fisher?'

'Wisher.'

'Disher? Beach,' cried Lord Emsworth, as a click from afar told him that the man of mystery had hung up, 'a Mr A. L. Fisher or Disher -I did not quite catch the name — says that an attack is to be made upon the Empress tonight.'

'Indeed, m'lord?'

'Almost immediately.'

'Indeed, m'lord?'

'Don't keep saying 'Indeed, m'lord', as if I were telling you it was a fine day! Can't you realize the frightful — ? And you, Connie,' said Lord Emsworth, who was now in thoroughly berserk mood, turning on his sister like a stringy tiger, 'stop sniffing like that!'

'Really, Clarence!'

'Beach, go and bring Pirbright here.'

'He shall do nothing of the kind,' said Lady Constance sharply.

'The idea of bringing Pirbright into the library!'

It was not often that Beach found himself in agreement with the chatelaine of Blandings, but he could not but support her attitude now. Like all butlers, he held definite views on the sanctity of the home and frowned upon attempts on the part of the outside staff to enter it — especially when, like Pirbright, they smelt so very strongly

310

of pigs. Five minutes of that richly scented man in the library, felt Beach, and you would have to send the place to the cleaner's.

'Perhaps if I were to convey a message to Pirbright from your lordship?' he suggested tactfully. Lord Emsworth, though dangerously excited, could still listen to the voice of Reason. It was not the thought of the pig-man's aroma that made him change his mind — the library, in his opinion, would have been improved by a whiff of bouquet de Pirbright -but that deep, grave voice had said that the attack was to take place almost immediately, and in that case it would be madness to remove the garrison from its post even for an instant.

'Yes,' he said. 'A very good idea. Much better. Yes, capital. Excellent. Thank you, Beach.'

'Not at all, m'lord.'

'Go at once to Pirbright and tell him what I have told you, and say that he is to remain in hiding near the sty and spring out at the right moment and catch this fellow.'

'Very good, m'lord.'

'He had better strike him over the head with a stout stick.'

'Very good, m'lord.'

'So we shall wind up the evening with a nice murder,' said Lady Julia. 'Eh?'

'Don't pay any attention to me, of course. If you like to incite pig-men to brain people with sticks, it's none of my affair. But I should have thought you were taking a chance.'

Lord Emsworth seemed impressed.

'You think he might injure Parsloe fatally?'

'Parsloe!' Lady Constance's voice caused a statuette of the young David prophesying before Saul to quiver on its base. 'Are you off your head, Clarence?'

'No, I'm not,' replied Lord Emsworth manfully. 'What's the use of pretending that you don't know as well as I do that it's Parsloe who is making this attempt tonight? The way you let that fellow pull the wool over your eyes, Constance, amazes me. What do you think he wheedled you into inviting him to dinner for? So that he could be on the premises and have easy access to the Empress, of course. I'll bet you find he has sneaked off while you were not looking.'

'Clarence!'

'Well, where is he? Produce Parsloe! Show me Parsloe!'

'Sir Gregory left the house a few minutes ago. He wished to take a walk.'

'Take a walk!' This time it was Lord Emsworth's voice that rocked the young David. 'Beach, there isn't a moment to lose! Hurry, man, hurry! Run to Pirbright and say that the blow may fall at any moment.'

'Very good, m'lord. And in the matter of the stick — ?'

'Tell him to use his own judgement.'

Lord Emsworth sank back on his settee. His mental condition resembled that of a warrior who, crippled by wounds, must stay in his tent while the battle is joined without. He snorted restlessly. His place was by Pirbright's side, and he could not get there. He put his foot to the floor and tentatively leaned his weight upon it

312

but a facial contortion and a sharp 'Ouch!' showed that there was no hope. Pirbright, that strong shield of defence, must be left to deal with this matter alone.

'I'm sure everything will be quite all right, Clarence,' said Lady Julia, who believed in the methods of diplomacy, silencing with a little gesture her sister Constance, who did not.

'You really feel that?' said Lord Emsworth eagerly.

'Of course. You can trust Pirbright to see that nothing happens.'

'Yes. A good fellow, Pirbright.'

'I expect that when Sir Gregory sees him,' said Lady Julia, with a steady, quelling glance at her sister, who was once more sniffing in rather a marked manner, 'he will run away.'

'Pirbright will?' said Lord Emsworth, starting.

'No, Sir Gregory will. There is nothing for you to worry about at all. Just lie back and relax.'

'Bless my soul, you're a great comfort, Julia.'

'I try to be,' said Lady Julia virtuously.

'You've made me feel easier in my mind.'

'Splendid,' said Lady Julia, and with another little gesture she indicated to Lady Constance that the subject was now calmed and that she could proceed.

Lady Constance gave her a masonic glance of understanding.

'Julia is quite right,' she said. 'There is no need for you to worry.'

'Well, if you think that, too . . . ' said Lord Emsworth, beginning to achieve something like that delightful feeling of *bien-être*.

'I do, decidedly. You can dismiss the whole thing from your mind and give me your attention again.'

'My attention? What do you want my attention for?'

'We were speaking,' said Lady Constance, 'of this money of Ronald's and the criminal folly of allowing him to have it in order that he may make a marriage of which Julia and I both disapprove so very strongly.'

'Oh, that?' said Lord Emsworth, the glow beginning to fade.

He looked at the door wistfully, feeling how easy a task it would have been, but for this ankle of his, to disappear through it like an eel and not let himself be cornered again before bedtime.

Cornered, however, he was. He leaned back against the cushions and women's voices began to beat upon him like rain upon a roof.

★　★　★

Down at the Emsworth Arms, Monty Bodkin had just decided to make a small alteration in the plan of action which he had outlined for himself. It had been his original intention, it may be recalled, to follow Lord Tilbury to the trap which he had prepared for him, so that, lurking in the background — probably with folded arms, certainly with a bitter sneer of triumph on his lips — he might have the gratification of witnessing his downfall. But when, wearying of the Wisher-Fisher-Disher controversy, he hung up the receiver and left the telephone booth, he

314

found this project looking less attractive to him.

A man who is by nature a light baritone cannot conduct a conversation for any length of time in a deep bass without acquiring a parched and burning throat. Monty came out of the booth feeling as if his had been roughly sandpapered, and the thought of that two and a half mile walk to the Castle and its little brother, the two and a half mile walk back, intimidated him. The more he thought of it, the less worthwhile did it seem to him to go to all that fearful sweat simply in order to see the scruff of Lord Tilbury's neck grasped by a pig-man. Far better, he felt, to toddle along to the bar-parlour and there, over a soothing tankard, follow the scene with the eye of imagination.

Thither, accordingly, he made his way, and presently, seated in a corner with a stoup of the right stuff before him, was lubricating his tortured vocal chords and exchanging desultory chit-chat with the barmaid.

For himself, gripped as he still was by that melancholy which torments those who have loved and lost, Monty would have preferred to be allowed to meditate in silence. But as he happened to be the only customer in the place at the moment, the barmaid, a matronly lady in black satin with a bird's nest of gold hair on her head, was able to give him her full attention, and her social sense urged her to converse. On such occasions she very rightly regarded herself as a hostess.

They spoke, accordingly, of the weather, touching on such aspects of it as the heat before the storm, the coolness after the storm, the violence of the storm, its possible effect on the crops and what always happened to the barmaid's digestive organs when there was thunder. It was after she had finished a rather lengthy description (one which would, perhaps, have interested a physician more than a layman) of what she had suffered earlier in the summer through rashly eating cucumber during a storm that Monty happened to mention that he had been caught in the downpour.

'Not reely?' said the barmaid. 'What, were you out in it?'

'Absolutely,' said Monty. 'I got properly soaked.'

'But what a silly you must be, if you'll excuse me saying so,' observed the barmaid, 'not to have took shelter in a shop or somewhere. Or were you taking one of those country hikes?'

'I was in the park. Up at Blandings.'

'Oh, are you up at the Castle?' said the barmaid, interested.

'I was then,' said Monty, with reserve.

The barmaid polished a glass.

'There's a great to-do up there,' she said. 'I expect you've heard?'

'A to-do?'

'About his lordship's pig. Eating all that paper.'

'Eh?'

'Oh, you haven't heard?' said the barmaid, gratified. 'Oh, yes, his lordship is terribly upset. I had it from Mr Webber, the vet., who stepped in for a quick one on his way up there. He'd just

316

been phoned for, extremely urgent. About half an hour ago, it was.'

'Paper?'

'That's what Mr Webber said. Somebook his lordship's brother had been writing, he said, and somehow, he said, it had got into this pig's sty, and the pig had eaten it. That's what he said. Though how a book could have got into a pigsty, is more than I can tell you.'

The barmaid broke off to attend to a customer who came in for a stout-and-mild, and Monty was able to wrestle in silence with this extraordinary piece of news.

So that was why Pilbeam had been so urgent in demanding cash in advance! From the confused welter of Monty's thoughts there emerged a clear realization that there must be a lot of hidden good in Percy Pilbeam that he had overlooked. A man with the resource and initiative to extract a thousand pounds from Lord Tilbury for a piece of property which he knew to be in the process of being digested by a pig was surely a man of whom one wished to see more, a fellow one would like to know better. As he reviewed that scene in the writing-room and remembered the confidence with which the detective had stated his terms, the gallant nonchalance of that take-it-or-leave-it of his which had sent Lord Tilbury scrambling for his cheque-book, something very like a warm affection for Percy Pilbeam began to burgeon in Monty. He did his hair in a pretty gruesome way, and there was no question but that that moustache of his was a bit above the odds

— nevertheless, he definitely felt that he would like to fraternize with the man.

He saw now — what had puzzled him before — why that cheque-tearing stuff had gone so big. At the moment of the cheque's destruction, Monty, like Ronnie Fish on another occasion, had intended merely the great gesture. Even while his fingers were busy, he was feeling that he was accomplishing little of practical value, because all the fellow had to do was to go and get another cheque from Lord Tilbury. But this news put an entirely different aspect on the matter. Obviously, Lord Tilbury would not do any more cheque-writing now. The great gesture had landed Pilbeam squarely in the soup, he realized, and, oddly enough, he felt remorseful.

He could now see the thing from Pilbeam's point of view. With a sum like a thousand pounds at stake, could the fellow be blamed for stooping to some fairly raw work? Was he not almost justified in going a bit near the knuckle in his methods? Absolutely, felt Monty as he sipped his tankard.

What with this dawning of the big, broad outlook and the excellence of the Emsworth Arms draught ale, he began to be conscious of an almost maudlin change in his attitude towards the investigator. Anyone who could send Lord Tilbury two and a half miles on a fool's errand was Monty's friend. More like a brother the detective now seemed than the tripe-hound he had once supposed him.

At this moment, just as he was at his

mellowest, the man in person came into the bar-parlour.

'Good evening, sir,' said the barmaid in her spacious way. As with so many barmaids, there was always a suggestion in her manner of being somebody who was bestowing the Freedom of the City on someone.

'Evening,' said Pilbeam.

He caught sight of Monty in his corner, and frowned. If Monty had begun to warm to him, it was plain that he was nowhere near warming to Monty. He eyed him sourly. His intention had apparently been to consume liquid refreshment in the bar-parlour, but the sight of the person who had so recently impaired his finances made him change his mind. One does not drink in an atmosphere poisoned by a man who has just robbed one of a thousand pounds.

'I want a double whisky,' said Pilbeam. 'Send it into the writing-room, will you?'

He stalked out. The barmaid, whose manner during their brief conversation had shown impressment, jerked a rather awed thumb at the door.

'See that feller?' she said. 'Know who he is? Mr Voules, the chauffeur up at the Castle, was telling me. He runs a big detective agency in London. Employs hundreds and hundreds of skilled assistants, Mr Voules says. Sort of spider, if you get my meaning, sitting in his web and directing the movements of his skilled assistants.'

'Good gosh!' cried Monty.

'Yes,' said the barmaid, pleased at his emotion. She polished a glass with something of an air.

But Monty's emotion had been caused by something of which she was not aware. Where she beheld a good-gosher who good-goshed from sheer astonishment at her sensational information, this young man's good-goshing had not been due to surprise. It was that bit about the skilled assistants that had wrenched the ejaculation from Monty's lips. Those two words had given him the idea of a lifetime.

Thirty seconds later he was in the writing-room, the detective looking up at him like a startled basilisk.

'I know, I know,' said Monty, rightly interpreting the message in his eye. 'But I've got a bit of business to talk over. I can do you a spot of good, Pilbeam.'

It would be too much to say that the investigator's eye melted. It still looked like that of a basilisk. But at these words it became that of a basilisk which reserves its judgement.

'Well?' he said.

Monty prepended.

'It's a little difficult to know where to begin.'

'As far as I'm concerned,' said Pilbeam, his feelings momentarily overcoming his business instinct, 'you can begin by getting out of here and breaking your ruddy neck.'

Monty waved a pacific hand.

'No, no.' he urged. 'Don't talk like that. The wrong attitude, old soul. Not the right tone at all.'

At this moment there entered a lad in shirt-sleeves bearing the investigator's double whisky. The interruption served to enable Monty

320

to marshal his thoughts. When the lad had withdrawn, he began to speak fluently and with ease.

'It's like this, my dear old chap,' he said, paying no heed to an odd noise which proceeded from his companion, who appeared not to like being called his dear old chap. 'I seem to recollect mentioning to you this afternoon that as far as my affairs were concerned there were wheels within wheels. Well, there are. Not long ago I became betrothed to a girl, and her ass of a father won't let me marry her unless I get a job and hold it down for a year. And, dash it, my every effort to do so seems to prove null and void, if null and void is the expression I want. No,' said Monty, gently corrective, 'it isn't a bit of luck for the girl. It's very tough on the girl. She loves me madly. On the other hand, being a sort of throwback to the Victorian age, she won't go against her old dad's wishes. So I've got to have that job. I tried being assistant editor of *Tiny Tots*. No good. The boot. I became secretary to old Emsworth. Again no good. Once more the boot. And this is the idea that struck me just now, listening to the conversation of that female who works the beer-engine out there. You run a detective agency. You employ hundreds of skilled assistants. Well, come on now, be a sport. Employ me!'

The only reason why Percy Pilbeam did not at this point interject a blistering comment on the proposal thus put before him was that three such comments entered his mind simultaneously, and in the effort to decide which was the most blistering he drank some whisky the wrong way. Before he had finished choking. Monty had gone on to speak further. And what he went on to say was so amazing, so arresting, that the investigator found himself choking again.

'There's a thousand quid in it for you.'

Percy Pilbeam at last contrived to clear his vocal chords.

'A thousand quid?'

'Oh, I've got packets of money,' said Monty, misreading the look in those watering eyes and taking it for incredulity. 'I'm simply ill with the stuff. If money had been the trouble, there never would have been any trouble, if you follow what I mean. That hasn't been the difficulty. What's been the difficulty has been the extraordinary mental attitude of J. G. Butterwick. He insists . . .'

An astonishing change had come over the demeanour of P. Frobisher Pilbeam. One has seen much the same thing, of course, in the film of Jekyll and Hyde, but on a much less impressive scale. His scowling face had melted into a face that glowed as if lit by some inner lantern. Aesthetically, he looked equally unpleasant whether scowling or smiling, but Monty was far from being in the frame of mind to regard him from the austere standpoint of a judge in a Beauty Competition. He saw the smile, and his heart leaped within him.

Pilbeam had still to wrestle with his emotions for a moment before he could speak.

'You'll pay a thousand pounds to come into my Agency?'

'That exact figure.'

'For a thousand pounds,' said Pilbeam simply, 'you can be a partner, if you like.'

'But I don't like,' said Monty urgently. 'You're missing the idea. This has got to be a job. I want to be a skilled assistant.'

'You shall be.'

'For a year?'

'For ten years, if you want to.'

Monty sat down. There was in the simple action something of the triumph and exhaustion of the winner of a Marathon race. He stared in silence for a moment at a framed advertisement of Sigbee's Soda ('It Sizzles') which was assisting the wallpaper to impart to the room that note of hideousness at which hotel-keepers strive.

'Butterwick's her name,' he said at length. 'Gertrude Butterwick.'

'Yes?' said Pilbeam. 'Where's your cheque-book?'

'Her eyes,' said Monty, 'are greyish. And yet, at the same time blue-ish.'

'I bet they are,' said Pilbeam. 'In one of your pockets, perhaps?'

'About her hair,' said Monty. 'Some people might call it brown. Chestnut has always seemed to me a closer description. She's tallish, but not too tall. Her mouth . . . '

'I'll tell you,' said Pilbeam. 'Let me get a sheet of paper.'

'You want me to draw you a picture of her?' said Monty, a little doubtfully.

'I want you to write a cheque for me.'

'Oh, ah, yes, I see what you mean. My

323

cheque-book's upstairs in my suitcase.'

'Then come along,' said Pilbeam buoyantly, 'and I'll help you unpack.'

★ ★ ★

Beach sat in his pantry, sipping brandy. And if ever a butler was entitled to a glass of brandy, that butler, he felt, was himself. He rolled the stuff round his tongue, finding a certain comfort in the fiery sting of it.

His heart was heavy. It was a kindly heart, and from the very first it had been deeply stirred by the stormy romance of Mr Ronald and his young lady. He wished that life were as the writers of the detective stories, to which he had become so addicted, portrayed it. In those, no matter what obstacles Fate might interpose in the shape of gangs, shots in the night, underground cellars, sinister Chinamen, poisoned asparagus and cobras down the chimney, the hero always got his girl. In the present case Beach could see no such happy ending. The significance of the presence in the library of Lady Constance Keeble and Lady Julia Fish had not escaped him. He feared that it meant the worst.

Eighteen years of close association with Clarence, Earl of Emsworth, had left the butler with a very fair estimate of his overlord's character. He wished well to everyone — Beach knew that. But where viewpoints clashed and arguments began, a passionate desire for peace at any price would undoubtedly lead him to decide in favour of whoever argued loudest. And eighteen years of close association with Lady Constance Keeble told Beach who, on the present occasion, that would be.

He saw no hope. Sighing despondently, he helped himself to another glass of brandy. Usually at this hour he drank port. But port to him was a symbol. He never touched it till dinner was over and the coffee served, and it signified that the responsibilities of his office were at an end and that until the morrow should bring its new cares and duties his soul was at rest. Port tonight would have been quite unsuitable.

Sighing again and about to start sipping once more, he became aware that he was no longer alone. Mr Ronald had entered the room.

'Don't get up, Beach,' said Ronnie.

He sat down on the table. His face had a pinkness deeper than its wont. There was a repressed excitement in his manner. The butler was reminded of that other occasion, ten days ago, when this young man had come into his pantry looking much the same as he was looking now and, having announced that he intended to steal his lordship's pig, had proceeded to cajole him into becoming his accomplice and helping him to feed the animal. The weighing machine in the servants' bathroom had informed Beach that he had lost three pounds in two days over that little affair.

'Bad show, this, Beach.'

Beach stirred mountainously. Solicitude shone from his prominent eyes. It has already been mentioned that Beach in the drawing-room and

Beach in his pantry were different entities. He was now in his pantry, where he could cast off the official mask and be the man with whom a younger Ronnie had once played bears on this very floor.

'Extremely, Mr Ronald. Then you have heard?'

'Heard?'

'The unfortunate news.'

'You were there when I heard it. In the hall.' The butler rolled his eyes, to indicate that there was something much more Stop Press than that. 'The Empress has eaten Mr Galahad's book, Mr Ronald.'

'What!'

'Yes, sir. Somebody apparently left it in her sty, and she was devouring the last of it when his lordship found her.'

'Pilbeam!'

'So one would be disposed to imagine, Mr Ronald. No doubt he had employed the sty as a hiding-place.'

'And it's gone?'

'Quite gone, Mr Ronald.'

'And Aunt Constance knows about it?'

'I fear so, Mr Ronald.' Ronnie's face became a little pinker.

'Well, it doesn't make much odds. There was never any chance of recovering it from Pilbeam. That's why I . . . I think I could do with a spot of that brandy, Beach.'

'Certainly, sir. I will get you a glass. Why you . . . you were saying, Mr Ronald?'

'Oh, just a sort of decision I came to. This is good stuff, Beach.'

'Yes, sir.'

'A sort of decision,' said Ronnie, sipping pensively. 'I don't know if you noticed that I was a bit quiet at dinner?'

'You did strike me as somewhat silent, Mr Ronald.'

'I was thinking.'

'I see, sir.'

'Thinking,' repeated Ronnie. 'Doing a bit of avenue-exploring. I came to this decision with the fish.'

'Indeed, sir?'

'Yes. And I think it will work, too.'

Ronnie swung his legs for a while without speaking.

'Have you ever been in love, Beach?'

'In my younger days, Mr Ronald. It never came to anything.'

'Love's a rummy thing, Beach.'

'Very true, sir.'

'Sort of keys you up, if you understand me. Makes you feel you'd stick at nothing. Take any chance. To win the girl you love, I mean.'

'Quite so, sir.'

'Go through fire and water, as you might say. Brave every peril.'

'No doubt, sir.'

'Got another dollop of that brandy, Beach?'

'Yes, sir.'

'Well, there it is,' said Ronnie, emptying his glass and holding it out for fresh supplies. 'Half-way through the fish course I made up my mind. Now that that manuscript has gone, I'm up against it. At any moment Aunt Constance will be at Uncle Clarence, telling him not to give me my money.'

The butler coughed commiseratingly.

'I rather fancy, Mr Ronald, that her ladyship was in the act of doing so when I entered the library not long ago.'

'Then by this time she has probably clicked?'

'I very much fear so, Mr Ronald.'

'Right!' said Ronnie briskly. 'Then there's nothing left but strong measures. The time has come to act, Beach.'

'Sir?'

'I'm going to steal that pig.'

'What, *again*, Mr Ronald?'

Ronnie eyed him affectionately.

'Ah, you remember that other time, then?'

'Remember it, Mr Ronald? Why, it was only ten days ago.'

'So it was. It seems years. Not that I can't recall every detail of it. I haven't forgotten how staunchly you stood by me then, Beach. You were splendid.'

'Thank you, sir.'

'Wonderful! Marvellous!' continued Ronnie in an exalted voice. 'I doubt if there has ever been anybody who came out of an affair better than you did out of that one. A sportsman to the finger-tips, that's what you showed yourself. And don't,' said Ronnie earnestly, 'think that I didn't notice it, either. I appreciated it very much, Beach.'

'It is very kind of you to say so, sir,' said the butler, his head swimming a little.

'You're a fellow a fellow can rely on.'

'Thank you, sir.'

'Through thick and thin.'

'Thank you, sir.'

'When I got this idea of stealing the Empress this second time, Miss Brown said to me, 'Oh, but you can't ask Beach to help you again.' And I said, 'Of course I can. Apart from the fact that Beach and I have been pals for eighteen years, he's devoted to you.' And she said, 'Is he?' and I said, 'You bet he is. There's nothing in the world Beach wouldn't do for you.' And she said, 'The darling!' Just like that. And you should have seen the look in her eyes as she said it, Beach. They went all soft and dreamy. I believe if you had been there at the moment she would have kissed you. And I shall be greatly surprised,' said Ronnie, with the air of one offering a treat to a deserving child, 'if, when everything is over and you've been as staunch as you were before and chipped in and done your bit again, as you did then, she doesn't do it.'

All through this moving address the butler had been shaking and rumbling in a manner which would have reminded an eyewitness irresistibly of a volcano on the point of finding self-expression. His eyes had bulged, and his breathing was coming in little puffs.

'But, Mr Ronald!'

'I knew you would be pleased, Beach.'

'But, Mr Ronald!'

Ronnie eyed him sharply.

'Don't tell me you're thinking of backing out?'

'But, sir!'

329

'You can't at the last moment like this, after all our plans have been made. It would upset everything. I can't act without you. You wouldn't let me down, Beach?'

'But, sir, the risk!'

'Risk? Nonsense.'

'But, Mr Ronald, his lordship was notified on the telephone in my presence not half an hour ago that an attempt was to be made upon the Empress tonight. I have only just returned from seeing Pirbright and conveying his lordship's instructions to him to be on his guard.'

'Well, that's fine. Don't you see how this fits in with our plans? Pirbright will be waiting for this chap. He will catch him. And then what will he do, Beach? He will march him off to Uncle Clarence, leaving the coast absolutely clear. While he's gone we nip in and collar the animal without the slightest danger of inconvenience.' The butler puffed silently.

'Think what it means, Beach! My happiness! Miss Brown's happiness! You aren't going to go through the rest of your life kicking yourself at the thought that a little zeal, a little of the pull-together spirit on your part would have meant happiness for Miss Brown?'

'But if I were detected, sir, my position would be so extremely equivocal.'

'How can you be detected? Pirbright won't be there. Nobody will be there. I only need your help for about five minutes. This isn't like the last time. I'm not planning to hide the Empress somewhere and feed her. This is the real, straight kidnapping stuff. Just five minutes of your time,

330

Beach, just five little minutes and you can come back here and forget all about it.'

Strong tremors continued to shake the butler's massive frame.

'Really only five minutes, Mr Ronald?' he said pleadingly.

'Ten at the outside. I forgot to tell you, Beach, that one of the things Miss Brown said about you was that you reminded her of her father. Oh, yes, and that you had such kind eyes.'

The butler's mouth opened. Lava might have been expected to flow from it, for his resemblance to a volcano had now become exceptionally close. But it was not lava that emerged. What did so was a strangled croak. This was followed by a remark which Ronnie did not catch.

'Eh?'

'I said 'Very good,' Mr Ronald,' said Beach, looking as if he were facing a firing squad. 'You'll do it?'

'Yes, Mr Ronald.'

'Beach,' said Ronnie with emotion, 'when I'm a millionaire, as I expect to be a few years after I've put my money in that motor business, the first thing I shall do is to come to this pantry with a purse of gold. Two purses of gold. Dash it, a keg of gold. I'll roll it in and knock off the lid and tell you to wade in and help yourself.'

'Thank you, Mr Ronald.'

'Don't thank *me*, Beach. You're the fellow who's entitled to all the gratitude that's going. And, talking of going, shall we be? There isn't a moment to lose. Shift ho, yes?'

'Very good, Mr Ronald,' said the butler in a strange, deep, rumbling voice, not unlike that of Mr A. L. Disher on the telephone.

# 17

Lady Julia Fish gave a little yawn and moved towards the door. For ten minutes she had been listening to her sister Constance express her views on the subject under discussion, and she was not a woman who accepted contentedly a thinking role in any scene in which she took part. If Connie had a fault — and off-hand she could name a dozen — it was that she tended to elbow her associates out of the picture at times like this. Standing by and acting as a silent audience bored Lady Julia.

'Well, if anybody wants me,' she said, 'they'll find me in the drawing-room.'

'Are you going, Julia?'

'There doesn't seem much for me to do round here. I feel that I am leaving the thing in competent hands. You speak for me. The voice is the voice of Constance, but you can take the sentiments, Clarence, as representing the views of a syndicate.'

Lord Emsworth watched her go without much sense of consolation. It is better, perhaps, to have one woman rather than two women making your life an inferno, but not so much better as to cause an elderly gentleman of quiet tastes to rejoice to any very marked extent.

'Now, listen, Clarence . . . '

Lord Emsworth stifled a moan, and tried — a task which the deaf adder of Scripture apparently found so easy — to hear nothing and give his mind to the things that really mattered.

He shifted restlessly on his settee. Surely soon there ought to be news from the Front. By this time, if Mr Disher was to be believed, the assault should have been made and, one hoped, rolled back by the devoted Pirbright.

Musing on Pirbright, Lord Emsworth became a little calmer. A capital fellow, he told himself, just the chap to handle the emergency which had arisen. Not much of a conversationalist, perhaps; scarcely the companion one would choose for a long railway journey; a little on the 'Ur' and 'Yur' side; but then who wanted a lively and epigrammatic pig-man? The point about Pirbright was that, if silent, he had that quality which so proverbially goes with silence — strength. The door opened.

'Well, Beach?' said Lady Constance with queenly displeasure, for nobody likes to be interrupted in moments of oratory. 'What is it?'

Lord Emsworth sat up expectantly. 'Well, Beach, well?'

A close observer, which his lordship was not, would have seen that the butler had recently passed through some soul-searing experience. His was never a rosy face, but now it wore a pallor beyond the normal. His eyes were round and glassy, his breathing laboured. He looked like a butler who has just been brought into sharp contact with the facts of life.

'Everything is quite satisfactory, m'lord.'

'Pirbright caught the fellow?'

'Yes, m'lord.'

'Did he tell you what happened?'

'I was an eye-witness of the proceedings, m'lord.'

'Well? Well?'

'Oh, Clarence, must we really have all this now?'

'What? What? What? Of course we must have it now. God bless my soul! Yes, Beach?'

'The facts, m'lord, are as follows. In pursuance of your lordship's instructions, Pirbright had placed himself in concealment in the vicinity of the animal's sty, and from this post of vantage proceeded to keep a keen watch.'

'What were you doing there?'

The butler hesitated.

'I had come to lend assistance, m'lord, should it be required.'

'Splendid, Beach. Well?'

'My cooperation, however, was not found to be necessary. The man arrived . . . '

'Parsloe?'

'Clarence!'

'No, m'lord. Not Sir Gregory.'

'Ah, an accomplice.'

'Oh, Clarence!'

'No doubt, m'lord. The man arrived and came to the rails of the sty, where he remained for a moment . . . '

'Nerving himself! Nerving himself to his frightful task.'

'He seemed to be manipulating an electric torch, m'lord.'

'And then — ?'

'Pirbright sprang out and overpowered him.'

'Excellent! And where is the fellow now?'

'Temporarily incarcerated in the coal-cellar, m'lord.'

'Bring him to me at once.'

'Clarence, do we want this man, whoever he is, in here?'

'Yes, we do want him in here.' Beach coughed. 'I should mention, m'lord, that he is considerably soiled. In order to overpower him, Pirbright was compelled to throw him face downwards and rest his weight upon him, and the ground in the neighbourhood of the sty had been somewhat softened by the heavy rain.'

'Never mind. I want to see him.'

'Very good, m'lord.'

The interval between the butler's retirement and reappearance was spent by Lady Constance in sniffing indignantly and by Lord Emsworth in congratulating himself that a sense of civic duty and a lively apprehension of what his sister would say if he resigned that office had kept him a Justice of the Peace. Representing, as he did, the majesty of the Law, he was in a position to deal summarily with this criminal. He would have to look it up in the book of instructions, of course, but he rather fancied he could give the chap fourteen days without moving from this settee.

The door had opened again.

'The miscreant, m'lord,' announced Beach.

With a final sniff, Lady Constance dissociated herself from the affair by withdrawing into a corner and opening a photograph album. There was a scuffling of feet, and the prisoner at the bar entered, trailing like clouds of glory Stokes, first footman, attached to his right arm, and Thomas, second footman, clinging like a limpet to his left.

'Good God!' cried Lord Emsworth, startled out of his judicial calm. 'What a horrible-looking brute!'

Lord Tilbury, though resenting the description keenly, would have been compelled, had he been able at the moment to look in a mirror, to recognize its essential justice. Beau Brummell himself could not have remained spruce after lying in four inches of mud with a six-foot pig-man on top of him. Pirbright was a man who believed that a thing well begun is half done, and his first act had been to thrust Lord Tilbury's face firmly below the surface and keep it there.

A sudden idea struck Lord Emsworth.

'Beach!'

'Did Pirbright say if this was the same fellow he shut up in the shed yesterday?'

'Yes, m'lord.'

'It is?'

'Yes, m'lord.'

'God bless my soul!' cried Lord Emsworth.

This pertinacity appalled him. It showed how dangerous the chap was. None of that business here of the burned child dreading the potting-shed. No sooner was this fellow out of that mess than back he came for a second pop, as malignant as ever. The quicker he was put safely away behind the bars of Market Blandings' picturesque little prison, the better, felt Lord Emsworth.

He was interrupted in this meditation by a voice proceeding from behind the mud.

'Lord Emsworth, I wish to speak to you alone.'

'Well, you dashed well can't speak to me alone,' replied his lordship with decision. 'Think I'm going to allow myself to be left alone with a fellow like you? Beach!'

'M'lord?'

'Take that thingummajig,' said Lord Emsworth, indicating the young David prophesying before Saul, 'and if he so much as stirs hit him a good hard bang with it.'

'Very good, m'lord.'

'Now, then, what's your name?'

'I refuse to tell you my name unless you will let me speak to you alone.'

Lord Emsworth's gaze hardened.

'You notice how he keeps wanting to get me alone, Beach.'

'Yes, m'lord.'

'Suspicious.'

'Yes, m'lord.'

'Stand by with that thing.'

'Very good, m'lord,' said the butler, taking a firmer grip on David's left leg.

'Hallo,' said a voice. 'What's all this? Ah, Connie, I thought I should find you here.'

Lord Emsworth, peering through his pince-nez, perceived that his brother Galahad had entered the room. With him was that little girl of Ronald's. At the sight of her Lord Emsworth found his righteous wrath tinged with a certain embarrassment.

'Don't come in here now, Galahad, there's a

good fellow,' he begged. 'I'm busy.'

'Good God! What on earth's that?' cried the Hon. Galahad, his monocle leaping from his eye as he suddenly caught sight of the mass of alluvial deposits which was Lord Tilbury.

'It's a horrible chap Pirbright found sneaking into the Empress's sty,' explained Lord Emsworth. 'Parsloe's accomplice, whom you warned me about. I'm just going to give him fourteen days.'

This frank statement of policy decided Lord Tilbury. For the second time that day he thought on his feet. Passionately though he desired to preserve his incognito, he did not wish to do so at the expense of two weeks in jail.

'Threepwood,' he cried, 'tell this old fool who I am.'

The Hon. Galahad had recovered his monocle.

'But, my dear chap,' he protested, staring through it, 'I don't know who you are. You look like one of those Sons of Toil Buried by Tons of Soil I once saw in a headline. Are you somebody I've met?' He peered more closely and uttered an astonished cry. 'Stinker! Is it really you, my poor old Stinker, hidden away under all that real estate? I can explain all this, Clarence. I think first, perhaps, though, it would be as well to clear the court. Pop off, Beach, for a moment, if you don't mind.'

'Very good, Mr Galahad,' said Beach, with the disappointed air of a man who is being thrown out of a theatre just as the curtain is going up. He put down the young David and, collecting eyes like a hostess at a dinner-party, led Thomas and Stokes from the room.

'Is it safe, Galahad?' said Lord Emsworth dubiously.

'Oh, Stinker — Pyke, I mean — Tilbury, that is to say, is quite harmless.'

'What did you say his name was?'

'Tilbury. Lord Tilbury.'

'*Lord* Tilbury?' said Lord Emsworth, gaping.

'Yes. Apparently they've made old Stinker a peer.'

'Then what was he doing trying to kill my pig?' asked Lord Emsworth, perplexed, for he had a high opinion of the moral purity of the House of Lords.

'He wasn't trying to kill your blasted pig. You came after that manuscript of mine, eh, Stinker?'

'I did,' said Lord Tilbury stiffly. 'I consider that I have a legal right to it.'

'Yes, we went into all that before, I remember. But abandon all hope, Stinker. There isn't any manuscript. The pig's eaten it.'

'What!'

'Yes. So unless you care to publish the pig . . .'

There was too much mud on Lord Tilbury's face to admit of any play of expression, but the sudden rigidity of his body told how shrewdly the blow had gone home.

'Oh!' he said at length.

'I'm afraid so,' said the Hon. Galahad sympathetically.

'If you will excuse me,' said Lord Tilbury, 'I will return to the Emsworth Arms.'

The Hon. Galahad took his soiled arm.

'My dear old chap! You can't possibly go to

any pub looking like that. Beach will show you to the bathroom. Beach!'

'Sir?' said the butler, manifesting himself with the celerity of one who has never been far from the keyhole.

'Take Lord Tilbury to the bathroom, and then telephone to the Emsworth Arms to send up his things. He will be staying the night. Several nights. In fact, indefinitely. Yes, yes, Stinker, I insist. Dash it, man, we haven't seen one another for twenty-five years. I want a long yarn with you about the old days.'

For an instant it seemed as if the proud spirit of the Pykes was to flame in revolt. Lord Tilbury definitely drew himself up. But he was not the man he had been. Every man, moreover, has his price. That of the proprietor of the Mammoth Publishing Company at this moment was a hot bath with plenty of soap, a sprinkling of bath-salts, and well-warmed towels. 'Kind of you,' he said gruffly.

Like the mountain reluctantly deciding to come to Mahomet, he followed Beach from the room.

'And now, Connie,' said the Hon. Galahad, 'you can put that book down and come and join the party.'

★   ★   ★

Lady Constance moved with dignified step from her corner.

'I suppose,' said the Hon. Galahad, eyeing her unfraternally, 'you've been nagging and bullying

341

poor old Clarence till he doesn't know where he is?'

'I have been giving Clarence my views.'

'You would. I suppose the poor devil's half off his head.'

'Clarence has been listening very patiently and attentively,' said Lady Constance. 'I think he understands what is the right thing for him to do in this matter — a matter which I must say I would prefer to discuss, if we are going to discuss it, in private.'

'You mean you don't want Sue here?'

'I should imagine that Miss Brown would find it less embarrassing not to be present.'

'Well, I do want her here,' said the Hon. Galahad. 'I brought her specially. To show her to you, Clarence.'

'Eh?' said Lord Emsworth, jumping. He had been dreaming of pigs.

'To show her to you, I said. I want you to take a look at this little girl, Clarence. Get those dashed pince-nez of yours straight and examine her steadily and carefully. What do you think of her?'

'Charming, charming,' said Lord Emsworth courteously.

'Isn't she just the very girl any sensible man would choose for his nephew's wife?'

'My dear Galahad!' said Lady Constance.

'Well?'

'I cannot see what all this is leading to. I imagine that nobody is disputing the fact that Miss Brown is a pretty girl.'

'Pretty girl be dashed! I'm not talking about

her being a pretty girl. I'm talking of what anybody with half an eye ought to be able to see when he takes one look at her — that she's all right. Just as her mother was all right. Her mother was the sweetest, straightest, squarest, honestest, jolliest thing that ever lived. And Sue's the same. Any man who marries Sue is in luck. Damn it all, the way you women have been going on about him, one would think young Ronnie was the Prince of Wales or something. Who *is* Ronnie, dash it? My nephew. Well, look at me. Do you mean to assert that a fellow handicapped by an uncle like me isn't jolly lucky to get *any* girl to marry him?'

This sentiment so exactly chimed in with her own views that for once in her masterful life Lady Constance had nothing to say. She seemed vaguely to suspect a fallacy somewhere, but before she could investigate it her brother had gone on speaking.

'Clarence,' he said, 'take that infernal glassy look out of your eyes and listen to me. I realize that you hold the situation in your hands. You can't have been hearing Connie talk for any length of time without knowing that. This little girl's happiness depends entirely on what you make up your woolly, wobbly mind to do. Nobody is more alive than myself to the fact that young Ronnie, like all members of this family, is worth about twopence a week in the open market. He's got to have capital behind him.'

'Which he won't have.'

'Which he will have, if Clarence is the man I take him for. Clarence, wake up!'

'I'm awake, my dear fellow, I'm awake,' said Lord Emsworth.

'Well, then, does Ronnie get his money or doesn't he?'

Lord Emsworth looked like a hunted stag. He fiddled nervously with his pince-nez.

'Connie seems to think . . . '

'I know what Connie thinks, and when we're alone I'll tell you what I think of Connie.'

'If you are simply going to be abusive, Galahad . . . '

'Nothing of the kind. Abusive be dashed! I am taking great pains to avoid anything in the remotest degree personal or offensive. I consider you a snob and a mischief-maker, but you may be quite sure I shall not dream of saying so . . . '

'How very kind of you.'

' . . . until I am at liberty to confide it to Clarence in private. Well, Clarence?'

'Eh? What? Yes, my dear fellow?'

'It's a simple issue. Are you going to do the square thing or are you not?'

'Well, I'll tell you, Galahad. The view Connie takes . . . '

'Oh, damn Connie!'

'Galahad!'

'Yes, I repeat it. Damn Connie! Forget Connie. Drive it into your head that the view Connie takes doesn't amount to a row of beans.'

'Indeed! Really! Well, allow me to tell you Galahad . . . '

'I won't allow you to tell me a thing.'

'I insist on speaking.'

'I won't listen.'

'Galahad!'

'May I say something?' said Sue.

She spoke in a small, deprecating voice, but if it had been a bellow it could scarcely have produced a greater effect. Lord Emsworth, in particular, who had forgotten that she was there, leaped on his settee like a gaffed trout.

'It's only this,' said Sue, in the silence. 'I'm awfully sorry to upset everybody, but Ronnie and I are motoring to London tonight, and we're going to get married tomorrow.'

'What!'

'Yes,' said Sue. 'You see, there's been so much trouble and misunderstanding and everything's so difficult as it is at present that we talked it over and came to the conclusion that the only safe thing is to be married. Then we feel that everything will be all right.'

Lady Constance turned majestically to the head of the family. 'Do you hear this, Clarence?'

'What do you mean, do I hear it?' said Lord Emsworth with that weak testiness which always came upon him when family warfare centred about his person. 'Of course I hear it. Do you think I'm deaf?'

'Well, I hope you will show a little firmness for once in your life.'

'Firmness?'

'Exert your authority. Forbid this.'

'How the devil can I forbid it? This is a free country, isn't it? People have a perfect right to motor to London if they want to, haven't they?'

'You know quite well what I mean. If you are

firm about not letting Ronald have his money, he can do nothing.'

The Hon. Galahad seemed regretfully to be of this opinion, too.

'My dear child,' he said, 'I don't want to damp you, but what on earth are you going to live on?'

'I think that when he hears everything, Lord Emsworth will give Ronnie his money.'

'Eh?'

'That's what Ronnie thinks. He thinks that when Lord Emsworth knows that he has got the Empress . . .'

Lord Emsworth rose up like a rising pheasant.

'What! What? What's that? Got her? How do you mean, got her?'

'He took her out of her sty just now,' explained Sue, 'and put her in the dicky of his car.'

Even in his anguish Lord Emsworth had to stop to inquire into this seemingly superhuman feat.

'What! How on earth could anyone put the Empress in the dicky of a car?'

'Exactly,' said Lady Constance. 'Surely even you, Clarence, can see that this is simply ridiculous . . .'

'Oh, no,' said Sue. 'It was quite easy, really. Ronnie pulled -and a friend of his pushed.'

'Of course,' said the Hon. Galahad, the expert. 'What you're forgetting, Clarence, what you've overlooked is the fact that the Empress has a ring through her nose, which facilitates moving her from spot to spot. When Puffy Benger and I stole old Wivenhoe's pig the night of the Bachelors' Ball at Hammer's Easton in ninety-five, we had to get her up three flights of stairs before we could put her in Plug Basham's bedroom . . . '

'What Ronnie says he thinks he'll do,' proceeded Sue, 'is to take the Empress joy-riding . . . '

'Joy-riding!' cried Lord Emsworth, appalled.

'Only if you won't give him his money, of course. If you really don't feel you can, he says he's going to drive her all over England . . . '

'What an admirable idea!' said the Hon. Galahad with approval. 'I see what you mean. Birmingham today, Edinburgh tomorrow, Brighton the day after. Sort of circular tour. See the country a bit, what?'

'Yes.'

'He ought to take in Skegness. Skegness is so bracing.'

'I must tell him.'

Lord Emsworth was fighting to preserve what little sanity he had.

'I don't believe it,' he cried.

'Ronnie thought you might not. He felt that you would probably want to see for yourself. So he's waiting down there on the drive, just outside the window.'

It was not at a time like this that Lord Emsworth would allow a trifle like an injured ankle to impede him. He sprang acrobatically from the settee and hopped to the window.

From the dicky of the car immediately below it the mild face of the Empress peered up at him, silvered by the moonlight. He uttered a fearful cry.

'Ronald!'

His nephew, seated at the wheel, glanced up, tooted the horn with a sort of respectful regret, threw in his clutch, and passed on into the shadows. The tail-light of the car shone redly as it halted some fifty yards down the drive.

'I'm afraid it's no good shouting at him,' said Sue.

'Of course it isn't,' agreed the Hon. Galahad heartily. 'What you want to do, Clarence, is to stop all this nonsense and give a formal promise before witnesses to cough up that money, and then write a cheque for a thousand or two for honeymoon expenses.'

'That was what Ronnie suggested,' said Sue. 'And then Pirbright could go and take the Empress back to bed.'

'Clarence!' began Lady Constance.

But Lord Emsworth in his travail was proof against any number of 'Clarence's!' He had hopped to the desk and with feverish fingers was fumbling in the top drawer.

'Clarence, you are not to do this!'

'I certainly am going to do it,' said Lord Emsworth, testing a pen with his thumb.

'Does this miserable pig mean more to you than your nephew's whole future?'

'Of course it does,' said Lord Emsworth, surprised at the foolish question. 'Besides, what's wrong with his future? His future's all right. He's going to marry this nice little girl here; I've forgotten her name. She'll look after him.'

'Bravely spoken, Clarence,' said the Hon. Galahad approvingly.

'The right spirit.'

'Well, in that case . . . '

'Don't go, Connie,' urged the Hon. Galahad. 'We may need you as a witness or something. In any case, surely you can't tear yourself away from a happy scene like this? Why, dash it, it's like that thing of Kipling's . . . how does it go . . . ? 'We left them all in couples a-dancing on the decks. We left the lovers loving and the parents signing cheques, In endless English comfort, by County folk caressed. We steered the old three-decker . . . ''

The door slammed.

'' . . . to the Islands of the Blest',' concluded the Hon. Galahad. 'Write clearly, Clarence, on one side of the paper, and don't forget to sign your name, as you usually do. The date is August the fourteenth.'

# 18

The red tail-light of the two-seater turned the corner of the drive and vanished in the night. The Hon. Galahad polished his monocle thoughtfully, replaced it in his eye, and stood for some moments gazing at the spot where it had disappeared. The storm had left the air sweet and fresh. The moon rode gallantly in a cloudless sky. The night was very still, so still that even the lightest footstep on the gravel would have made itself heard. The one which now attracted the Hon. Galahad's attention was not light. It was the emphatic, crunching thump of a man of substance.

He turned.

'Beach?'

'Yes, Mr Galahad.'

'What are you doing out at this time of night?'

'I thought that I would pay a visit to the sty, sir, and-ascertain that the Empress had taken no harm from her disturbed evening.'

'Remorse, eh?'

'Sir?'

'Guilty conscience. It was you who did the pushing, wasn't it, Beach?'

'Yes, sir. We discussed the matter, and Mr Ronald was of opinion that on account of my superior weight I would be more effective than himself in that capacity.' A note of anxiety crept into the butler's voice. 'You will treat this, Mr

Galahad, as purely confidential, I trust?'

'Of course.'

'Thank you, sir. It would jeopardize my position, I fear, were his lordship to learn of what I had done. I saw Mr Ronald and the young lady go off, Mr Galahad.'

'You did? I didn't see you.'

'I had taken up a position some little distance away, sir.'

'You ought to have come and said good-bye.'

'I had already taken leave of the young couple, sir. They visited me in my pantry.'

'So they ought. You have fought the good fight, Beach. I hope they kissed you.'

'The young lady did, sir.'

There was a soft note in the butler's fruity voice. He drew up the toe of his left shoe and rather coyly scratched his right calf with it.

'She did, eh? 'Jenny kissed me when we met, jumping from the chair she sat in.' I'm full of poetry tonight, Beach. The moon, I suppose.'

'Very possibly, sir. I fear Mr Ronald and the young lady will have a long and tedious journey.'

'Long. Not tedious.'

'It is a great distance to drive, sir.'

'Not when you're young.'

'No, sir. Would it be taking a liberty, Mr Galahad, if I were to inquire if Mr Ronald's financial position has been satisfactorily stabilized? When I saw him, the matter was still in the balance.'

'Oh, quite. And did you find the Empress pretty fit?'

'Quite, Mr Galahad.'

'Then everything's all right. These things generally work themselves out fairly well, Beach.'

'Very true, sir.'

There was a pause. The butler lowered his voice confidentially. 'Did her ladyship express any comment on the affair, Mr Galahad?'

'Which ladyship?'

'I was alluding to Lady Julia, sir.'

'Oh, Julia? Beach,' said the Hon. Galahad, 'there are the seeds of greatness in that woman. I'll give you three guesses what she said and did.'

'I could not hazard a conjecture, sir.'

'She said 'Well, well!' and lit a cigarette.'

'Indeed, sir?'

'You never knew her as a child, did you, Beach?'

'No, sir. Her ladyship must have been in the late twenties when I entered his lordship's employment.'

'I saw her bite a governess once.'

'Indeed, sir?'

'In two places. And with just that serene, angelic look on her face which she wore just now. A great woman, Beach.'

'I have always had the greatest respect for her ladyship, Mr Galahad.'

'And I'm inclined to think that young Ronnie, in spite of looking like a minor jockey with scarlatina, must have inherited some of her greatness. Tonight has opened my eyes, Beach. I begin to understand what Sue sees in him. Stealing that pig, Beach. Shows character. And snatching her up like this and whisking her off to London. There's more in young Ronnie than I suspected. I think he'll make the girl happy.'

'I am convinced of it, sir.'

'Well, he'd better, or I'll skin him. Did you ever see Dolly Henderson, Beach?'

'On several occasions, sir, when I was in service in London. I frequently went to the Tivoli and the Oxford in those days.'

'This girl's very like her, don't you think?'

'Extremely, Mr Galahad.'

The Hon. Galahad looked out over the moon-flooded garden. In the distance there sounded faintly the plashing of the little waterfall that dropped over fern-crusted rocks into the lake.

'Well, good night, Beach.'

'Good night, Mr Galahad.'

★ ★ ★

Empress of Blandings stirred in her sleep and opened an eye. She thought she had heard the rustle of a cabbage-leaf, and she was always ready for cabbage-leaves, no matter how advanced the hour. Something came bowling across the straw, driven by the night breeze.

It was not a cabbage-leaf, only a sheet of paper with writing on it, but she ate it with no sense of disappointment. She was a philosopher and could take things as they came. Tomorrow was another day, and there would be cabbage-leaves in the morning.

The Empress turned on her side and closed her eyes with a contented little sigh. The moon beamed down upon her noble form. It looked like a silver medal.

# SPECIAL MESSAGE TO READERS

**THE ULVERSCROFT FOUNDATION**
**(registered UK charity number 264873)**
was established in 1972 to provide funds for
rese~~~~~~~~~ses.

- The Children's Eye Unit at Moorfields Eye Hospital, London
- The Ulverscroft Children's Eye Unit at Great Ormond Street Hospital for Sick Children
- Funding research into eye diseases and treatment at the Department of Ophthalmology, University of Leicester
- The Ulverscroft Vision Research Group, Institute of Child Health
- Twin operating theatres at the Western Ophthalmic Hospital, London
- The Chair of Ophthalmology at the Royal Australian College of Ophthalmologists

You can help further the work of the Foundation by making a donation or leaving a legacy.
Every contribution is gratefully received. If you would like to help support the Foundation or require further information, please contact:

**THE ULVERSCROFT FOUNDATION**
**The Green, Bradgate Road, Anstey**
**Leicester LE7 7FU, England**
**Tel: (0116) 236 4325**

**website:** www.foundation.ulverscroft.com

000002207263